Indigo
Alien Hunting Grounds Book 1
Kyla Breene

Ree

"There was no saving them."

She might be right, but facts haven't helped ease the ache in my chest.

With each breath, the pain reminds me of failure. We did everything we could for the man, and while it seems wrong to shove the thought of him aside, I can't let images of him linger in my mind.

And yet they still do.

The long hours of a double shift aren't helping. My limbs are leaden now that I'm no longer in motion, and my mind is losing some of the careful barriers I usually keep in place for moments like these.

I let out a breath and sink farther down into my uncomfortable chair. "Yeah. It's harder when they're young."

I drag a hand across my burning eyes as Tamina lets out a low hum of agreement. I yawn so wide my jaw cracks and when I open my eyes, she is glaring at me.

"You need to stop covering for Sherry. You can't keep up this pace, Ree. ER work is hard enough as it is."

It's a frequent admonishment, and while I should have had plenty of time by now to perfect my response, I don't have a ready argument. It might have something to do with her position being unassailable, but there's no way I'm telling her that. I let out a sigh and run a finger across one of the gouges in the breakroom table to help center my mind.

Unfortunately, nothing pithy bubbles up from the slow morass.

"I know."

"You won't stop, will you?"

I go back to pressing my eyes with the heel of my hands and don't bother responding. She knows the answer.

She lets out a disgusted huff. "Fine. Burn out, then."

I realize she means well, but she never did like Sherry. "She just signed the divorce papers, Tam. Give her a little grace."

"Hell no. She needs to open the sparkle cave and go wild for a nice long weekend. Not mope around while you kill yourself taking her shifts."

I let out a choking laugh. "Sparkle cave? Are you serious?"

She purses her lips and gives me an exaggerated once-over with comically wide brown eyes and raised eyebrows. "I can tell by your tone that yours needs some attention."

She's always had a knack for jolting me out of unhelpful moods, sometimes forcefully if she thinks the situation calls for it. The corners of my mouth lift thinking of some of her more comical tirades.

Well, comical now. Not so much then.

"I love you, Tam, but we aren't talking about my sparkle cave." A groan rises up my throat and to the front of my mouth in self-rebuke. "I can't believe I just said that."

I startle when a deep voice speaks from behind me. "Is that what they're calling it these days?"

A blush spreads from my cheeks down to my chest as Asad walks over to the fridge and pulls out a bottle of water. His muscles flex and not even scrubs can hide how much time he must spend at the gym.

We rarely share shifts, thankfully, because I would constantly make a fool of myself.

He's got those dark, bottomless eyes you can fall down into forever and a smile that promises sin and long nights.

He leans back against the counter and tilts his head back as he takes a drink. I'm mesmerized by the movement of his throat and the shadow of beard against his copper skin for a moment before I make myself look away.

I definitely could do with more of that type of long night.

I turn back to Tamina. She's smirking and I know I'm in for it as soon as he leaves the room. I widen my eyes at her, silently pleading.

She rolls hers, but bails me out. "Did you file that report?"

"Killjoy," he shoots back. "Nice to see you, Ree."

"Uh. Y-Yeah. You too."

I enjoy the view as he walks away, then lean forward to rest my forehead on the back of one hand.

"Girl. You have no game. All these years of coaching and... still. Nothing."

"I know," I say again, this time drawing out the last word. "You are right about e-ver-y-thing."

She snickers. "Well, at least I taught you something."

I swing my leg forward, hitting her ankle just hard enough to let her know what I think of her humor. She narrows her eyes at me and there's an answering sting on my own.

Our lips quirk up, but I still see the worry etched on her face. I resolve to say no the next time someone asks me to cover their shift, the feeling of purpose reclaiming some of the space freed up by the slowly retreating ache of failure.

Her face falls into a more serious expression, and I know what advice is coming next.

"You can't keep letting him mess up your head, Ree. You are a great person, and you deserve happiness."

I try to keep looking her in the eyes, but the mere mention of my ex-husband makes my eyes skate away. Then my heart races and my mind shies away, too.

She's right, of course. She always is, but I married when I was young and dumb. I didn't recognize the damage until it was well past already done.

My career I can handle. Finishing my abandoned degree after I found the courage to leave him helped ground me. The past few years working as a nurse has been incredibly fulfilling.

I've also used it as a reason to avoid facing the issue. At the same time, I yearn for companionship and a healthy relationship. What does that even look like? Can I trust myself to recognize it?

My ex seemed great. Until he wasn't.

Interacting with men seems permanently linked to trauma and his voice in my head. It would be really convenient to be attracted to women, dammit.

She doesn't push me anymore, thankfully.

She knows this isn't the time or place. Instead, she begins rattling off her weekend plans with her wife. She always knows just what I need to ease out of being triggered.

Shared moments of peace are hard to find and predictably we're right back to the insanity soon after.

Per usual, I find energy reserves I didn't realize existed to meet each new challenge. After a blur of activity, I'm heading out to my car, my fatigue pulling me down and each step making my aching head pound.

I'm making my way through the covered walkway between buildings when a buzz tickles my hip. I fish my phone out and see a message from Sherry.

Can't face work yet. Not sleeping. Can u cover again?

I tap back an instant reply, my heart aching for her.

Of course! Self-care is important! :)

I cringe as I slide the phone back into my pocket. Tamina is going to pin me with one of her famous scathing looks tomorrow. The verbal lashing will be even worse.

I groan, then keep walking so I can finish my post-shift routine.

As always, I imagine all the horror sloughing off as I take the long walk through the hospital annex and make my way out into the night. The weight can't come home with me or it will disrupt every part of my life.

It would make me less useful to the next person. Or the next.

Sometimes they don't make it. Sometimes it's a life cut entirely too short. If I let myself think of all the pain each passing causes their family and friends, it would be a constant torment.

With each step I feel lighter. Instead of continually recreating scenarios in my mind that might have ended differently, I think of what I'm going to eat tonight. Pad Thai sounds amazing, but I'm too tired to bother ordering ahead.

Not to mention the idea of interacting with anyone else today makes my head spin.

Seems like it'll be another night of staring at a frozen dinner making small circles in a microwave as Sammy twines around my legs, yowling at me for leaving him so long. No doubt berating me for not fluffing his dried food and skipping his tuna treat.

I'm almost to where I parked my car under the flickering lights. The beep of the doors unlocking chirps at the same moment I'm plunged into darkness.

My heart skips a beat and I stop abruptly, hoping to give my eyes time to adjust. There's a scuffing sound from behind me and I whirl. I don't make it far before I'm grabbed in a steely grip and pushed into a nearby car.

My ribs protest the abuse and my heart races.

I try to push away, but a solid wall of muscle and the paunch of an aging man blocks my way. Like almost everyone, he is much larger than me and smells like stale beer, sweat, and cigarettes. I struggle against his forceful grip, a scream cut off by a rough hand over my mouth.

It smells like acetone.

The fumes and jostling make my head throb and my stomach roil.

"It's not working. Ow! Stay still, bitch."

The man's voice sounds petulant under a veneer of hardness. As if I'm the one who started all of this.

The second man's voice is pure menace, and it sends ice racing along my skin. "Just give it time. She'll be down soon enough."

The whiner has me wrapped in a bruising grip, but my lower body and legs are free.

Adrenaline is making it hard to think clearly, but I figure out what they're talking about as I continue to writhe. The idiots are trying to use chloroform and expect it to work instantly.

The side effects rise from memory. Starting with organ damage and ending with hepatitis and I kick even more wildly. It hurts when I connect with the car in front of me, but it gives me an idea.

I keep kicking the side of it until the alarm blares.

"Just... stop. Fuck!"

"What the fuck, man? Get her under control."

They seem unconcerned with the alarm and simply yell over it. I'm getting dizzy and fight harder. Each panicked breath I take fills my lungs with noxious fumes.

"I'm trying to not break anything."

"The slimes don't care, asshole. Do your fucking job."

"Fine."

He grabs the arm I was using to rake gouges into his hand as he curses me and twists it painfully behind me. As a result, his hand is away from my mouth and I take in a ragged breath to scream. My lungs are burning and my mind is on fire.

I let out a screech, but it's cut off by the seizing of my abused lungs.

"You're fucking useless."

I scream again, and fingers dig into the back of my neck. The man with the menacing voice slams my head into the car in front of us, effectively cutting off my cry for help. The intense sensation overtakes me and I hang limp.

Though my mind is still urging me to get away, my body isn't following commands as they drag me across the rough concrete and throw me into the back of a van.

I groan at the added injuries, my back and hips on fire, but shakily try to rise.

In the muted light of the van, I'm able to see one of them for the first time. He's masked and his eyes promise incoming pain. He pins me down and stuffs a gag in my mouth as the van moves. It tastes like engine oil and my throat convulses trying to expel it.

Combined with the heady stench of his cheap cologne it makes me heave.

"You're going to pay for that, bitch."

"Leave off, Jeff. You know they won't take her if you do it."

"It might be worth it with this one."

I'm frozen now, hopelessness and dread overtaking my fight response. Locking my limbs down and making my lungs burn as

I hold my breath. My tears are no longer ones of rage and are building into a torrent.

It blurs his baleful visage.

"Fuck no. You can find someone else. I've got bills to pay."

The man straddling me curses, lifts my upper body, and slams me back down. There's a shot of pain that reverberates through my skull and then darkness.

***

My dreams are horrific.

Bright lights. Straps and machines. Something forced inside my ear. Glimpses of gray skin with pink slime oozing down it on the other side of a glass window.

Robotic arms holding me down. Needles with tubes of liquid.

Just as I gain enough control of my facilities to resist, I'm being forced into a silver container that looks like a high-tech coffin with a red lining.

My defiance and screaming are useless against mindless machines.

Their bruising metal grip positions me so I'm facing out, and then a glass door slides across, trapping me inside. I'm about to pound on it when I get my first full view of what's watching from another room.

Naked gray skin with oozing salmon-colored liquid. Black bulging eyes that stare back at me.

"This harem should do well on Zentrea."

Aliens.

My mind is still trying to catch up with the fact that I can understand them as needles stab into the back of my neck. A hiss of air and I'm swirling down into oblivion, my limbs still stiff with shock.

2

Thivoll

I always forget just how peaceful it is out here in the dark.

No shift change announcements, none of the usual hissing, popping, and clanging that comes along with being an air technician. Just the gentle thrum of the engine as it propels me out to fix a broken satellite.

It isn't my post, but Shaltann just delivered her first kit and it's an easy enough fix that anyone handy can take care of it.

I let my muzzle settle down on the padded headrest and my hands and paws dangle from where the long bench supports my chest and belly. I'm normally in constant motion, but I must admit the forced stillness is nice.

Though it's only a welcome reprieve if it doesn't last very long or my limbs will twitch and my tail dance with the need to expend energy.

For now, I close my eyes and enjoy the rare silence.

It's interrupted a few short moments later with the rumble of an incoming call. I let out a growl and crack open one eye. As much as I'd like to go back to basking in the silence, there's no ignoring it without losing parts of my scaled hide next time she sees me.

"Accept."

Instead of her usual luminous eyes and dainty features, I see the side of her head. She has one rounded ear swiveled toward me and the other oriented the way she is facing. Her short fur is as immaculate and glimmering as always, but her movements betray her agitation. Her scaled hands flutter around her neck, the two thumbs of one of them twitching, like she's trying to grasp at something unseen.

I've rarely witnessed my dam in such a state and my breath comes faster.

"What's wrong?"

She turns toward me, a muffled vidfeed in the background the only sound between us. From the drone of the voice, I assume it's a newscast.

She was never one for mincing words. "The slimes took more women. Do you remember Veentann? Her entire research team is gone."

The fur on my neck rises. Veentann is the smartest person I've ever met and should have been better protected instead of wasting away in captivity.

"There were no males?"

"There was only one. He was found with a few dead genali around him. He didn't survive."

"Venom bliss?"

"No. He was an Abstainer."

My long tail wraps around me at the mere mention of the sect, though I stop just short of hugging the tip to me like I did when I first learned about their beliefs.

They remove the end of the tail, which includes the venom delivery system, from their male kits at birth. The goal is to take away the temptation along with a male's most formidable weapon.

For every male outside their sect, it is our worst nightmare.

I wonder how many of the Abstainer kits internally rage at the disfigurement. Though of course no one would dare call it that.

Even those who disagree.

"Have you been taking the extra supplements I sent you?"

The change in subject gives me mental whiplash and I blink several times to clear my thoughts. I'm also not thrilled with the topic choice, although it shouldn't surprise me.

She lets out a displeased mew. "Your mane is looking darker than usual."

I'm quite certain my mane is the same fiery orange it has always been, but I know she's trying to take her mind off the pressing fear of the genali threat by focusing on her only kit.

Though I've long since grown past the need for hovering.

"Greetings to you as well, my dam," I tell her, ignoring her question and needling her about her notorious lack of social niceties by returning to what she left out of the very beginning of our conversation.

She narrows her golden eyes at me, leaving two small gold and orange slits and despite the distance between us I shiver at the implied threat.

She might be half my size, but no one would ever underestimate her.

"Let me see your claws."

I suppress a growl, but hold up my hands. I extend my claws, making sure she has a good view of both sets of black thumb claws by pivoting my wrists, and then I retract them again.

My superiors frown upon random scratches left on equipment and so it's best to keep them tucked away.

I wiggle all eight of my long fingers in front of my face while pushing my whiskers forward, since I can't help myself from returning to the habits of my youth.

She hums, ignoring my juvenile attempt to get a rise out of her. "What about your paws?"

I've had enough of humoring her. I'm certain she has enough information that she won't use back channels to access my medical records.

Somewhat certain.

I sigh. She already put it on her mental list for the day, I'm sure.

There's no rancor in my mind, however. Considering how many long cycles she spent waiting to find out if my sire was still alive, just to have her worst fears confirmed, I can't blame her for worrying.

"I'm perfectly healthy."

The old guilt tries to resurface and I remind myself that I couldn't have stayed planet-side. It would've been a slow death to not be moving toward something new. Though I admit I've made little progress in my goal to see more of the universe since taking my station post.

It might have something to do with this being a compromise between what I want and what will cause her the least amount of pain.

She growls at me, but there's no bite promised in it. "Are you on the station?"

"No, I'm in a small vessel headed to make repairs."

"With slime in the system? I need to talk to your station lead."

"I'm sure there's a patrol around."

She huffs out her disbelief. "As if the Thorisian Sentinels have enough resources to patrol that far."

"Well, people like me should join so they do."

It's a common argument for us and her fur stands on end. "Absolutely not, Thiv. You owe me at least another fifty years of being safe and boring for the first fifty you put me through as a kit. These last forty haven't been nearly enough to heal the emotional scars left from random disappearances and near drownings."

My whiskers push forward at the memories her chiding provokes. "Every adventure was worth it."

Her whiskers twitch. "For you, possibly. For me? Why was I stuck with the oddest kit to grace the pride?"

I puff out my long mane in mock outrage. "I am an altogether normal male."

After a moment of holding the expression, we both break out in chuffing. Hers has a manic edge to it infused with her disbelief.

As usual, I own up to nothing.

She huffs out a breath and the weight of recent events shows on her face again. It strikes me that for the first time I can see signs of aging. The light purple around her muzzle isn't as vibrant as it once was and more of her black scales than normal show through her short orange and green fur.

I don't want to stress her further, but reality is harsh these days. "I understand your wishes, my dam, but at some point we'll have to defend ourselves. That means people like me need to do more than clean vents."

She slumps. "I know, Thivoll. I just don't want you to get hurt."

My jaw drops open, and for a moment no response comes to me. There must be more going on than she shared. I've been discussing joining since I was a young kit of thirty, but it always felt like that one step too far to push my harried dam.

I take in a breath but a proximity warning interrupts my response. I freeze when I see it. There's a weight in my chest and my limbs shake as I work through what's about to happen.

I almost tell her, then take the coward's way out.

"I'll have to return your call after my shift."

She hums in agreement. "Be safe," she orders me as the display fades.

If she only knew. "Call central command."

After an indicator boop, the call is connected.

"Central."

"A genali cruiser is inbound to my location."

"Notifying Sentinels. Standby for instructions."

I tune them out. Nothing they can do will help. The only protection would be fully funded Sentinels, which we won't have until they stop endlessly debating it in Session.

Abstainers are a formidable presence and their fear of males devolving into raving, venom-addicted beasts is greater than the genali threat.

In their view it is better to mutilate kits and ignore the abduction of women than return to our ancient empire seeking days.

Most of us don't agree with them, not fully, but few have effectively taken on our most vocal minority.

At least not until recently.

Reports that nearly half of our female population is dead or missing has caused a backlash, but not soon enough to protect me.

Or Veentann and the many women like her.

My mouth tastes sour and my heart pounds. We always think we'll have so much time and leave so much undone and unsaid. After a moment's hesitation, I open another call with my dam. She looks surprised when she answers.

I waste no time in voicing what needs to be admitted. "I was a terror, and I deserved every punishment."

Her whiskers droop. "You're scaring me, Thiv. You've never admitted that."

"You were the best dam anyone could ever ask for and I wish my sire could see how beautiful you are after all these years."

Her muzzle is pale, and her fur is quaking. "The slimes..."

She can't finish so I do it for her. "There was a proximity alarm. No one is in range to help."

The sound of them locking on to the hull joins her outraged, heartbroken roar. It only takes a few moments for them to cut through the thin membrane and a canister to drop in. It pulls my eyes away from her. Why would they even attempt gas on our species?

But then I can feel it taking effect.

I turn back to her precious face. It's a good view before death. She is stoic now, her usual impressive emotional control in place.

"I've always been proud. You never conformed and I wish I let you follow your sire's path into the Sentinels."

I can't leave her with that regret. "I did what I wanted, and this was it. Tell someone the slimes made a new... compound."

I'm struggling to stay awake. "I love you," I say as my eyes drift closed.

Her responding roar fades to static as I succumb to the darkness.

3

Ree

There are women scattered in front of me like bright jewels and I'm to be their keeper.

After years of working one of the hardest jobs imaginable I'm not thrilled to be thrust into the role of brothel madam. Nine of them. All mine to keep in line, but right now they can't even fucking talk to me.

"Boredom is preferable to death," I mumble to myself, ensuring I'm only mouthing the words and not vocalizing.

No need to draw unneeded attention in this hell.

I'm locked into a tiny room of alien design, one side taken up by a viewing area for our captors. The walls and floors gleam like an ultramodern, sleek hotel, but appearances don't change the fact that it's a cell and we are captives. In a small hall connected to my glass cell are nine upright cryogenic chambers with women inside of them.

They face each other in pairs, with the one behind them offset just enough so the camera mounted at the back of my cell can see their full, naked bodies.

The only clothing we have is a thin band of black around our waists we aren't allowed to use. The women rest against the soft red fabric in what looks like peaceful slumber. At the end of the row another stands, as if waiting to be seated at the head of a table.

None of it matches the horror of our reality.

None of them know what I've learned. My jaw clenches as I think of trading places with them, but as their leader I am the one who is always awake with no reprieve from the terror.

I hate thinking of them as colors, but they're unable to tell me their names. There are ten of us in total. I'm Indigo, since it only seems fair to reduce myself to a color if I'm to do the same to them.

Some day soon I hope to find out each of their names and tell them my own.

Ruby, Azure, Emerald, Navy, Coral, Citrine, Diamond, Silver, and Amethyst. Each with skin tones chosen to best compliment their added shades. Making the pops of color of their long hair and the patch of pubic hair draw the eye.

The small triangle of the latter leaves little doubt where our alien 'artists' were trying to lead a wandering gaze.

Nine women I would have never met, but now we share a cell in a spaceship hurtling along through the universe. To where, I don't know, but I'm quite certain it will be very far from earth. Our abductors told me just enough to help keep my fellow harem-mates in line when the slimes wake us for our new master, but not a location.

That's right. We are to be sold at auction at the end of this space voyage to who knows where, to who knows what alien species as the highest bidder.

From what I've gathered, the slimes are opportunistic middle men who cater to any kind of taste, especially if it involves slaves. Judging by the constant string of comments on the live feed of my cell, they have no shortage of clients.

Ones that really enjoy it when the sticky bastards torture me, if the ratings ticker is any indication.

Fucking perverted pieces of...

I'm pulled from further musing by today's visit. The hatch creaks open in the observation room and I focus on keeping the tension it causes from showing. It seems our captors are back for more gloating and entertainment.

I drift in a slow turn as the squelching sounds of their footfalls across the floor causes a shiver to race down my spine.

This time it's only one of them.

I don't recognize which one. Just another amorphous gray blob with bulging black eyes.

They have a viscous pink substance always trailing down their skin and dripping onto the floor. The sight of it makes my stomach turn and I'm once again relieved to have a barrier between us so I can't smell them.

They are repugnant.

Nothing about them is the least bit attractive, as I realized from my very early impressions, but now my body reacts to the sight of them like they are somehow the epitome of all things sensual.

My skin is flushed and I'm getting wet and I fucking hate them for it. The rage steals my breath and my hands want to clench, but I force myself to remain relaxed.

At least on the outside. I can't do much about the roiling thoughts inside my head.

His disgusting eyes are roving over the women behind me as he settles into the control panel chair with a sickening squeak as his bare, wet skin contacts the surface. His body sags over the edges and his short legs jut out.

All of it dripping.

It's a struggle to keep my thoughts off my face. He moves his gaze to me, his nictitating membrane sweeping across his eyes from the side, roaming over my naked body and down to my thighs.

"I know you want me, whore, but you won't get me today."

He's confusing what my body is doing with motivation, but of course I don't correct him. There's bile at the back of my throat as I consider the disconnect between what my mind thinks and what my body is telling me.

I no longer trust it and it's yet another layer of violation.

He shifts so the camera can see him better and starts talking in his salesperson voice. It makes my skin crawl, but it's the only way I've gained useful information so I listen intently.

"We loaded this harem with a wide range of immune system boosting nanites that will keep them healthy, help them adapt to new environments, and slow aging."

Well, that explains why I now look to be in my early twenties instead of thirty-four. My twenties aren't an age I'd revisit of my own free will. I doubt anyone would pay this price to look young again.

"They will stay clean and smelling exquisite with our upgrades, regardless of how much seed you put into them, or whatever else you would like to stuff them full of. And you will absolutely love this special announcement..."

He leaves a dramatic pause while I try not to gag.

"Once you pump your way to ecstasy the first time, your harem will change in the most wondrous ways! Each tailored to your own genetic makeup. Be warned, however, that if you want to share them among friends of another species, you should be sure to break them in yourself first. Unless of course you want to think of a special friend each time you find a hole to fill."

He makes their honking version of a laugh, then continues.

"This species has plenty of cavities to choose from! And of course you can make more of your own thanks to the healing upgrade. You told us healing was an important base feature, and we listened. But don't you fear. There is no need to make further changes. The pocket between their delightful legs will always stay wet for you once you claim them. And although you can share them freely, they will be utterly devoted to you."

Well, that's false advertisement. I suppose for their purposes it doesn't matter, but I take my mental freedom as a minor victory.

Then that small voice of doubt whispers to me.

It's afraid he might be right.

The back of my neck prickles and my head swims when I picture myself mindlessly looking up at our new master with adoration in my eyes. I can't keep the slight tremors from my hands and have to clasp them in front of me.

He pulls up a recording on his console. It's a slime with a human woman and I dart my eyes away. The terror on the woman's face from the last video has haunted my dreams during the few times I've been able to rest. I needed to know what I was up against if they raped me, but the information came at a cost.

I make myself loosen my white-knuckled grip and take a slow, deep breath.

I think back over the caution to not share us with friends. It explains the clean room barrier. They must not be able to reverse whatever they did, and it's protecting us from rape. On this ship at least. Exposure to genetic material must start the changes he mentioned and they can't make it a targeted thing.

The thought of even more unwanted changes to my body makes my chest ache.

A feminine scream and a honking laugh interrupts my thoughts. I need a better distraction from the disturbing sounds of the video.

I turn to Silver, where she stands at the end of the hall, wishing I could talk to her and sort this all out. I don't know why, but something about her face makes me think she would be a great listener. She is beautiful, with gleaming ebony skin that sets off the silver of her long, curly hair. It falls around her in wavy cascades of shimmering light.

Like all of us, it extends well down her back.

I assume her eyes will be some shade of silver to match her hair, or maybe the hint of green it shows at certain angles. It will be striking on her, but I'm sure she'll hate the change as much as I hate my own. Just like all the other women I'm in charge of will despise it.

No one should have their body modified without their consent.

Not that consent plays much of a role in all of this but knowing something logically and not railing against the unchangeable anyway is impossible. It's a human curse. Human women must be a sought-after commodity in the universe and so we are doubly cursed. It brought the slimes to us, after all.

Vultures don't descend unless there is something to gain from it.

I blink, my mind wanting to provide a better example but I shake my head and move on.

I should have paid more attention to all those crazy shows about aliens. Maybe they had some advice for moments like these. My mind's spinning out and I realize I need to get myself under control. Three breaths in and out as I stare at Silver's lovely face and I'm more settled, if not calm.

The sound of the video cuts off and I dart my eyes back to the control panel.

"Well, enough of that. I realize many of you have been hoping to see more of this special collection moving around. We'll get some of those exciting bits bouncing for you in just the right ways!"

This is not good.

Whenever they talk about something being exciting, it means punishment.

Their form of entertainment involves either telling me how they would rape me, how vicious their clients are, showing videos of any version of the former, or flooding my room with tear gas. A glance down to the vents along the floor rules that out.

A sound from behind me makes me spin around.

Emerald's chamber is open.

There is a beep and then she falls. I don't make it to her in time and she crashes to the ground. Then I'm down with her, coughing and trying to wipe the streaming tears from my face so I can see her. She's still prone and is trying to expel the gas from her lungs.

Thankfully, the vent system whirs to life and I can breathe again and also make out the slime's words.

"Aren't they so delightfully powerless?"

My eyes clear enough to see her shaking form. She's looking around in shock as his grating voice breaks in again.

"Just imagine them bent over like that for your own purposes."

And with that, she's screaming. I can't blame her, but I also know where that path leads so I rush forward, put my hands on her shoulders to keep her in place, and put my mouth right next to her ear. "They won't stop pumping gas in here until you stop screaming. Just..."

I don't get to say more before we are coughing again.

When it clears, she is only making terrified moans, though I can tell by her wild eyes another scream is right under the surface. The slime keeps droning on about our body parts and where a buyer can put theirs as I pull her into my arms and whisper to her.

"I have you. I know this is terrifying, but it only gets worse if you seem scared. They like it."

Tears are streaming down both of our faces now, and not just because of the gas. "Wh-Where are we? What is that?"

"On a spaceship. Those aliens captured us."

The last prompts her to consider her surroundings. She does a double take when she sees the other women, then looks at me again.

"What did they do to your eyes?"

I hold back a groan.

I once had nearly black irises, but now they're aquamarine.

They must have decided that a human iris didn't make enough of an impact because my almond-shaped eyes are now, except for black pupil, completely blue. There is no more white sclera, and it's unsettling.

I don't tell her that her own eyes are a lighter version of her long green hair.

She's had enough of a shock.

She moves on to another question before I can answer her. "Why can I understand it?"

That one is easier to address. The slimes covered it in a very early advertising session.

"They put nanites in us that do lots of things, including somehow letting us understand and speak other languages."

What I leave out is that they loaded us with all the known languages in the universe, even those from species unlikely to be among our buyers. Their reasoning is that we can double as interpreters on pleasure cruises or invasions.

Such a waste of a hard-earned education. Brothel madam with an upgrade to allow for more enjoyable alien pillaging.

This has become my life.

She's shaking and crying and it's steadily eroding the careful control I've built up in order to not fall apart. That's the last thing she needs from me right now, so I push the rising panic back down.

"There's a live feed running at all times and they like it when we watch it. Don't look at it because you'll be able to read the comments," I warn her.

Of course it makes her look and I feel guilty even though I realize she would have found it anyway. Mostly I've ignored it, but in the long hours with nothing to do I haven't always been able to stop myself from seeking some sort of break in the mind-numbing sameness of it all.

I have regretted it every single time.

She shakes harder. "That's anatomically impossible."

I let out a mirthless chuckle. "I'm a nurse and so I was sure to point that out to them. They started showing videos of how buyers have sex. Avoid talking about it. Trust me."

She gulps, then nods. "My name's Olivia."

"I'm Ree."

The telltale hiss of an incoming punishment is our only warning before the torture begins anew. Once we gain control of our bodies again we cling to each other. Her arm is wrapped around my waist and mine around her shoulders as tears stream down our faces.

"You have no names until your buyer gives them to you," the slime says to us in a nasty tone.

He goes back to his salesperson voice. "That concludes our special session. We will bring another of the harem out to play soon."

He turns back to us, his eyes focused on me. "Put the green whore back in her chamber."

Our refusal ends up being futile, of course.

After multiple rounds of yelling out our defiance and choking on gas leaves our lungs aching, Olivia climbs back in. Tremors wrack her body, but we don't look away from each other.

Neither one of us flinch at the despair written in every anguish painted groove of skin.

We are both sobbing as the chamber closes and then she's still again and I'm trying to put the broken pieces of myself back together.

Feeling more alone than I ever thought possible.

4

Thivoll

Their stench is the first thing I notice as I awaken.

My hands and paws are bound like I'm livestock and my head is pounding from whatever mixture they used to knock me unconscious. I try to move my body but it isn't responding. My eyelids are too heavy to lift and my breathing is labored.

From the squishing sounds they make as they move around me I can tell there are several of them.

The slick blobs are a complete plague on the known universe. Willing to do anything for credits, which they use to indulge in their taste for mind-altering substances and raping women of as many species as possible.

There is a depressingly large intergalactic demand for both and so their efforts to keep finding ever more exotic products and slaves are well-funded.

I still don't know how they captured me, aside from it being some sort of new drug cocktail. It shouldn't have worked, and it won't work for very long, but that doesn't really help me right now. One of my toes twitches and a wave of relief follows.

At least whatever it is isn't a permanent paralytic.

Their wet footfalls come closer and I'm overwhelmed by their acrid, musty odor. There are rustling sounds, then they start speaking. I learned enough of their language back when I still had hopes of joining the Sentinels that I can understand their gurgling.

"I don't like the look of his vitals. Move faster with the straps."

"If you want us to move faster, why don't you come help?"

"No... uh... I'll just keep monitoring him."

"Dried out old coward," one of them near me says in a low voice.

A sudden pain flares across my flank from something raking along me with enough force to tear the flesh under my protective layer of scales.

The scent of my blood fills the room. Through the burning throb I can feel something shift against my body. It must be a strap, which is confirmed when it starts tightening.

I continue to unsuccessfully urge life back into my limbs.

Too much more of this and it will trigger the rage that always lurks below the surface. While it might help burn through the rest of the chemical they used, it would also take away rational thought. I had better get myself out of this before my subconscious catches up to the fact that I'm trapped.

"Did you see that? Desiccated testicles! He just moved."

"His tail is contained. You'll be fine."

Another breath in and I can detect their fear.

They should be afraid. I'm going to rip out their Thela-cursed throats.

Just as soon as I get my body to respond. The sensation of every one of my claws extending from their sheathes is almost sexual. The rumble of my growl fills the room along with wet screeches of terror.

I must be right on the edge and try to pull myself back from it.

"We aren't equipped for this," one of them yells. "I'm not some disposable bot. I'm done with plans made by shriveled dung holes."

"No! Get him strapped."

"No amount of credits is worth this. Let me out to get a pistol, sand humper!"

"And have the captain kill us? He's worth too much. Get him in the chamber, you withered member."

I feel flecks of their slime flinging on my fur as they scramble around me and continue to hurl insults at each other.

There's another pain along my upper body and a strap starts to tighten around my shoulders. I force my eyes open. My vision is swimming, but I can make out the wide terrified eyes of a genali.

He is easily within range of my claws and although I am slow and stupid from the drug I'm still plenty fast enough to reach my bound hands forward and slice four gashes across his almost nonexistent throat. He lets go of the strap he was holding, his webbed hands darting up to try to contain the gushing torrent of gray blood.

He gurgles out a sound of disbelief and despair and a purr rumbles to life in my chest for a moment before reality reasserts itself.

The strap continues to tighten as the screams of the remaining slimes echo even more loudly off the slick white walls. Their impersonal aesthetic makes me as sick and enraged as it always has. Ever since I was old enough to research my sire's killers.

A nearly powerless species, but made strong by their seemingly endless numbers.

Like the swarms of insects that flow in undulating, deadly waves on my home planet: easy to squash alone or in pairs, but if you're caught without proper protection they'll pick your bones clean long before anyone can assist you.

I don't have easy access to any other slimes and my tail is held tight against me. It wriggles where it's wrapped multiple times around my waist, just above my sheathe. Another strap must be around it. I shakily lift my head, my mane disheveled enough to block one eye.

I can still make out another genali.

He must think he's out of range and obviously knows nothing about the way my people fight. Everyone focuses on our tails and teeth.

Few think of our paws.

I kick out my back legs. The claws that extend from just below the knob at the back of my knee rake across his soft, wet stomach. I roar an inarticulate battle cry as his entrails start to puddle on the floor and he sinks down to join them. He continues screaming, the wound fatal but one that leaves him with plenty of time to fear his impending death.

I feel a rush of satisfaction, but then I'm rising and not of my own will.

The straps cut into me as they take my weight, my flexible spine making it so my side is the last to leave the blood soaked floor. I still don't have enough control of my body to resist, let alone keep them from raising me up like a trussed up, limp bundle of fur.

The genali across the room at the controls is shaking violently. A puddle of liquid under him betrays the depths of his fear.

I roar at him, promising a violent end as soon as the rest of my paralysis lifts. Then I start to swing sideways, the movement spinning me away from him.

I see what I'm headed for and wriggle as much as I'm able, pulling my tied-together limbs back as far as I can in an attempt to slice through the straps.

They've cobbled together a cryogenic chamber large enough to hold me. It's one of the very few ways to trap our species, though even fewer have been able to force a male into one. Ironically, it works because we were the ones who designed them.

One of the most essential tools of our abandoned empire, now one of our few cages. Fitting.

This one looks like a death trap of hastily printed and assembled parts. Clearly they didn't expect to capture me and they plan to put me in an untested chamber.

I'm snarling in rage as the genali moves me above it.

The sight of it is enough to break the last vestige of control over the bubbling fury. It wipes away rational thought. The straps creak under my maddened flailing, but don't give way. My roar turns into a long cry of pure outrage.

I must escape or die trying and I'll kill anything that tries to stop me.

As I spit and thrash, one of my claws catches the strap around my flank. The bottom part of me crashes down into the unlined chamber, flares of pain darting through my rump and up my spine from the impact.

Then I drop all the way in with just a nanosecond between my fall and the glass sliding closed above me.

I try to escape but all I manage to do is leave long scores in the cover before the needles push between my scales and the hiss of the gasses start. I let out another roar, which is almost deafening in the small space.

Then... darkness.

5

Ree

I'm studiously avoiding looking at the feed and considering laying on my bed, which is really just a cryocoffin laying down instead of standing upright like it is for the rest of the harem, when the slimes make their appearance.

There's no predicting when they will pop into the tiny room to the left of my bed. I think they like the idea of throwing me off balance and so the time between their visits has never settled into a recognizable pattern. It wasn't worth the exposure to the comment feed to look at the time stamps to try to figure it out.

There really are a bunch of sick bastards out in the universe and access to a galaxy-wide internet hasn't made them any less prone to trolling.

An image of an alien troll—complete with far too many horns and a vicious sneer—bubbles up after that thought and I can't help a small shiver. Hopefully their actual buyers are more refined?

I let out a huff of breath. Unlikely.

This seems like one of the visits where they haven't really come to talk to me directly, just to get away from other parts of the ship.

There is a surprising amount of overlap between the types of conversations they tend to have when coming around to shoot the breeze and what I've overheard young human males talking about.

Except in this case, the sexual jokes are downright nasty and the casual discussion of violence fits everything I've come to assume about their culture. They have very little regard for the suffering of others and seem to actually derive a great deal of pleasure from it.

I have yet to hear any of them speak to each other with affection or respect.

It must be a horrible way to live.

It might be speciesist of me, but I can't tell one slime from another. They all look like blobs and it doesn't help that they continually change shape. I'm sure they have some obvious ways they tell each other apart, but for me it's a non-starter.

There are two of them this time. Ooze flings off of them as they walk across the floor toward me on their three limbs that remind me of tiny, sticky elephant legs.

Bile rises to the back of my throat at the sight of them, but I can feel my skin heating and moisture pooling between my legs soon after they open the hatch and enter the small observation room. Though hate burns through me like fire and ice, I don't let it show on my face.

They won't get that sort of satisfaction from me ever again.

"Shentrea cabal should have never been allowed to rise," one of them comments.

"We're on a live feed, arid dung," shoots back the other as they settle into the seat of the controls.

The one who spoke before thinking is quaking, their body wiggling in their apparent terror, membranes sliding across their eyes repeatedly.

"I... I d-don't think t-that! How could you say such a thing? Taken out of context—Someone might—"

He clears his throat in a long gurgle. "I was speaking about what is said by the uninformed masses. Of course! No one on this ship has anything but incredibly deep, undying respect for Shentrea."

I realize my eyebrows are raised as he fumbles along and I wipe my face clean of expression. Then I move to the middle of the cryochambers in case they plan to bring a woman out of stasis.

My heart's pounding with more than just fear.

I vacillate between hoping they will leave the women alone and longing for company.

"How about you just start the entertainment so our slick and fabulous Shentrea viewers can see just how unique this harem is?"

When the glass of Silver's chamber slides open I can't help a surge of happiness, then feel sick I could ever feel something positive when a woman is about to have whatever dreams she held close shattered beyond repair.

But my heart's a traitor and for better or worse it has latched on to her.

Unlike Olivia, she doesn't fall, and I look back to the slime at the controls. He's slumped back in his chair like a drooping pile of phlegm. The other one is still trembling and jiggling in fear, though his eyes have mostly returned to normal.

I stand in front of her with my arms poised to catch her just in case.

My mouth is dry and I'm moving my weight rapidly between each leg. Will she like me?

What a stupid thing to focus on right now.

She is going to hate every moment of this, with no understanding of just how much whatever happens right now will mean to me. I hate myself for it, but I can't keep shouldering all of this alone. I need some of them to take the burden.

I know it's selfish. It changes nothing.

Silver still hasn't fallen. The frightened slime looks over to the other and starts speaking in a petulant voice, drawing my attention.

"Just pull her out already so they can have their show. You made your star-baked point."

A gasp brings my gaze back to Silver.

Her light green eyes are wide open and I can tell by the way her muscles are tensed that she is trying to pull herself away from the chamber. It holds her fast and a moment later she is screaming. Next, I'm on the ground hacking, but she is still stuck in her upright position.

When the gas clears she is still coughing, her body wracked with it, but she's unable to move into a position better suited to helping her lungs expel the fumes.

I scramble back up, grabbing one of her hands. "Please don't scream. They hurt us when we scream."

She whimpers, tears running down her face, but she stays quiet. Her hand trembles violently and I grab the other one and squeeze them both gently.

"Shut up, parched hole. I like it when the whores scream."

Apparently he isn't scared anymore now that there's someone new to terrorize.

The one at the controls sits forward. "Now, now. I see we have questions rolling in about the state of the indigo one's channel. I assure you it is anything but dry. In fact, we can—"

He's interrupted by the hatch opening and another slime stepping in. They pull an odd-looking gun from behind them and shoot the slime closest to the door.

Silver lets out another screech and this time I join her.

He falls with a sickening splat, then shudders before falling still. Slimes must have minimal bone structure because his body slowly sinks until he is spread out across a surprisingly extensive area and only rises about six inches off the floor.

The one at the controls grunts. "Was he really worth a frangible?"

"Yes. Compliments of Shentrea."

I don't know who the hell Shentrea is, but they are clearly not to be messed with or even talked about. I shudder as it occurs to me that the monsters in front of me are likely a pale shadow of some broader, far more dangerous political structure.

It's too much to even consider and my vision swims.

Gray blood seeps out around the dead slime and Silver starts dry heaving next to me. I turn my back to them and try to get her to focus on me.

"Hello. I'm Indigo. If I share my real name, they will punish us. I've been calling you Silver. Sorry."

She's staring past me, her body trembling and still trapped against the red fabric of the cryochamber. From the sounds behind me, I can tell they are working on cleaning up the mess and that there are now multiple slimes in the observation room.

"Hey. Hi. Why don't you just look at me, huh? Yes, that's right. Where are you from?"

"C-Congo."

"Oh, that's lovely. I've never been. They gave us translators, which is why we can understand each other."

Her brow furrows. "I'm speaking English."

I'm making a terrible first impression at the absolute worst time. I thought they spoke French or something.

"Wow. I'm a complete ass, sorry."

"No, it's okay. W-Why can't I move?"

"To be honest, I'm not really sure. All I know is the alien at the controls is making it happen. I'm so sorry this is happening to you, Silver. I wish I could change it."

My eyes fill with tears and she looks at me closer, likely just now having enough mental bandwidth to notice that they are freakish. Then her eyes dart to my hair, then down to my naked body before looking at her own.

I hate that I feel a prickle of shame that I'm like this now, but she doesn't comment about my body.

She gulps hard and her tremors become more violent. "Trafficking?"

I nod and she sobs, once again trying to heave herself away from the hold the chamber has on her. I scramble to think of something to help her feel better. There is nothing. Absolutely nothing. Anything I could say would be empty.

Or a lie.

Best to stick to facts, then. I open my mouth to tell her about the things I've learned but I'm interrupted by one of the slimes.

"Move back."

Silver tries to cling to my hands but I pull hard to break her grip so I can do what he says.

I won't put her through any more rounds of torture than necessary.

When her chamber closes and she screams, it's like a knife to my heart. I can't keep the tears from pouring down.

The loneliness is like a crushing weight and it's hard to breathe.

"Now, what was I saying? Right. We can most certainly prove the indigo one is sufficiently moist for whatever use you have in mind. I was always partial to some knife play to add some additional juices to the mix. Not to mention the delectable screams each time I push in, but you chose your own pleasure."

I take a long breath and roughly wipe the tears from my eyes. I won't survive this if I let myself fall apart.

And where would that leave Silver?

"Show our good viewers what they have to look forward to."

I turn back to him, afraid I know what he wants, but hoping there is a way around it.

I stare and hold my breath, willing him to see another comment on the feed that tells him to torture me some other way. The thought makes me glance over and I see comments with images that make me look away just as fast.

"I can always bring that one back out and have her do it."

I stride forward, turn around so my back is to the camera and get down on my knees. As I tilt forward onto my hands to ensure they have the best view possible, I think of gray blood creeping across the floor.

It's the first time I've smiled in a very long time.

Thivoll

I wake up to pain.

It pulses through my body, pounding in my skull with an insistent rhythm. I groan, hoping the cryosickness wears off soon. I've read about it, but never thought I'd ever experience it. It's so typical of the genali to steal our tech and never bother to access our upgrades.

We fixed the pain response issue generations ago.

Then it occurs to me they likely use the improved version for themselves and intentionally use this one to torture people.

Thela curse them. I somehow feel complicit even though I wasn't even alive yet when we invented it.

I hear a beep next to my ear and awkwardly shift my bound limbs around so I can look toward it. A screen is flashing a completed countdown.

That's odd.

A moment later the transparent cover slides back and a petrichor scented breeze wafts in. The sounds of insects and small animals hum through the air. I haven't heard the rustling of leaves in years and this isn't the context I would have chosen to become reacquainted.

Clearly I'm on a planet.

I take in a long breath and confirm it's not one I've ever been to before. Which means we aren't in manticorid space. So there could be many unknown dangers out there and I'm tied up like a tasty offering. I reek of genali blood from where it's caked in my fur, causing it to pull uncomfortably.

Nothing like a blood cocktail to invite predators.

The blood was well earned. A growl rumbles through my chest, and I bare my teeth remembering their deaths.

Except, it also feels wrong.

It goes against the beliefs of my people. We had our bloody millennia of galactic empire. Leaving it behind was no small feat and no one wants to revisit those days. And yet... if we don't we aren't going to survive.

Reality is rubbing up against idealism and the friction is painful.

Even after all those years I spent imagining what it would be like to be on the Sentinels it's hard to accept that I so violently took lives.

I huff out a breath. Best to not think of that right now and get myself out of here.

I can't quite get my hands high enough to unbind them with my teeth. So I set about the painful process of repositioning and bending around until I'm able to pull up a leg and use one of the claws on my left paw to slice through the cord binding my hands. I hiss as I catch the inside of my right wrist.

The blood soaks into my chest as I unwrap the rest of the cord.

From there it's a simple matter to free my tail, which is pounding to let me know I've been blocking blood flow by laying on it. I'm still bleeding heavily as I pull myself out of the chamber, my purple blood smearing across the chamber as I leverage myself up and out.

My vision swims as I look around. There is a heavy canopy of bright green above me, the long brown tree trunks with rough bark leading down to an understory of mostly purple plants.

I swivel my ears, listening for any of the telltale wet sounds of genali, but only hear a variety of fauna. I take another long breath to confirm that none of the slimes are nearby, then look at the forest surrounding me. There are broken limbs, wheel marks, and what look like the footfalls of a heavy animal between them.

My whiskers droop as I try to work through it, but I'm distracted by the flow of blood dripping from my fingers.

It's an awkward process, but it doesn't take me long to cut a strip of the strapping and tie it around the wound. That should speed up my scales shifting.

As I bind the wound, an image of the genali's horror-filled eyes flits through my mind.

It should bother me that I killed them.

Shouldn't it?

My mind pulls away from the thought of killing, like a practiced response. And yet there is no niggling horror or the tremor of regret passing through my limbs. I'm at peace with causing their deaths.

Which is what bothers me, of course.

I wonder what my sire felt when he killed them? It's a thought process that has plagued most my life and as always, there is no answer.

For now, I can simply avoid the slimes and leave philosophical issues for later.

I keep listening for sounds of the enemy but it's a lack of sound that I suddenly notice. I turn back to the cryochamber and confirm that I no longer hear its gentle hum.

Did they really put me in a chamber without a backup power source?

It's a simple matter to puncture the thin metal with my claws and rip off the protective paneling to find out. After a quick inspection, I confirm it has all the usual components. There's simply no power to keep the nanites active now that I'm no longer in it. Typical crude slime manufacturing.

But what if it isn't?

There are several known planets where technology is rendered inoperable—for a variety of reasons I never bothered to research. Could this be one of them?

I try to narrow down the options. My eyes unfocus as pieces of overheard conversations filter through my mind. I remember the many calls with my mother where she shared her latest vidfeed-induced fear for my safety. Then I remember the slime talking about how valuable I was.

I let out a snarl as I figure it out. I'm on their Thela-forsaken hunting ground.

7

Ree

I'm in front of Silver's chamber again. It's becoming a habit. One I know I must break or the slimes will notice and use it against me.

Or worse, use it against her.

But somehow she's become my anchor. The one keeping my mind from fracturing, even though I know it isn't logical. Even though I know it's an unfair burden to place on her.

Our brief conversation wasn't nearly enough to help ease the intervening days of being alone with my terror. I'm not sure why they let so much time go by between waking another of the women. Or why they have only woken up two so far. Or even what the point is of only having me awake.

Maybe the goal is for me to be lonely. If so, they've been wildly successful.

I desperately need someone to talk to.

The ever-present guilt surges when I think about how horrific it is each time one of the women is woken up, and yet I can't help but ache for their company.

For someone to share this hell with me and for once maybe to have someone tell me it's going to be alright.

I choke up on that thought, the despair so big it leaves no room for breath or clear thinking. I make myself walk away. It isn't Silver's responsibility to protect me.

It's mine to protect her. To protect all of them, just like I've always done.

It's just another day in the ER, Ree, I tell myself. That's a far better form of horror and a soothing sort of pretend.

The realization brings clarity and enough purpose to crowd out the lurking hopelessness. To wallow is to let the slimes win and that would be intolerable.

If they weren't such a persistent presence in my mind I would say the thought summoned them.

The creak of the observation room hatch pulls my attention. Three have come for today's entertainment. The slime on the left lets his eyes roam over me and I stare back dispassionately.

It has long since stopped bothering me.

"You aren't being interesting, human," says Left Slime. "I know you're doing it on purpose, so if you want to avoid another round of gas you need to provide our viewers with more entertainment."

I nod at him, letting him know I heard him.

I learned early on that it's best to not respond verbally unless I must, but to not respond at all just invites pain.

I doubt that's the reason they came in here. Usually when they make threats like that it turns out to be just a pretense. An excuse to talk about something else and ignore me.

Sometimes they flood my chamber with gas; sometimes it's just an idle threat.

When Left Slime turns away from me to Right Slime, I have my answer. "Open the pink whore's chamber."

I keep the grimace off my face, but I can't avoid the surge of self-reproach. Careful what you wish for, as they say.

I hasten to the front of Coral's chamber and have just enough time to help ease her fall before both of our bodies are wracked with coughing.

The woman rubs her eyes once the gas is vented out and looks around. For the first time, there is no screaming.

I reach forward and touch her arm. "I know you're scared. I'm here. We were abducted. They took us," I say as I jerk my chin toward them.

Her fully pink eyes sharpen on the three slimes, then return to me. "They do that to you?"

I nod, knowing she means my eyes and hair. "Yours are pale pink."

She scoffs, then looks down to the soft coral waves tangled up in her naked limbs, the color a striking contrast to her cinnamon skin tone. She picks up one long lock and then flings it away. "Couldn't even get the texture right."

I blink, surprised at how calm she is. "I'd share my name, but they punish us with the gas when I try. I've just been calling you Coral and myself Indigo"

"Fuck that shit. My name's Kira."

I cringe, but I like her spirit.

Thankfully, the slimes seem to be ignoring us. "I'm Ree. It's a relief to not think of you as a color anymore."

She lets out a muted dark chuckle. "Oh, I'm used to that."

I'm too agitated to fully appreciate her dark humor, though she reminds me a bit of Tamina. If Tam was a complete badass.

I look back over to the slimes as a wave of homesickness passes over me.

They must be distracted today, or we'd be coughing by now. They're sharing nasty jokes and Kira wrinkles her nose.

"They aren't speaking English."

I shake my head. "No, we have translators."

"What else?"

I take a deep breath. "We heal faster. Adapt to new environments. We'll keep changing, somehow, depending on who we're around. Who, uh, buys us."

She pulls a face, but doesn't comment and I go on. "That belt around your waist will expand to clothes but if you do it they punish you. You'll be aroused and can't control it. There's a live feed."

I look toward the camera and she follows my gaze. The three slimes let out a chorus of honking laughs after a particularly gruesome joke and both of us focus on them again.

The slime in the middle moves forward to press against the glass, leaving disgusting blush-colored mucus smudges in order to get a better look at the rest of the women.

I assume that's the one who seems to have a particular interest in Ruby. Like all the women, she is beautiful and her red hair sets off her porcelain skin to good effect. She is tall and willowy. The type of woman I assume is a dancer or a model.

The slime on the right seems bored and is picking at the short claws rising from his webbed fingers.

I wonder if the rest of the ship is full of water, since their features suggest they are at least partially aquatic. I have seen no evidence of gills, but since my xenobiological experience is nil, I recognize that means very little.

Left Slime turns to Middle Slime. "We're nearing the hunting grounds."

This causes Middle to shift his bulbous eyes away from Ruby to join the conversation. "I hear they stocked it with a whole new range of species this year."

Left seems to shiver in excitement. Or something. I don't really know if I understand their non-verbal communication, even after dozens of observations.

Right sounds less impressed, but still shares what he knows. "They did. After rumors started up about how easy the prey was they focused on much deadlier challenges this season for the southern hemisphere. Some of the most terrifying and grotesque they could find."

Left breaks in, no longer able to contain his excitement. "I heard they caught a manticorid."

"You lie," shoots back Middle, which earns him a gurgling hiss from Left.

"There was a vidfeed about it," whines back Left. "Apparently the beast took out two traders trying to sedate it in transit. They placed it in the southern continent along with the rest of the more dangerous prey."

"Won't it just kill all the rest?" Right asks this with the same bored tone I had picked up from his body language.

Maybe I'm getting better at reading them after all. Kira and I share a look.

Left rises and his voice sounds annoyed. "Is your head dry? Don't you watch any of the feeds? They are loaded with blocks against killing other prey. No one wants to pay millions of credits to capture and transport them just to have them destroy each other before they can be taken as a prize."

Right makes their equivalent of a grunt in response. "They made a mistake adding a manticorid. What stops them from forming an army?"

That seems like a reasonable question.

It causes a lull in the conversation when none of them can answer it. For the first time since finding myself in this miserable cell, I'm actually excited about what the fiends have come in to talk about.

I mean, that it's a planet they use for blood sport is disturbing, but something killing them is extremely satisfying. I can tell Kira is just as interested by the strength of her gaze.

I love the idea of something scaring them, since I certainly never will. I'm small and completely untrained in any sort of self-defense. I went into medicine because I enjoy helping, not harming.

Had I known the slimes existed I might have reconsidered a few life choices.

"It has never happened," Left continues after a long pause. "They are all taken from primitive planets and don't speak each other's languages."

"Manticorids are technologically advanced," points out Right. "We get most of our tech by stealing from the dry headed, limp dick pacifists. Not to mention I doubt any blocks placed on them will work very long. If at all."

That piques my interest.

I hope that means there are even more species in the universe who might be advanced enough to crush these bastards like the leeches they are. I work hard to keep the look of disgust off my face and must manage it or we would be choking on gas right now.

Middle makes a dismissive sound. "I'm sure they would take away its technology, and without it they are just like any felidae. Just a giant version of a tasty snack."

I feel sick when I realize he's talking about cats. I love cats. I think of my sweet, demanding brown tabby. I'm sure someone has found him in my apartment by now, but I miss him with a sharp jolt in my heart.

I have to blink rapidly to keep tears from falling.

"Except with venom," scoffs Right, the gurgling puff of wind causing slime to fleck away from him and land on the floor. "A pacifist wouldn't have killed those traders."

A huge venomous cat sounds like just the enemy they deserve. I look over to Kira. The small smirk on her lips and the narrowing of her eyes makes me think she agrees with me.

I'm fairly sure the look Middle shoots Right is one of annoyance, though it's hard to tell since their faces look like melting wax over whale blubber and the only clue is how much their eyes bulge.

"But how do we really know what happens down there? The same interference that makes location technology useless, and of course the hunt more exciting, makes recording impossible."

Middle says this like they find the last highly disappointing.

"How do we even know they actually hunt the prey at all? There is never any actual evidence and for all we know they can get trophies by poisoning prey."

"Hunters die every year," points out Left. "I'm sure you've seen the feeds of the ones that have been recovered. Ripped to shreds, torn apart, pieces missing. And those are just the few they ever find."

I don't like how excited he sounds, but just imagining these three meeting such a well-earned fate makes me want to smile. To think me, a nurse, would be driven to the point of wanting to grin over some monster tearing someone's limbs off...

But if any species has earned it, the slimes have.

Middle turns back to us. "The pink one is poor entertainment. Ratings are going down. Bring out the red one."

"The purple one is on the schedule next," says Right.

Middle lets out a whine. "I'll take a third of your next shift if you bring out the red one."

"Half."

Middle deflates, but agrees. "Go back to your chamber, pink slut."

She lifts a middle finger at him. "Fuck you."

Right Slime presses down on the control to punish us.

She refuses two more times as I hack and cry right along next to her. I'm proud of her, despite the pain. They are demanding her obedience again as I wipe the tears from my eyes.

Kira looks over at me. I can see the question on her face.

"I'll support whatever you decide," I tell her.

Then we are choking again.

When it lets up she looks at me, looks at the slime and his flipper hand poised over the controls and rises. There's a stillness about her and a calculation in her eyes that makes me think this woman is dangerous.

The exact type I want on my side.

"You're dead," she promises Right Slime.

She turns to me as they start up a round of honking laughs. "I'll see you soon," she tells me.

It's the closest anyone's come to comforting me in a very long time and I choke on the rising swell of emotion it causes.

Then she stands up, climbs back in, and engages the controls herself before the slime can do it. There's a hiss of gasses and then she is still. I stare at her sleeping form in shock.

I don't think I could make myself do it, but I admire her for taking that little bit of power away from them.

"I wonder if the captain would take a detour," says Left in a wistful tone and I take a moment to realize they are back to talking about the hunting grounds.

"I'm sure the captain is going to skirt well around the interference and we will be past the planet in a few more minutes," comments Middle. Left deflates. Literally. His mass seems to pull tighter, and he shrinks closer to the ground.

Right blows a very wet raspberry. "Don't you think the conglomerate might notice if the harem's tracking devices all turned off at the same time?"

Great. We have tracking devices.

Nothing about this news is a surprise, really. That doesn't mean hearing it feels any better. I'm distracted by the news and as a result don't move to Ruby's chamber fast enough to help her transition to her new reality. She is screaming after a moment of taking in the environment.

There is no choking gas to interrupt her.

"Delicious," moans out Middle.

I attempt to console her but she pushes me away. She falls to the floor with a sick thud, mewling in pain.

Middle is still making his disgusting noises of appreciation. Left is still whining.

"It's just such a shame to be this close and not be able to pop down to the planet. I hear the resort on the island has any sort of low-tech distraction you could ever—"

He never finishes his sentence.

The ear-splitting alarm that interrupts him makes me startle and look around wildly. The slimes move as soon as they hear it. Left and Right hustle back toward the hatch.

Middle turns to me. The strobing red lights are disorienting, but he has an expression I've never seen on them before.

"She will die if you don't get her back in," he yells at me over the sound of the alarm and Ruby's continual screeching.

A shudder rocks the ship and I believe him.

I turn to her. She's pushed back up against the base of her chamber, her fully red eyes wide and terrified. I try to move toward her again, but she's much taller than me and has horror infusing her limbs and lending her strength.

I go sprawling when she pushes me a second time.

Another shudder and the slime yells out again. "I'll leave her to die."

I scramble up, this time moving fast to get past her flailing arms. I slap her across the face as hard as I can. She stops screaming, startled.

"Stand up," I yell at her in between the sounds of the klaxon blaring.

She does and I push her with all my strength so she falls back into her cryochamber, then I barely move out of the way fast enough to avoid getting my hands crushed by the glass covering.

She throws her hands onto it, pounding and screaming curses at me, but then falls still once again.

"Get in your chamber, human," the slime orders me. "You're too valuable to be lost."

Then he exits from the hatch, closing it behind him.

8

Ree

I'm still standing in shock as the door closes behind him and the first shuddering explosion rocks through the ship.

It knocks me into my cryobed, then I bounce back off and fall heavily onto the slick floor. Pain shoots up my left knee from the impact, then my body is flung down the passage where the rest of the harem is stored. I crash into the cryocoffin at the end, immediately feeling the telltale ache of cracked ribs.

The spike of pain that follows my next breath confirms it.

"The hell! We're in space," I complain, not understanding what could cause these shifts if the ship itself supplies artificial gravity.

But physics was never a strength of mine.

Right now I feel pinned to the floor. Is the ship malfunctioning? From the sounds I assume it's being attacked, even though I don't really have any obvious reference points based on experience. The blaring alarm seems to confirm it.

As much as I don't enjoy following the slime's orders, it seems like the best course of action is to get back to my cryocoffin-cum-bed and close the protective glass.

Or whatever it's made of, since glass would have cracked under the force of me hitting it, but the chamber I collided with shows no sign of damage. I'm glad, since I would have then had to figure out how to move Silver out of her damaged chamber and into my own.

And then, judging by the shuddering explosions I feel, the rest of this ship would truly be my coffin.

The heavy weight pinning me to the floor suddenly eases.

I crawl down the passage toward the relative safety of my chamber as fast as I can, trying to ignore the pain radiating from my ribs and knee. The ship continues to shudder, then I'm abruptly lifted off the ground, weightless. This improves my pain levels, but leaves me spinning in the air wildly until I can get a hand solidly around one of the chamber handles.

It's Azure's chamber that I grab and it doesn't seem possible that someone could be so still and unconcerned with such pandemonium all around them.

I take a moment to get my bearings and for the dizziness to pass and I realize I need to reverse directions and get my feet spun around toward the floor. The process of turning myself is excruciating and my ribs are on fire, but I do it anyway.

I move myself through the air by pushing myself from one chamber handle to the next, not realizing until I push off from the last one that I'm moving too fast out of their hallway and into my small cell.

I brace my arms in front of me, which helps absorb some of the impact as I collide with the wall that holds the camera. My right arm braces more effectively than my left because I'm at a bit of an angle, which starts me on a spin toward the left of the cell.

I ping-pong off the wall after hitting it with my back, my foot catches on the bed and I spin again, with my feet moving toward the ceiling. I grind my teeth against the pain and shoot out my arms, successfully snagging the edge of my cryocoffin.

The hated camera catches my eye.

"I hope you enjoyed the show, assholes," I yell at it.

I take a few moments to get myself properly oriented, then I use the internal handles of the chamber to pull myself into a lying position.

For the first time since waking up in this cell, I appreciate one of my harem's upgrades, since it allows me to read the text on the touch screen.

I stab a finger at the 'close' option, relieved when the cover extends and snicks closed.

I feel a sudden pressure on my back as I'm pulled tight against the soft lining of the chamber. The intense feeling of claustrophobia I get is improved slightly when I realize I can still move my arms.

After witnessing Silver's terror and paralysis, I haven't been able to get anything but fitful rest when using this thing as a bed.

Nightmares of waking up and not being able to move have plagued me ever since.

There are no straps and I have no idea how the chamber is managing it, but I'm being held in place so I don't ricochet around.

I carefully avoid touching anything else for fear of accidentally putting myself to sleep. I'll admit that I have begged the universe to let me have a break from the terror, but this is not the time. I'm breathing heavily and shaking. Each breath is like being stabbed with thousands of knives and so I focus on getting my panic under control.

As I do, I rethink the nickname I gave these cryocoffins now that I'm in one and feeling far safer than I did just moments ago.

It helps that I was the one who put myself in here. I look out to the other women in their chambers. They look exactly the same. Long hair draping over their upright bodies. Eyes closed like they are sleeping peacefully.

I can still feel shudders, even now that I'm in my chamber and held in place.

Several long minutes later, just as my breathing is no longer elevated so the stabbing pain happens at a more controlled spacing, the shuddering gets far worse. Rather than intermittent explosions, the shaking is constant and is steadily increasing in violence.

When a giant fissure opens up in the ceiling of the long cryochamber hallway, I understand why.

The outside of the ship is on fire.

Considering we were just flying through space and there is no oxygen to burn out there, we must be crash landing on a planet. I have a moment to appreciate my penchant for science fiction movies helping me make that deduction before my mind shuts down that train of thought in sheer terror.

The fissure widens, mostly staying along the ceiling.

The cryochambers are holding in place, but have started to shudder. When the opening extends down the wall toward one of the chambers, whatever was holding Navy's chamber down loses the battle to stay affixed.

She hurtles toward the jagged edge of the hole and it shatters the protective covering, then in another blink she disappears out the burning opening.

It feels like a shot to the heart, and I let out a keening cry.

Although it all happened too fast for me to see exactly what happened, I'm certain Navy is dead. I assume these chambers were designed to withstand damage, but that clearly exceeded their parameters.

Tears stream down my face when I realize I'll never know the woman's name. Or anything else about her.

Losing her is like a gaping wound in my mind.

She may not be the only one to die.

My chamber isn't shaking yet, I assume because of the relative protection of my slightly offset room, but others are moving more violently. Olivia's chamber shoots out the opening and I cry out again in anguish. The fire clears a moment later.

I'm pretty sure hers was still intact as she flew out.

"Please, please let her be alive," I sob out.

I can only hope that the chambers were made to survive a crash landing on their own.

Soon after, the ship spins and I catch glimpses of heavily forested land, then the sky, then back to the land. I make myself stop looking because the force of the spin and the rapidly changing colors is making me sick. Still, I have to keep opening my eyes to check on the rest of the women.

One by one, more of the chambers break loose and fly out of the opening.

The only chamber, aside from my own, that is still in the ship is Silver's. It's currently wedged against a jagged edge of the ceiling or it would have already been ejected.

I have this inane moment of panic at the thought of her leaving me alone, then our plummet comes to a sudden, violent halt.

Silver's chamber crashes forcefully to the floor.

I'm dazed for an unknown amount of time following the impact. Even with the chamber to protect me, it felt like my brain tried to flatten out when the ship met the unforgiving ground.

I take a quick stock of how my body feels. My ribs and knee still hurt, but I assume the nanites have been at work because the pain levels are diminished.

I don't seem to have picked up any additional injuries.

When I look back out, I see that Silver wasn't as lucky.

Her chamber is on its side, the protective glass shattered and she looks like a rag doll, bent at the waist and partially hanging out of it. The glass is cutting into her stomach and blood is seeping from a large gash in her forehead, mixing with the silver of her hair.

"No, no, no, no!"

I scramble to get out to help her, initially unable to remember how I got inside to begin with.

"Get your shit together!"

9

Ree

My hand is still trembling as I press the touchscreen 'open' option, but my mind is back under control.

I take a relieved, painful breath when it allows me to exit. After being stuck in a cell for weeks, the thought of being trapped in an even smaller space is terrifying.

I push myself out, gritting my teeth against the pain and then hobble over to Silver, my heart breaking when she continues to lay still. Then I see the slight movement of her breathing as I keep moving toward her and let out a relieved whistle.

I don't like the idea of moving her without knowing if she has spinal injuries, but her weight is steadily making the broken glass-like material of the chamber cut deeper and deeper into her stomach.

It goes against my training, but it's better to risk permanent spinal injury than to leave her to die to gravity. I put my arms under hers, then lift with all my strength.

She slips out and I tumble backwards under her weight, then shift her off of me.

I feel terrible when I see the deep scores I've left down her hips and legs because I wasn't able to fully lift her body off the jagged edge.

Then it occurs to me that considering how much larger she is than me, deep scrapes are a small price. She's a tall, curvy woman. I'm not even sure how I could lift her at all.

In fact, now that I no longer have that spike in strength, I struggle to drag her away from her chamber so I can lay her flat.

I have to take a moment to catch my breath and steady my shaking hands, then I ensure her neck is stabilized. Her stomach and head are bleeding heavily and I have nothing to use to staunch the blood flow. Nothing to use to stitch it up.

Her pulse is still steady and her breathing is even. It's possible her nanites will heal this, but I have no proper way to know.

I look around wildly, already knowing there is nothing here to help me, but still hoping.

There is no longer any light coming from the ship, with just our chambers providing internal illumination. I look up at the ceiling, noting that there is some muted natural light coming from above. It's a miracle we landed upright.

I'll have to figure out a way to get up there and see where we are, but that will have to wait.

I feel sick at how helpless I am.

I'm a trained professional, but I'm used to having a hospital and all its many tools available to me. I know that without them I can do very little to save this woman.

I jerk my head toward my cryochamber, realizing it's her best option. I hate the idea of putting her back into what equates to a jail cell. After her last experience, they are probably her absolute worst nightmare.

I hope she'll know that my intent differs greatly from the slimes when they put her in the one that lays broken open behind us.

I clench my jaw against my pain, hoping I'm not about to cause her further injury, and then start dragging her the few feet needed to get her to the base of my chamber. I step on broken glass, hissing in pain but simply keep pulling.

I doubt she has much time.

When I get her there, I'm unsure how I can get her in it.

I try to heave her up, but the small burst of strength I had in order to save her from the broken chamber doesn't come a second time.

"Think, dammit!"

I haven't been this rattled in years, but there is a process to follow and tools to use in an ER.

Here I have nothing and living in terror for weeks has left me frayed.

The amount of blood pooling on the ground lets me know I need to figure something out very, very quickly. The flow seems to have slowed, but I know she can't afford to lose much more. I look around, but there's nothing I can use to leverage her weight.

I panic, then remember the touch screen of the chamber.

My hand smears blood across it as I tap through different settings. I ignore 'close,' 'freeze,' and 'open.' When I see 'load' I jab it quickly, then yelp when I lift off the ground.

A quick glance lets me know Silver is also being raised into the air. I throw my arms out, bracing myself against anything I can find, which really just comes down to squeaking along the wall.

Luckily this slows my movement down just enough for the chamber to get Silver mostly lifted into it ahead of me.

Suddenly we're unceremoniously dropped. I bang my jaw on the edge of the chamber, then fall hard on my left elbow and hip. I only allow myself a moment to process the new layers of pain this adds before pushing myself to my feet.

She is only partially in the chamber and I have to heave her legs inside, a small scream trying to bubble up from the pain it causes me.

I don't know how much time she has and so I press 'freeze' as quickly as I can.

The glass door moves sluggishly and I help it snick into place with shaking hands. I take a relieved breath when it fills with a mix of different colored gas. A moment later they clear and I can see Silver resting within.

Blood is no longer flowing and I let out an explosive puff of air.

Then groan from the pain.

"Fuck."

With that task done, my energy plummets and my back slowly slides down the glass of the observation room. I take a moment to yank out the shard of glass embedded in my foot and with that, I complete the only task left to drive me and help me keep it together.

The thought of slimes coming in right now turns my trembling to violent shaking, but for the moment my body is not responding. Recognizing the symptoms of shock doesn't help me overcome it any faster, unfortunately.

Not only that, but I also suddenly realize that I opened my chamber with no idea if the air was breathable.

All I know about bacteria and viruses bubbles up uninvited. My brain burns from an overload of fear and my breathing is ragged for several long minutes.

Eventually I push all the unhelpful thoughts down and slouch in a daze.

I'm not positive how long I take to collect myself, but no slimes come in to check on me. I hope they're all dead, but if they provided us chambers to protect us I highly doubt they didn't have as good of protection, or better.

I really need to get out of here while I still can.

I look over to Silver, feeling extremely guilty. If I couldn't even lift her, there's no way I'll be able to take her chamber with me. There are no doors. Only a jagged hole in the ceiling. I can't figure out how to get her out, but the thought of leaving her is heart-wrenching.

It's just plain wrong.

But there's no real choice. I wouldn't want her to stay because of me, though I would hope that she would return if she could. I'll come back if I can figure out a way to heal her or get her chamber out of this hellish place.

"I-I'll return for you, Silver. I promise."

That decided, I make myself stand, which hurts like hell, but now that I've decided to leave, I don't want to stay here a moment longer.

I can't.

My throat is raw from how fast and harsh my breathing is and I take another moment to center myself. Then I look back up and see the hatch that has opened dozens of times, bringing torment with it, and I'm locked in place by remembered terror.

My heart is pounding and my vision is blurred.

"Fucking move, bitch," I growl at myself.

I lick my parched lips, tasting the sweat that is beaded on my lip, then pull a shaky hand across my forehead to prevent more of the stinging liquid from getting in my eyes.

I move jerkily, with great pain, toward the edge of the room to a ladder. Before the crash it went to a locked access tube. Now I'm able to use it to raise myself, one trembling step up at a time, just high enough to grab ahold of the shredded remains of the ship's hull.

The realization that less than a foot of different layers of metal once separated us from outer space is terrifying to know. The giant gash in the hull is a testament to how unsafe the voyage had been, but it seems like a species that could invent cryochambers that just survived flying through the sky should be able to keep their ship together.

What do I know? I'm no engineer.

When I finally manage to scramble up, I get a good view of the ship. We're in a small remaining hunk of it. Or at least I assume there must have been more of it than what now seems to amount to not much more than my cell, the hallway the other women were stored in, and the observation room.

Where we were severed from the ship looks like a surprisingly clean, straight cut.

From the shape, I assume we were in some sort of outer wing. There are burn marks and it's obvious the ceiling lost structural integrity because our entire section split off from the rest of the vessel. Had it stayed intact we would have all remained together. After a moment of regret that the other women were scattered to who knows where, I realize that without this tear we would have also been trapped.

Likely simply waiting here until we were recovered and sent along to auction.

"But how can I possibly protect them now?"

Who am I kidding? I can't even get Silver to safety.

The stark reality of just how fucked up all of this is doesn't remove my sense of duty.

I'm the only person who knows where they are. Well, kind of knows where they are. Either way, I guarantee no one else on this planet will consider them as anything but slaves.

Which is probably a best-case scenario.

Aside from maybe Kira, I doubt any of the women were awake and aware long enough to have the same sense of responsibility. And she seemed like a hard woman who might not consider it a worthwhile risk to search for them. I let out a broken, mirthless laugh.

If I'm their only hope, lord help them.

I have to keep wiping away tears as I look out to the forest surrounding us.

I don't think it's just because I live in a city that it seems particularly thick and wild. It feels completely untamed. And now that I know we aren't attached to the rest of the ship, where I assume all the slimes were, I'm wondering if my plan to leave is wise.

From the brief conversation I overheard, I assume we've crashed on an alien hunting ground, where their prey are likely to be as deadly to me as the hunters.

Can I believe what the slimes said about our tracking devices not working on this planet? What dangers lurk in that forest if hunters—who I assume don't come here if they aren't confident they can survive—get torn to pieces out there?

I bite my lip until I taste blood and continue scanning, hoping that something about the view will help me decide.

10

Thivoll

When I see the ship hit the atmosphere and break apart I know right away it's a genali cruiser.

Genali technology, or any technology, doesn't work well on this planet. Anything that relies on external power inputs doesn't function. Some power sources react explosively to the atmosphere, which might explain the damage done to the ship.

I don't feel any sympathy for them.

Just like I haven't been able to dredge up any for the ones I killed, regardless of how ambivalent I feel about it in relation to everything I was taught as a kit.

When you wake up and realize you've been abducted, it's hard to stamp down the instinct to rip out something's throat, even if most of your time in life has been spent cleaning vent systems.

I wonder how much the genali hunting me for sport would appreciate knowing that the prey they spent millions of credits to be allowed on this planet to track is essentially a janitor. I tip my head back and let out a chuff at the thought.

My mane shifts against my ears and I flick them forward, then back to ensure I'm still carefully listening to my surroundings.

I'll likely have numerous hunters hoping to add me to their trophy wall.

A quick image of my ugly face, purple lips pulled back in a snarl, black teeth bared, some poor semblance of my golden eyes flashing and mounted to a wall makes me chuff again.

Let them come.

They will quickly realize they are outmatched.

I look down, realizing those thoughts made my claws extend. I carefully sharpened them on a fallen log this morning, then flipped it over to hide the evidence. They are naturally sharp, but I never had any reason or motivation to remove the outer claw layers to make them into deadly razors—aside from keeping my index claws honed to help clean vent edges.

The two claws that extend from the thumbs on each side of my hands I have only used a few times in my adult life, and those times just out of curiosity. They are designed for latching on. My ancestors used these to keep an enemy stationary long enough to violently whip their tails around and deliver a load of venom.

From all accounts, the process floods a manticorid with a sense of euphoria, which explains why it took us so long to move past that stage in our social evolution.

I suppose as a species we'll soon be finding out how we can reconcile battle euphoria with our peaceful social mores. I avoid thinking about how I'll react.

I wonder how many of us the genali will move to their hunting grounds before whatever method they used stops working.

Not that they would place me anywhere near any of my fellow manticorids, so I suppose it doesn't matter.

I twitch my tail in irritation even thinking about the genali having a momentary advantage over us, since their sheer numbers are already enough of a menace.

My tail spikes respond to my emotional state by extending. I don't bother to look, since I'm certain they're dripping venom. Too bad—for them at least—the disgusting things never developed an antidote, let alone any immunity to it.

If they come for me, I will be prepared.

11

Ree

The only thing the forest tells me after scanning for long minutes is that it's getting dark and it looks just as thick, wild, and dangerous as ever out there.

After brief consideration, I decide it would be best to wait until morning before I go out into the trees. Hopefully, by then some of my injuries will have healed enough to make it safer.

I continue to stare out into the forest, which looks quite a bit like Earth, except for where I would expect to see leaves it looks more like bristly feathers. The greens of the plants are all so much brighter than I'm used to, but at least they are green.

I'm not sure what I would expect when being on an alien planet, but it makes me feel better that these plants clearly photosynthesize. I hope the night here won't last too long. As I'm thinking about that, a breeze picks up, making the feather-like leaves rustle.

Even the sound is distinct.

It's funny how after an event as disturbing as a crash landing it's that one minor detail that makes me most unsettled.

I doubt situations like these really hold up to any clear mental process to help a person make sense of it, and I know enough about shock to know I'm still suffering from it.

Everything I see seems to take on an overlay of menace. I know it's the fear of the unknown, which is pretty damn reasonable. And yet I know I will soon be out in it because I fear the slimes far, far more.

The breeze brings with it a cool air that raises goosebumps along my body. I look down at myself, surprised to see I'm still naked. I suppose it wasn't really at the top of the priority list.

Still, after spending weeks wishing I could be dressed, I find it weird that it took me so long to realize there was nothing stopping me anymore.

I concentrate on the desire to be covered, and just like it did that first day I woke up to this nightmare, the strip of fabric around my waist quickly expands to cover the rest of my body. I can feel the material becoming thick at the soles of my feet because it raises me slightly higher.

I found out early that it responds to my desire to be covered by expanding out into a black bodysuit, but it was made very clear that if I wanted to avoid any more of the stinging gas that invaded my small cell and left me hacking on the floor with my eyes streaming I wouldn't do it again.

The sleeves extend down to my hands, forming fingerless gloves and I can feel the material snug around my neck.

I experiment with another thought, imagining that the material covers my fingers, and it responds. That might be useful, for sure. For now, I focus on imagining the material stopping at my wrist, and it shrinks back.

I panic and nearly fall off the ladder when I let an errant curiosity about if it will cover my entire body flit through my mind. The black fabric covers my eyes and mouth for a moment before it occurs to me to imagine my face uncovered.

Well, that answers that not fully realized question. "Real smart," I grumble.

I'm surprised the slimes gave us something so incredibly useful. Or that it responds to mental commands. Then it occurs to me that if I can respond to my thoughts, it could respond to others, and so it's likely a package upgrade.

It's not as if I wasn't quickly trained that I wasn't allowed to clothe myself without permission.

"Like a good little bitch."

My self-loathing tries to crawl out of my skin and become a physical presence. If it did, it would probably kill me. That's just what I would need as the cherry atop this fucked-up sundae.

I shake my head, flinging off the inane thoughts.

"Just focus on what you can do right now."

Being dressed is an improvement, so that feels like a step forward.

The material of the suit helps some, but I can still feel the cold seeping through. This makes my previous decision to remain with the broken ship for the night seem like an even better idea.

All I can hope is that the slimes don't come in the middle of the night, but since night vision clearly wasn't one of my upgrades, I wouldn't accomplish much if I left now.

I descend the ladder and return to Silver. She is just as I left her, and I feel another pang that I don't have the supplies to help her.

I would also very much like someone to talk to and strategize with right now.

I can tell it's rapidly getting darker outside because the small amount of ambient light starts to disappear. I can still see by the light of the cryochambers, though I should probably see if I can power off Silver's broken chamber, just in case it might be useful later. I don't know how long their charge will last without the feed from the ship.

The thought of it being even darker in here makes the back of my neck prickle and my heart beat faster, so I leave it alone for now.

Speaking of feeds, I realize that I'm now cut off from my food and water supply.

I glance over to the dispenser I once drank out of like a giant gerbil. My movements are stiff as I go over to it. I lean down and position my mouth under it and push the button. I get a small mouthful before it gurgles and stops.

Even though it hurts to keep myself in place, I linger to make sure I suck in every drop.

I'll need to find water as soon as I can in the morning.

That I don't really know how to find anything in a forest isn't a comforting thought. I've never had to think of that before, since I've always lived in large cities.

The list of what I don't know and likely need to in order to survive this experience is completely overwhelming.

I'm depleted and give in to the overwhelming desire to sleep by laying down on the gray floor at the base of Silver's new cryochamber.

The light of her old chamber winks out, leaving me feeling like I'm blind in addition to helpless to any threat. Exhaustion quickly overtakes it all.

Even my shivering isn't enough to keep me awake, and I feel myself drifting into unconsciousness.

12

Thivoll

I've been walking in the dark for some time now.

Periodically, I readjust my trajectory so I can keep myself headed toward the direction I saw the closest ship piece fall. I'm walking on my back paws, making sure my tread is silent and ready to tip forward at any time for a burst of quadruped speed.

For now, I like the added perspective gained at this height.

This leg shape makes walking on two limbs somewhat ungraceful, but when I tip forward onto my hands, with my back claws extended and ripping into the soil, I'm able to run at impressive speeds.

I wish I could do so now, since I haven't experienced the joy of running like that for years. Space station floors don't hold up to the abuse and it's frowned upon.

I'm sure there will be reason enough to do so soon, but for now I would only leave deep furrows in the ground that would make it easy to track me.

So easy that even rich genali playing at hunters could manage it. I suppose at a slow run I'll leave almost no trace.

I tip forward so I can make faster progress.

I assume the season must have just started here or I would have already come across hunters. I've yet to find a place that seems worth trying to create a den. A cave would be nice, but only if it had more than one exit.

So far the land has been fairly flat, with a few natural clearings, but mostly heavily wooded.

I was lucky enough to be in one of those clearings when the genali ship crashed or I wouldn't have been able to get a good bearing on the direction it was falling.

I'm thankful for my species' ease in navigating terrain. I'm certain the genali are finding it much more difficult. It's actually surprising any of them would subject themselves to the challenge considering how few natural advantages they have when technology is no longer available.

Thinking of them must have brought them to me, because I suddenly smell their acrid scent. The wind has been brisk tonight and moving from the west.

It's possible the ones I smell aren't hunters at all, but are instead crash survivors, but I'm going to assume anything I come across on this Thela-cursed planet is hostile.

That should improve my chances.

The scent is faint and intermittent. I decide it would be best to rest for a while, rather than go out seeking my prey. I walk a while longer, looking for a good tree. One that will be comfortable and also effectively hide my presence.

I haven't climbed one since my youth. The trees suited to growing in a space station are nothing like these tall, imposing figures with their fluffy plumes of light green.

I come across a suitable candidate, with a thick trunk that leads to a heavy canopy. It's tempting to dig my claws in and scramble up the tree as I did when I was young, but I can't risk leaving evidence. Instead I hook my arms around the tree and carefully find places to insert my claws between bark pieces. I brace by back paws against the trunk and scoot myself up the tree in that manner.

I lash my tail imagining how I must look.

Mane fluffed out, arms grasping the tree in an embrace, the toes of my back paws splayed as I slowly hop-wiggle my way up the tree. I push my whiskers forward in amusement, thinking of how much my friends would chuff at me right now. I doubt I'll see them again and the thought brings my whiskers back toward my face.

I try to avoid thinking about people I won't get to speak to again as I continue climbing.

I'm pleased with my tree choice once I get into the dense canopy. The leaves extend down past a thick, almost horizontal branch. I pad my way out, then lay my body along it, hands and paws dangling down. I double check to ensure my tail, which dips down much lower than my back paws, is still well hidden, then tuck the whiskers on the left side of my face close to my cheek and rest my muzzle on the branch.

Just to be extra cautious, I wrap my tail a couple times around the branch so the bright orange and purple plumes at the end of it don't attract attention.

It will remain coiled like that as I sleep.

The wind picks up, sending a pleasant breeze to ruffle my fur. I've spent a lot of time in vents and so I appreciate the hard work that goes into keeping station air scrubbed and fresh. It simply cannot approach the quality of air and lovely weather of this planet.

If only this could be a pleasant vacation instead of me being on the cusp of having to fight for my life.

***

My limbs are looser and my mind clearer when I wake up.

After carefully listening to my surroundings I descend part way and then hop down out of the tree. I follow the smell of water to a nearby stream and drink my fill. A few more minutes of careful waiting and a quick darting of my claws and I have a wriggling prize in my hand.

Soon after, I'm tossing back a few of the planet's aquatic creatures as a morning snack.

Although I should make haste to the crash site, I still take the time to scoop water out of the stream to wash my face, then extend the tips of my claws so I can run them through my long mane.

I might strike more fear into the hunters if I didn't, but I have my pride and in no way will they find me looking bedraggled or out of sorts.

I can't do anything about the missing fur in two long stripes on my shoulder and flank. Nanites can only do so much and scars are inevitable.

I'm playing by my own rules on this planet, not theirs.

That task done, I use my inner ear compass to find my bearings, then pad off toward the crash site.

It's a beautiful morning on a lush planet.

Dappled sunlight filters through the trees, catching motes that are dancing in the air. Large insects and the avians hunting them swoop between branches of the thick undergrowth. The scents are complex and lively.

It really is a shame that it's now being used for sport hunting. Even with the limited technology on the planet, I'm sure the genali have already started polluting the environment with their love of chemicals.

I realize why that thought even occurred to me once I detect not only the scent of genali, but also of one of their favorite compounds used to keep slaves in line: a type of tear gas that makes anyone but a manticorid feel like their lungs and eyes are on fire.

It doesn't actually do any damage, but no one wants to feel it ever again.

It stopped working on us many years back. If they have that gas with them, they're not looking for me. Which means there is probably other prey in this area and they might be just as deadly as I am.

That gives me more pause than thinking of the hunters. I continue to pad toward them as I think it over.

Calculated risks are necessary to gain the upper hand.

Before I get closer, I take the time to more deeply analyze the scents, pulling up my lips so I can channel a steady stream of air over the roof of my mouth and the olfactory organ located there.

I gain little new information, except the addition of a number of polymers and what I assume to be the scent of the prey. They smell of salt, fear, and something utterly foreign, but distinctly pleasant.

If I had to guess, I would say female, but it doesn't align with what I've heard about the hunting grounds.

As far as I know, most, if not all, prey are males on this continent, though for plenty of species the largest and fiercest are the females.

Maybe this is one of those females?

To overcome the rampant misogyny of the genali she would have to be particularly grotesque. Any other females they sell into sexual slavery.

I love a good mystery and am eager to find out if I'm correct.

13

Ree

The temperature on this planet is downright awful at night.

After what feels like a blink of rest, I wake up shivering. There's no way to get any warmer.

I imagine my black suit becoming thicker and nothing happens. It stays the same skin-tight, thin fabric no matter how many images of fluffy pajamas, thick robes, winter coats, or blankets I send at it.

I also know it doesn't respond to at least thirty different curse words or insults.

I check Silver, who looks exactly the same as she did before I fell asleep. I don't let myself dwell on my anxieties about her health or my guilt over leaving her.

I'll come back, but I'll be no good to her if I'm weak and dehydrated.

The metal of the ladder is cool in my grip as I scramble up to pop my head outside of the ship. There are all kinds of sounds that my mind wants to associate with insects and birds, but they all just seem very wrong to my ears. It's unsettling, and that is the last way I want to feel when I'm staring out into a dark forest I'll soon be trudging through. I can see flitting creatures the size of birds, but with the flight patterns of insects.

I have to stop myself from thinking of all the dangerous or venomous animals and plants on Earth.

Humans spent millennia figuring out what in their environment was safe to touch and eat. The thought of traipsing out into a forest without any of that knowledge is panic-inducing and I have to focus on my breathing to keep it under control.

Gawking won't lead to finding water, so I climb as high as I can on the ladder and reach my hands to the outside of the ship, looking for a place to pull myself up with.

It's wet, I assume from overnight dew, but the surface is rough enough that I feel confident in my grip. There is scorching and scoring of the metal hull in enough places that I'm sure I can climb down.

I spend a few minutes figuring out the best angle to leverage my body past the few feet of ship hull between the ladder and the top.

I shift my hands around to a few different positions then pull myself up slightly, testing my weight on the handholds. When they hold, I heave myself up, my ribs protesting, but healed enough that it doesn't stop me. I scrape my legs and stomach as I go, but after a few moments of effort, I'm on top of the ship.

I spare a look down, then have to fight vertigo when I think of the process I'll have to go through to get back down.

A problem for later.

I slowly re-situate my body so I can sit up and use the greater height I gained to figure out the best way to climb down to the ground. To the right of me I can see the line of damage we caused the forest when we crashed. It's a carnage of broken trees and scored ground.

To my left, there are trees right up against the hull and stacked together, their feather-like leaves already drooping compared to the surrounding undamaged ones. I wince at the sight, not only because I never liked the idea of that sort of destruction, but also thinking of just how rough our landing was and how lucky I am to not only be alive, but to be moving around.

I decide to take the route that slopes down and away from where the rest of the ship was and also leads toward the undamaged forest.

I can always climb back up. Possibly use one of the trees if I need to.

With that decided, I angle my feet down, then carefully roll over onto my stomach.

After about fifteen minutes of slowly and carefully choosing my next hand and footholds, slowed down considerably by continually needing to move my hair out of my way, I come to a sharp ledge. I can't see over it, and judging by the view behind me I'm still at least fifteen feet from the ground.

I take several very long minutes to convince myself to continue over the ledge.

I move down until my waist dangles over, then panic when my feet can't find any purchase. This makes me tense up my arms, which are screaming at me by the time I kick farther in and find my first toehold.

The angle is extreme and I don't know if I have the upper body strength to descend it safely, but I know by the way my arms and hands feel, I need to get down as fast as I can.

I keep moving down, and once I'm able to see around the ledge, I can tell that I have about fifteen feet of a sharply underhung climb left. I only get about two more feet down before one of my feet slips and it makes my body swing out and away.

I try to swing my legs back toward the wall, but lose my grip with my left hand, then instantly lose grip with my right.

I have the presence of mind to roll when I hit the ground, which saves me from breaking my legs, but also causes me to slam into a tree.

My back takes most of the hit and I struggle to pull air back into my lungs.

I lay there for a few minutes, waiting for my muscles to stop telling me just how much they hate me. I'm pleasantly surprised once that wears off that I only added a few muscle strains to my injury list.

It's still very painful to lift myself up from the ground and I stifle a groan of protest.

I doubt my landing was quiet, but there's no sense in announcing my presence to predators. I look around. With no sense of how to navigate forests or find water, I can't make an informed decision on which way to go now that I'm on the ground.

I'm trying, and failing, to ignore just how similar, but alien, my surroundings are, with the bark of the tree in odd shapes, what looks like grass and moss in colors that just aren't quite the right shades of greens and blues. Purple bushes.

And a purple sky, which I thought was just the fading light last night, but seems to be the normal hue. It's disorienting and overwhelming.

At least the dirt and rocks that the ship section displaced look pretty much how I expect them to look.

With no way to know, I guess the best course of action is to just walk into the forest right next to me, and so I do it without letting myself think any more about it.

I'm so engrossed in the process of making myself take one more step after the other I don't think of how I'll return to where I was. The realization hits soon after, and my heart skips a beat.

That small moment of panic leads to a stutter-step over a root with my left foot, which ends up cascading into three more trips that make me tumble into a bush.

The hundreds of pinprick feelings across my body let me know it's the equivalent of a sticker bush and it takes several minutes and lots of muttered curse words to extract myself from my attacker.

"Well, I guess I was technically the attacker," I admit, by way of apologizing to the prickly plant.

If I was in different circumstances, I would better appreciate the comedic value of such an ungraceful tumble, but right now it just feels like I can't catch a break.

I look around me, quickly noting that I can no longer see the ship.

"Shit, Ree. Don't be so dense," I chastise myself quietly.

I'm smarter than this and I really don't want to die on some alien planet because of something as foolish as not marking which way I came.

Just looking at the surrounding trees it's clear that I won't ever be able to walk in a straight line.

I don't even know which direction I came from thanks to tripping.

My heart pounds when I think of not knowing where the ship is. It's likely not something I should be near anyway, but the thought of leaving Silver without knowing how to find her again just feels incredibly wrong.

After a moment's thought, I turn back to the bush, take careful note of where it's damaged, then use that angle to find my previous path.

Here and there along the way I find bent or damaged foliage and realize that if someone as clueless as me can track my progress and I'm on a planet full of hunters and their prey then I've been stupidly careless.

Soon after, I get my first glimpse of the ship section through the trees.

"How in the hell am I going to mark a way back in a way that doesn't also mark where I go?"

No one answers my rhetorical question, of course.

I feel rooted to the spot. I know I can't stay with the ship. I also know I won't be able to find it again if I leave because I can't mark my trail.

I take a moment to curse just how useless I am at navigating thanks to always having GPS at my disposal, then shut the thought down.

It isn't helpful.

As much as I would like to delude myself that I can somehow return to Silver, it would merely be a soothing lie.

The hard truth of it is that I'm going to have to walk away from this ship and find water or I'm going to die. I don't even have the option of placing myself in stasis because there's only one functioning cryochamber.

Not that it would be an appealing option, but it's the only one I can think of that would allow me to stay with her.

I still can't make myself move away.

It's one thing to consider leaving Silver alone for a brief period, but I'm not sure I can make myself just abandon her.

I have to admit it's not even my morals that are truly keeping me here. I don't know if I can keep my mind from shattering without her after so many weeks of treating her like some sort of living talisman.

"Fuuuuuuck."

14

Ree

I hear a crack of a branch breaking behind me and to the left and whip around toward it.

I can't see anything, but I hear more sounds.

Shit. Time to go.

I try to move as silently as possible to the right, which is back toward the broken trail of trees left by the crash.

My heart hammers in fear and my muscles quiver with the urge to just break out into a run. I know I can't do that quietly, though, so I force myself to maintain my current pace.

It isn't fast enough, or nearly quiet enough, because I hear a shout behind me.

I crane my neck back that direction and see what I assume to be slimes in some sort of hazmat suit. The shape is incredibly strange, but it matches their profile and I glimpse bulging black eyes and gray skin through a glass-covered face mask.

I can only see two of them, but have absolutely no interest in finding out if they have guns. Or heat seeking lasers or some other sci fi shit.

I run as fast as I can, but am quickly hampered by scattered debris and exposed tree roots.

There's a thumping sound in front of me and I glance up to see a silver canister break open with a hissing sound.

I can't see anything coming from it, but my eyes instantly start to burn and tear up, making it impossible to maintain my current speed. I try to hold my breath as long as possible as I scrabble away.

I trip over something, and the breath whooshes out of me as I hit the ground hard.

Although my lungs are screaming at me to take a breath, I continue to move away on my hands and knees. Moments that feel like hours later, I'm unable to stop myself from breathing in, then hack back out the breath in a sharp cough.

I can't see and can't get myself to move forward because of how debilitating the coughing fits are.

Whatever they're using feels even more concentrated than the torture gas from the ship. At any moment, I expect to be captured or shot, but instead hear a loud crashing sound, then a roar.

It startles me enough that I look back to the sound instead of trying to get my body to move away, but I can only make out a blurry image of bright green trees, the white blobs that must be the hazmat suits, and a streaking orange movement rapidly closing in on them.

I assume it's the source of the roaring, because it happens again, this time sounding closer.

The orange streak closes the gap with the white blobs, then I hear a whipping sound, followed by an impact, then a long, keening scream. The same process happens again, with the same screaming at the end, now doubled and I assume to be coming from both of the slimes.

Holy shit, I think between coughing fits.

Whatever it is appears to be more than a match for them.

I continue trying to cough up my lungs, swiping at my eyes in between and trying to clear them enough so I can see what in the hell is going on and if I'm going to be the next one screaming.

"I'm not... very... tasty," I tell it between coughs.

Another few moments later the screams die down to nothing and I'm the only one making noise.

I'm acutely aware of how bad an idea drawing attention to myself is, but have absolutely no control over my body as it tries to expel the gas. I know from previous exposure that once it dissipates I won't have any lasting damage from it.

Considering what I assume is one of the planet's apex predators is likely eying me up as a tasty dessert after it finishes with the slimes, that offers little comfort.

"Guar-anteed... indi-gestion," I say inanely.

I'm not sure why, but the predator simply stands still for several minutes as I continue to hack away. I try to move my body, but the seizing of the coughing just takes over and it's all I can manage, my lungs burning and my neck and stomach muscles straining from overuse.

I don't understand why the creature isn't eating them. Or coming over to see what is going on with me.

It just stays in the same position, though my eyes are too blurry to make out details. I try to speak again, but my lungs are cramping in agony now between coughs.

The orange blob goes from low and close to the ground to what I assume is a standing position and holds itself still for another few moments.

Then it turns toward me.

I don't have the air to scream, or I would do it loudly right now.

I tense my body, waiting for the same attack it used to such a quick and dangerous effect on the slimes. After weeks of terror and surviving a crash, it would be particularly cruel to die right now.

As orange, and now that it's closer, black and purple, fill my vision no attack comes. Instead, I hear a purring sound, then the feel of powerful hands under my shoulders and knees right before I'm lifted into the air.

I continue to cough as I'm gently pressed against soft fur and move away on an odd, shifting gait.

It only takes about a dozen steps before I feel the urge to cough diminishing, then a few more after that to feel like I can pull in a full breath.

Although I'm still terrified to move and draw attention to myself, I can't stand the thought of no longer being able to see. Between coughs I creep one arm up closer to my face until I'm able to swipe at my eyes.

When I look up, it's into luminescent golden eyes.

15

Thivoll

Dear Thela, when I turned to look at this small human with venom bliss pumping through me she looked like just the woman I needed to cage with my teeth and plunge my throbbing sex into.

Luckily, I got myself under control, though her scent is trying to tear down my hastily erected veneer of civility.

I shake my mane, chiding myself sharply. I will not be a ravening beast around a person who clearly has been abducted and treated poorly only to be sold in the galactic sex trade.

Not to mention, she is human.

That thought is enough to ease the pressure against my sheathe, though the woman still smells delectable for some inexplicable reason.

Before I approached her, I raised myself onto my back paws, not wanting to alarm the poor biped, not to mention needing my arms to carry her.

Now I'm struggling to keep us both upright. I keep having to whip my tail in different directions as a counterbalance so I don't come crashing down on top of her.

It's definitely worth it.

I pull in a deep breath of her personal scent. It's exotic and indescribable and the reason my purr continues to rumble through me like I'm a love struck dolt.

But I don't bother stopping it.

I have more important things to focus on, like the way she feels against me. She weighs almost nothing and is considerably smaller than me. From what I know about humans, she seems to be particularly petite, though has the full mammary glands that mark her as grown.

I'm quite certain her hair has been changed by the genali.

I'm endlessly curious and learning about other planets has always been a hobby. I don't remember there being many examples of hair this long among humans, but I find it captivating.

Manticorid females have beautiful, soft fur all over their bodies, but it's short.

Nothing you can really grab onto.

As I walk the woman away from the gas causing her so much distress, the long strands of it brushing against my scales and ruffling my fur make me swell again.

Our women would never let me carry them like this unless they were deathly ill or injured.

To attempt it, even in jest, would result in deep scores across your hide, if not worse. I don't believe human women are known for being quite as fierce, but just in case, I focus on the sensation of holding her slight weight and the feeling in my chest while it lasts.

I want to keep holding her small form to me as I shield her from the dangers of the world.

A spike of anxiety follows that thought. There are many, many dangers here for such a defenseless species.

She is already improving after only a small distance away. Her coughing diminishes rapidly, and she reaches her small hand, which only has five digits and is a pale white-pink, up to wipe her eyes.

Once she opens them, it confirms my suspicions of genali modifications.

Her eyes are a mesmerizing blue color that seems to draw me into their depths, even more so as they open wide to take me in.

Her lips part in surprise when she sees me, showing a delightful pink tongue and the blunt white teeth of an herbivore.

Utterly adorable.

16

Ree

I'm having a hard time processing what I'm seeing and go stiff with shock.

Holding me against them in what can only be described as a gentle embrace and staring at my face with intelligence in its gaze is one of the most beautiful and absolutely terrifying beings I have seen in my life.

Around its pupils of molten gold, which catch the light in a way that makes them seem to glow, is an orange, rather than white, sclera.

Its face reminds me somewhat of a lion, with the rounded ears as you would expect, and a long, flat nasal plate with a typically feline nose shape, but in a light blue color instead of pink.

From there, it defies easy comparison.

Its fur is a brilliant orange across most of its face, rising into a mane that plumes on the top of its head and sweeps down around its neck. The top and front part of the mane are orange. It has sections of fur in neon green, but only in small parts, like the women back home who like to highlight their hair.

It has a broader lower face than a lion with lips that on top are a pale blue, but then transition to a lilac color. The sides of its mouth have a puff of lilac fur extending from them in an arch and another lilac arc of hair below each of their ears that mimics the same shape, but is separated by a bright wedge of orange—like two crescent moons on either side of their face complementing each other.

Its chin is a rough-looking lilac skin that transitions to black scales before disappearing under a thick patch of fur.

Even though I know it just killed those slimes quickly and brutally, nothing about its features or demeanor suggest it's a threat. There is also a comforting rumbling sound, like a purr, coming from it.

Still, my instincts scream at me to get very far away as fast as possible.

A quick glance to my shoulder and legs and I see its black scaled hands, with far too many thumbs, are only resting lightly against me. Despite that, the lizard part of my brain wants me to get the hell out of here.

Luckily that part of my brain isn't in charge because everyone knows big predators chase anything that runs.

I realize my mouth has been hanging open when I gulp and shiver at that imagery.

Soon after that terrifying thought, I can feel my cursed nanites take over and while the sight of it is still strange and alarming, my pulse is now high for another reason altogether.

I feel a flush come over my cheeks and chest, then the slick heat building in my core.

The creature suddenly stops walking, takes a deep breath, and then raises its lilac lips.

This exposes a set of ebony teeth. My eyes widen at the sight of them and I'm thinking that maybe my lizard brain was the smarter one after all.

Thankfully, it doesn't use those teeth to tear out my throat.

The creature simply huffs out a breath, and the purring picks up in intensity until I can feel it resonating across my whole body. It suddenly occurs to me; it can smell that I'm aroused.

Does the purr mean it... likes it?

"Oh, shit..." I trail off, since nothing I could say beyond that really encapsulates how screwed up my life has become.

I startle when the rumble in its chest transitions to a harsh, coughing language.

Thanks to the slimes, I understand it.

"I don't know your language, small human, but something tells me that was a curse," it guesses

After one long blink, I realize what this means.

It's more than just intelligent, it's sapient. That means not an it. I glance at the puffy mane. A he?

I open my mouth to speak, then grab my throat as I feel a sharp stabbing pain in the back of it. Then, for lack of a better description, I feel a shift.

When I cough, it's in a much harsher tone than a human should ever be able to make.

"So they gave you translation nanites."

He makes a humming sound I assume from the context is commiserating or soothing. "Those things are rough, just give it a moment."

I feel gentle patting against my shoulder as the stabs of searing pain suddenly relent. I clear my throat experimentally and it sounds just as weird as before.

I don't filter what I'm going to say, it just spills out.

"What in the actual fuck was that!"

The harsh language that comes out of my mouth is one I have never spoken before and I sound very odd to my own ears.

I get a chuffing, gravelly sound in response. The increased sparkling in his eyes makes me suspect it's laughter.

I realize then that, unlike the slimes, while I find the way he looks strange, nothing about him is revolting. In fact, he's quite beautiful, with a certain allure that all apex predators have.

I was never one to beat around any bushes and have found that ever since I passed my thirtieth birthday, I've become more and more prone to simply speak my mind. Mostly it goes well, since I have a healthy dose of charisma and well-honed people skills.

Well, except for love interests, I suppose. With them I'm a train wreck.

I shake off that thought.

"Are you laughing?" I ask him.

"I most certainly am, little human. I'm not sure what fornication has to do with anything at this moment, but I find your phrasing entertaining. And your accent is simply adorable."

There's a gleam in his eye, but no smile.

"If I'm entertaining, does that mean you don't plan to do to me what you did to those slimes?"

"Please have no worries about that. I'm perfectly harmless, at least to you. In fact, those were the first beings I have ever killed. Well, fourth, actually," he says this in such a wide-eyed sort of innocence it's almost hard to believe he just dispatched two slimes in a few brief moments.

Almost.

"From the sounds of it, you are very good at killing."

I realize that could be rude and add a hasty amendment. "No offense meant, of course. They totally deserved it and I really don't like violence, so that's saying a lot."

"I agree, but I propose we vacate the area quickly and find a safer place to talk. I must admit that I have been in a bit of a daze dealing with the aftereffects of using my venom and I'm not making very sound decisions right now."

His ears swivel around and he moves his eyes away from me. "We shouldn't stay here."

I suddenly remember Silver when he mentions leaving.

"There's another woman inside the ship. She was injured, and I had to put her back in one of the cryochambers." His eyes turn back to me as I point. "The access is on the top of the ship."

He glances over to where I gesture.

"I'll need to return for her after I find a good hiding place for you," he replies.

It sounds reasonable, but I'm not sure I can leave her. "Will you be able to find the ship again?"

"Yes, easily," comes his confident reply.

My hands clench and unclench as I chide myself to leave it at that, but of course I don't. "Her safety is more important. I can just hide in a bush or something."

He growls, the sound rumbling through me. "I disagree. It won't take long until I can come back."

My heart pounds and I want to push the issue again, but what if he decides we're too much trouble?

My nails are digging into my palms so hard the nails are sending spikes of pain up my wrists and I focus on relaxing one finger at a time until I'm under control again.

It's hard to force the word out, but I manage. "Alright."

I realize then that I've decided to trust him.

This makes me uneasy, because I just met him, but it also brings a bigger feeling of relief that I won't be alone out among those trees with no actual idea what the hell I'm doing.

I push any analysis of my feelings aside and focus on logistics. "I can walk now, if you like."

He makes a soft rumbling sound and his hands tighten slightly on me before he shifts his body to gently place me on the ground. He gives me a pat on my butt, making my eyes widen, but he does it in such a nonchalant way I doubt he knows it isn't socially acceptable.

"Good. I should check the genali for anything useful."

I nod to him in response, then realize that the gesture may make little sense.

"That sounds like a good plan," I say instead.

I walk toward the slimes, or genali, I suppose, but he places a hand on my waist to stop me.

The feel of his scales through the thin fabric makes me shiver.

"I don't think you should be near that much venom. I won't take long."

I can't argue with that and stay put.

As he walks away, I'm able to observe his whole body. The same orange and green fur extends all over him, except for black scales near his hands, throat, and back paws. He isn't striped like a tiger but instead the green color is in a random swirling pattern. My eyes want to just keep following the mesmerizing trails and loops, but I resist.

As my eyes trail over him a sudden memory of the genali talking about a giant venomous cat comes back to me. "Are you a manticorid?"

He pauses and looks back at me. His whiskers aren't extending from his face anymore and hang limply toward his chest. "How did you know?"

"The slimes—I mean genali—talked about you."

"We call them slimes, too. It's a fitting name."

He moves away again and then suddenly whips back around toward me. "Wait. They didn't have you in cryo?"

I shiver and wrap my arms around myself as images try to bubble up right along with the acid in the back of my throat.

"No. I was the, uh... entertainment. N-not sexual, thankfully. Mostly torture gas and threats."

His mane puffs out, sharp black claws extend from his fingers, and a low growl sounds. "I should have taken my time with those two."

17

Ree

He should look terrifying. He has retractable claws and serrated teeth, for fuck's sake.

But I feel safer than I have in weeks.

"I am so sorry, little human. There are no words to express my regret."

I squeeze myself tighter and fight the tears that want to pour out of me.

I've waited so long to hear those words.

That they are coming from an alien who looks like a neon orange lion walking on two legs makes hysterical laughter want to bubble up right along with the tears.

If my life was a painting, Dali would definitely be the painter.

I blink rapidly to clear my mind. "Thank you. That means a lot."

He shakes himself and goes back to his task. I continue observing him as a way to stave off any embarrassing hysterics.

His long mane extends well down his back, coming to a tapered point a few inches away from where his tail starts. It looks just as elegant as you would expect in a feline's tail, shifting with him in graceful sweeps and bounces as he walks. It has a large black ovoid shape at the end that comes to a point, which is covered in the same shiny scales as his throat, arms, and paws.

Or would all four limbs have paws?

I suppose it doesn't matter, but I'll have to listen for how he refers to himself for clues.

His gait is awkward, just like any feline would look trying to walk on two legs, but his torso doesn't have the same shape as a cat.

His fur ripples as he walks and his tail dances along behind him. The muscle structures work in enough different ways that my mind is having a hard time pulling apart the differences.

I just know he looks absolutely deadly and utterly gorgeous.

"What's your name? Mine is Ree," I offer.

"Ree?"

When he says my name, it's with the sexiest gravelly purr. "Is that the right way to say it?"

No one has ever said it like that but no way in hell would I want to correct him. I feel another rush of heat between my legs and gulp, then realize I've let too much time pass.

"Y-yes, that's right," I say hastily.

"My name is Thivoll."

I test it out on my tongue, but don't say it out loud, feeling self-conscious even though I seem to be doing just fine communicating so far.

He rifles around the dead bodies, which makes me feel slightly guilty, but I'm far too practical to protest.

My gaze snaps back to him when it occurs to me that his limbs aren't bending as I would expect.

After a few more moments of observation, I realize he has an additional set of joints compared to a human. There's an elbow up close to his chest like a cat has, but then another halfway between it and his wrists.

Watching how he articulates his arms with an additional joint makes me feel queasy.

"There is nothing here of worth," Thivoll says after another few minutes.

I nod, then get annoyed with myself, relieved to have something to distract me by such a rude reaction to the natural way his body works.

"That'll be a hard habit to break," I grumble.

He hums again. "That gesture with your head? Just tell me what it means. No need to break a habit."

"Oh. Thanks. When I move my head up and down, it means yes. If I move it from side to side, it means no," I explain, moving my head the way I describe.

"Fascinating. I'll remember, and later I'll show you the equivalent from my culture. For now, let's move to safer ground, Ree."

Thivoll walks back over to me, then extends an arm out. I hesitate, then take his hand in mine.

It's huge, with fingers so long and thick I have to really stretch to thread mine between them. The black scales catch the light with a blue glow. They look raised and rough, especially starting at his wrists down, but are surprisingly soft.

His hand has two thumbs, and it's weird to feel them gently closing around my wrist from both sides. The black scales catch slightly when I shift my grip in a way that runs counter to how the scales lay against his skin.

"That is an interesting clasp, Ree," he says to me, looking down at our intertwined fingers.

I start to remove my hand from his, increasingly self-conscious, but he squeezes lightly.

"No, I like it. Very much."

Holding hands with a cat-lizard-scorpion-person as I walk turns out to be a somewhat bewildering, but very pleasant activity. We only take a few dozen steps before Thivoll pulls us to a stop.

I look up at him with a questioning look on my face.

"I hope this will not cause offense, Ree, but our trail will be very clear to any hunters if we continue on like this."

I think back to my brief foray into the woods earlier and realize I'm the weak link here. "I don't want to put you at risk because I'm with you. I can—"

I don't get to finish my thought before Thivoll starts shaking his big fluffy head. He wasn't joking when he said he'd remember the gesture.

Just that minor act makes me even more inclined to trust him.

He taps both thumbs against my wrist, the gesture soothing. "You won't bring additional risk, but I don't think you should be walking. I can carry you in my arms, but we will be faster and better prepared to flee as needed if you simply ride on my back."

"That won't be insulting?"

Once again, he shakes his head, then tips forward to place his hands on the ground. I'm disappointed to no longer be holding one.

My mind gets momentarily distracted thinking about how that works for him compared to a cat's paws. He pulls his fingers in like he's making a fist and his thumbs wrap around the fingers in a tight grip.

It reminds me of how a gorilla would run, except nothing else about him is like a primate.

I shake myself out of my staring and try to figure out how I'm going to scramble up on his back. Thivoll solves the issue by crouching down so his stomach is almost against the ground and sticking one of his fisted hands out to the side.

"Step on my arm and I'll boost you up," he offers and I move to comply, then freeze when a random memory flits into my head.

It was some old classic movie, *Star Trek* I think, where the alien's genitals were on its knee.

I feel like my life really must have turned into a complete joke if my mind is pulling up William Shatner to help me navigate.

"What's wrong?" Thivoll asks, his eyes intent on me, but ears suddenly swiveling around frantically.

I'm being weird.
"Oh, nothing. I just... uh..."
Now is not the time to explain, but some questions might help.
"What gender do you identify as?" I begin with, then cringe at how invasive it sounds.
"Male," he responds in a slow harsh drawl that lets me know he's confused.
His whiskers droop.
I feel my face getting bright red.
"I won't, um..." I clear my throat, resisting the urge to put my hands on my burning face. "You know, uh, smash any delicate parts?"
The last word is said in as much of a mortified squeak as one can manage in his rough language.
"No. Nothing delicate at all," he replies with a twinkle in his eyes and his whiskers pushed forward.
He seems to lose some sort of battle at keeping his composure and breaks into the chuffing sound he already admitted was laughter.
I scowl back at him, feeling silly, but also knowing it was a legitimate concern based on extreme ignorance.
"You really are so enchanting," he says. "We should leave now, Ree."
I shake myself out of my embarrassed outrage and unceremoniously grab some of his fur and clamber onto his back.
"You won't hurt me. Grab my mane and hang on tight."
I do as he asks a moment before he springs forward. My heart is in my throat for the first few strides, then I realize his gait is incredibly smooth.
Nothing like the few times I've ridden horses.
His body seems to flow from one stride to the next without feeling like his paws or fists impact the ground at all. I can see why he thought this would be better. It's almost as if we're floating instead of running.
When he speaks to me, I can feel the rumble all over.
"Do you feel secure?" he asks.
"Oh, yes. This is wonderful. You are amazing!"
I wish I had a better filter.
Because now I feel my face trying to burn off my cheeks again, though I can tell by the rumbling purr he liked hearing it.
"As are you, Ree. I have never met a human before. You are delightful."

I feel a glow in my chest, but it dims when I wonder if he simply means that I'm entertaining like some sort of bumbling tourist trying to order a pound of fish.

What an odd example. I feel so flustered right now.

The last time I felt like this was when Asad was talking about his plans for the weekend and I thought he might be about to ask me out. According to Tam, he likely was trying to ask me out before I panicked and started talking about needing to clean out Sammy's kitty litter.

Thankfully I'm interrupted before I can keep spiraling. I don't really want to think about how an alien has sparked my ridiculous social anxiety.

I'm officially far too old for it.

It needs to grow the hell up or something, dammit.

"We should wait to talk until we gain some distance from the dead slimes," he explains.

I breathe out in relief, hoping my addled brain will somehow find a calm, cool version of Ree so he thinks of me as an attractive sort of interesting instead of pitiful.

Whoa, whoa, whoa, there, I chide myself. *I just met this man. Lion thingy. Whatever! This is just the nanites at work,* I tell myself firmly.

But I know it's a lie.

My mind was totally on board with hating the genali. I'm in control of my thoughts and they say Thivoll is the most interesting being I have ever met.

I thrust those thoughts aside. I can't do anything about the lust pumping through me, but no need to trot out those thoughts and risk blurting them out.

I instead focus on trying to figure out what bone and ligament structure would lead to this type of movement.

The wind is blowing my hair behind me and I can't help but feel exhilarated by the speed. Not to mention the feel of his flexing muscles and the surprisingly silken feel of his fur in my hands.

Or the musky scent that smells better than any expensive cologne imaginable.

18

Thivoll

She's almost completely bald, her skin is the color of kit vomit, her legs bend the wrong way, and her species is deplorably socially primitive considering how many technological advances they've made recently.

She should be grotesque or at the very least I should chide myself for even thinking of anyone of her species as anything other than the galactic equivalent of children.

And yet I find myself intrigued and aroused.

Her aroma is trying to pull that primal part of myself I had to work so hard to squash right back up to the surface. I've seen enough images of humans to know she's been changed and feel guilty when I think about how much I love the modifications.

I doubt she feels the same.

Her fully blue eyes look so much more natural than the disturbing white eyes of her species. Her hair is the most glorious mane I could ever imagine. It's odd to see one on a female. The sensation of it rippling against me brings up all kinds of carnal thoughts one simply cannot share when first meeting someone.

I know she should repulse me, but no one ever said I was a normal male.

To be panting over a human is clear evidence, if any more was truly needed. There's a reason I ended up relegated to air scrubbers and paperwork.

That reminds me of ships and the fact that Ree was so close to a crash site. "You were in the ship when it landed?"

I feel a shudder pass over her body at the reminder and a prickle of guilt makes my scales itch. I shouldn't have brought it up.

I open my mouth to retract the question, but she responds.

"Yes. There were ten of us. I'm pretty sure one of us died, but the rest of them, except Silver of course, went flying out of the ship. Do you know if the chamber would have protected them?"

Out of respect, I take a moment to think of the unfortunate female, then respond. "Most likely. It really depends how they landed and how quickly the main power died when it hit the atmosphere."

She grips my fur so tight it hurts. "I need to find them."

"Well, let's get Silver settled and figure it out from there. I smelled laser burns when we were near the ship. Was it attacked?"

"I think so."

"I assumed it was an accident. I can't imagine pirates suicidal enough to target a cruiser so close to one of the few neutral grounds. Most of the more vicious species wouldn't risk losing access. I don't know who it could be."

"The slimes don't have enemies?"

"Sure. Plenty, but mostly people just focus on protecting their home systems."

"Huh. Why's it neutral ground?"

"For genali, the credits. For everyone else, access to hunt here and the pleasure resorts on the space station and habitable moon. Few planets are like this one. Billions of credits went into figuring out a stable space elevator to get past the atmosphere."

"Why?"

"Sorry. I'm used to everyone knowing these things. Technology doesn't work here."

"Shit! I need to get back to Silver. I put her in cryo to heal her."

"No, no. She's alright. I'm not doing well at explaining." I growl at myself and resolve to do better. "The primary power source would have died long ago, but nanites are the backup. The chamber will keep pumping nanites through her to harvest power."

"So she's the battery? Won't she run out of charge, or whatever?"

"Yes and no. It will have enough stored nutrients to keep her in stasis for a while. The chambers will fail after a while, but they're programmed to open before that point."

She makes a grunting sound and then falls quiet. I take the opportunity to better focus on our surroundings.

Maintaining a slow run and swiveling my ears for sounds of hunters feels surprisingly natural.

I suppose the philosophers were right when they said our species was only ever one small step away from reverting to our base natures. That's a mercy at the moment, though I know I was once caught up in the shared horror of losing our social progress.

I wonder how many of the Abstainers would wish for their venom back if they were here.

All of them, I bet.

The surge of instincts is especially nice since it gives me plenty of mental space to enjoy the sensation of Ree's lithe legs wrapped tight around me. I can feel the radiating heat from between her legs. The place reports indicate is the entrance to her reproductive organs.

I was never interested in alien sexual habits, so I have no idea if we would be compatible. I do hope we find out. No need to rush things, though.

The fun is in the stalking.

Well, no reason beyond imminent death.

I almost trip over a root when a good reason to not pursue her occurs to me. I might be wrong about what her scent means. She might also already have a mate. I'm not sure how to ask her without reminding her of what she's lost.

Maybe the key is to bring up my family.

"The slimes have been taking our women, too. I've lost cousins and good friends."

She loosens her grip with one hand and pats me. "That's terrible, Thivoll. I'm so sorry."

She doesn't quite get the guttural accent in my name correct and it's endearing. Her voice is sincere, hinting at a deep well of empathy.

I hadn't realized how much I needed to talk about it, but her words feel like a good soak in the sun.

"Thank you. I miss them, but I think it's worse for my friends who fear for their mates."

My nose twitches as I berate myself for being so obvious. Not to mention using such a heavy topic for the sake of my incessant curiosity.

I do believe that, but now that I've said it to find out if she is mated it feels wrong.

"I can see that. My parents would be devastated to find out I was missing if they were still alive."

I feel a pang of shared grief. "I share your grief. My sire was killed when I was a young kit. I rarely go long without thinking of him."

"Me too. It's crazy how something as simple as a *Vietnamese* restaurant will remind me of my dam and how she kept her culture alive through food. Or my sire and his love of sweets. What about your dam? Uh, *mother?*"

"Luckily my dam is safe. Or was, at least. She's likely contacted every member of Session tens of times by now about me. Our government, I mean."

She makes a low sound that isn't quite a chuff, but seems to have the same function. "I have a friend like that. Had? I'm not sure I'll ever see her again."

She sounds so lost and I wish I could offer better comfort. "I hope so, Ree."

I assume she has the same ache in her chest I do and it explains the lull in our conversation after that.

I think we have left a suitably confounding trail so I look for trees so I can comfort her. I look forward to talking with her about how we can manage her Silver's rescue.

I search for a perfect option, with a thick canopy, but a trunk structure that will provide a roomy nest for us.

But not too roomy.

I want Ree cuddled up against me as we talk through our next steps. I might be odd, but I enjoy cuddles as much as any of my species. I think I see a suitable candidate after we walk in silence for a short while.

Yes, this tree will do. "Go ahead and slide off, Ree."

She obliges, and the feel of her gliding along my fur is momentarily distracting.

She comes to stand in front of me while I'm still caught up in the pleasurable shivers that run down my spin and make my tail dance. I shake my mane to I gather myself, then assess her hands.

No claws, but I don't want to insult her so I don't make any assumptions.

I fall back on the formal politeness my grand sire taught me just in case. "Would you like to climb by yourself or would you prefer assistance?"

She responds by tipping her head back and letting out a melodious trill. Manticorid bodies could never make such a pure, high sound.

I'm transfixed.

When she speaks it's back to a lower register. "Oh, Thivoll, I couldn't make it a single step up this tree."

I'm trying to figure out why she added the extra sound to the front of my name when she starts speaking again.

"There's nothing to grab on to."

I look back at the tree, realizing what she means. When I look back at her, she is baring her teeth at me. I recoil on instinct.

"No need for violence! I'm sorry to offend," I say with as much regret as I can muster.

I hope she isn't too angry.

Her forehead wrinkles. "What? Oh! Uh, no. I thought it was funny. I was laughing at my own terrible climbing skills."

I realize her 'ohs' and 'uhs' must be vocalized pauses.
Adorable, but I'm still confused.
"Then why the threatened bite?"
I know something's been lost in translation, but the hair along my spine rises anyway.
"Oh! That was a *smile*, not a threat. Sorry," she says, her oddly flexible lips pulling the opposite direction as before.
Now I wonder what that lip movement means.
Dear Thela, humans are an odd species.
"When I *smile* I'm happy. Or trying to look friendly," she explains.
There is no translation for the word in my language.
Showing your teeth when happy is an odd concept. I try it. Ree's eyes get big, then she holds her stomach and lets out another long trill.
She moves her other hand over her mouth at the end, probably so I won't be threatened.
"This *smile* is confusing, but I very much like your lovely trill," I tell her. "We should climb, though, so we can be more comfortable."
She nods to indicate her agreement and I'm relieved.

19

Ree

Thivoll's attempt at a smile would've been one of the most frightening things I've ever seen had he tried it when we first met.

His ebony teeth are deadly sharp.

Except the combination of his lips trying to mimic a human's movement and the way he squints his eyes makes him look like a giant Cheshire Cat with black shark teeth.

Or maybe I'm feeling a bit too much like Alice and I'm projecting.

Either way, it's comical.

I can't contain another laugh and I'm relieved when Thivoll doesn't take offense.

I like the idea of getting more comfortable, especially after the terribly cold night and the stress of the crash landing. Not to mention that this is the first time I've felt a glimmer of hope that maybe I won't be sold off at auction.

That alone brings its own form of exhaustion on the heels of weeks of tension and terror.

"To answer your question, I would appreciate your help," I say.

"Excellent, I..." Thivoll trails off, his ears stop their constant swiveling, and he turns his head to his left. I hold myself still and quiet, wondering what he hears.

The forest around us stills and the hairs on my arms rise.

I startle when Thivoll pulls me to him, but I remain silent. My face is enveloped by the soft fur of his mane as he pulls me tighter against his chest with one arm. Then I feel us rise, a shot of panic at the speed of it causing me to wrap my arms around his thick neck.

After catching a quick glance of how far up we are I bury my face deep into his fur so I can't see and wrap my legs around his waist. It tapers at a different angle than a human, with no hips to catch my weight so I have to squeeze hard to remain locked against him.

We stop ascending not long after, and I feel the difference in gravity pulling me away from his chest instead of down toward his back paws. I hazard a look and am relieved when all I can see are twining tree trunks and thick leaves.

Thivoll pulls gently on my legs, letting me know he wants me to release my death grip. As I do, his arms wrap around me and he repositions me so he is holding my weight. It gives me the confidence to pull my face from his fur and inspect our surroundings.

We're on a relatively spacious platform created by the splitting of the main trunk into multiple massive snaking limbs. I can't see anything beyond that because not long after the trunk splits there are masses of smaller branches with thick feathery foliage.

Thivoll's body is still tense, and so I assume the danger hasn't passed, whatever it is.

I can't see his face, but his steady breathing suggests he isn't panicking or afraid. He moves us until he's sitting upright with his back legs folded under him. He wraps his long tail around a tree limb. Probably to provide stability since his arms are around me.

I have no proper sense of what dangers lurk on this planet.

Aside from the genali, of course. Thinking of them and their dark, bulbous eyes leering at my body for the past weeks makes me shudder.

Thivoll squeezes me to him gently, then runs one of his hands through my long hair in a soothing motion. He mostly stays near my scalp and the sensation is like no other. I always loved when my mother would play with my hair and it always brings back feelings of deep contentment.

I let out a long sigh, then return the favor by massaging my hands into the fluffy, thick fur of his mane, his scales against the tips of my fingers an interesting distraction from our precarious situation.

A gentle purr starts up in his chest soon after.

I get lost in the moment, enjoying the feel of his silky fur under my hands.

When his body starts to relax, I let out a relieved breath, but otherwise remain silent. My ears are useless compared to his and it would be reckless to speak without knowing it's safe.

"I don't hear them anymore," he tells me in a quiet voice, "but let's remain here for a short while just in case."

"Genali?"

"Possibly. They were too far away for me to say with accuracy."

"I heard them talking about this place before we crashed," I share. "This is some sort of holiday planet for terrible people, it sounded like."

"Yes. There are other species of hunters here," he explains. "Usually the type who've had lucrative careers terrorizing and enslaving. They train in ancient weapons and survival skills on the nearby moon."

"But why take the risk?"

"I assume they're bored with their usual methods of violence. It seems like the more hunters die here, the more popular it becomes. So many suicidal hunters and I'm meant to be one of the prey," he says with a chuff in his voice to let me know he finds it amusing.

Or I'm misinterpreting. "That's funny?"

"Yes, very much so. They'll realize their critical error soon enough."

I blink at that, not sure how to take his comment. "Uh, are you part of the military or something?"

"No, negative. I'm a vent cleaner."

I'm missing something. He's awfully confident, but I fail to see how cleaning has prepared him for this.

As usual, I lack a filter.

"I don't understand. Are cleaners also warriors on your planet?"

He chuffs in response, amused. "You are so delightful, Ree."

I feel my face coloring, but his tone lets me know he isn't making fun of me.

He hums, then explains. "Before we took the path of peace, my species was the dominant one in the known universe. Now we primarily make art, try to figure out our own mysterious biology, and keep ourselves mostly isolated to our home system."

I perk up about his mention of biology. "What's mysterious about your biology?" It occurs to me it might be too personal. "I mean, if you don't mind sharing, of course. I'm a nurse, so it's a particular area of interest."

"You take care of younglings? That must be a rewarding if not tiring profession."

"No, no," I correct him. "I think something was lost in translation there. I'm a medical nurse. I work in a hospital."

"I see. Medicine has been taken over by technology in my culture, so there are really only technicians left. The word must have lost that meaning at some point."

I blink slowly, absorbing the loss of an entire profession.

Everyone is always afraid of the newest form of technology and how it might replace their jobs. It sounds like there is some validity to that fear after all.

I open my mouth to ask another question, but he interrupts me. "I would love to discuss this more, but we should move out of the area and to another tree. I climbed in haste and so there will be damage to the bark."

"Yikes, we should definitely move then," I reply.

"I'm not sure what 'yikes' means, Ree," he says, his voice puzzled and his whiskers drooping slightly.

"Uh, well I'm not sure of the official definition, but I just use it when I think something sounds really important and I hadn't realized it."

He nods at me, the movement clearly not natural for him yet, but seeing him trying to communicate with me in my own gestures makes my chest feel full.

Not to mention it makes his fluffy mane move in a captivating way.

I realize I'm staring and shake myself out of it. "Is there a better way for me to ride you... um... er... no, that sounds wrong. A better way for me to hold on to you on the way down?"

I'm embarrassed about my slip of the tongue and hope he doesn't get the double meaning.

"I liked the way you held me on the way up," he says, his voice with an underlying purr that makes me think we are talking about more than just logistics now.

20

Thivoll

I wish I had done more than surface level research on humans, but how was I to know I would ever meet one?

There are countless species out in the universe and the odds I would meet any of them, let alone be attracted to one, were astronomical. Better information would have made trying to figure out why Ree's face keeps turning red much easier.

I hope it isn't related to some sort of medical condition, though I would assume if she worked in medicine they would have dealt with it.

Then I remember with a shot of panic that their technology is incredibly primitive.

It makes me speak before thinking.

"Are you healthy?"

"Well, yes. I think so?"

The redness from her face dissipates, but now there are odd wrinkles on her forehead. I once again have no way to know what the expression means. But there's no time for that now.

She's far too distracting.

I want to know everything about her as fast as possible.

"We should move now," I tell her again, then gently reposition her so she can clasp herself to me again.

The somewhat uncomfortable grip she had on my mane on the way up was a small cost for how lovely her embrace felt.

Manticorid anatomy would never allow a female to wrap her legs around me and it sent a thrill through me when she held on to me with such a firm double grip.

The same heady feeling rushes through me again and coupled with the ever-present scent I'm fairly certain must be arousal, I can feel myself swelling against the confines of my sheathe just thinking about it.

Confident I'll stay confined, I let myself enjoy the sensation and the heat of her core against my fur on the climb down.

Part of me wishes I could have climbed slower, but the other part of me that's firmly in charge knows I need to get her to safety as soon as I can.

I have to whip my tail out and wave it around to keep my balance on two feet. My species wasn't really designed to walk like this, let alone have a delightful little passenger pulling by balance forward.

It's a struggle to keep my body from doing that even without a burden.

Ree is still clutching herself tight to me after we stop descending, little shivers running through her letting me know she's afraid of the height. I would be too if I lacked my claws and strength.

Humans have no natural defenses, according to reports. It makes a frisson of anxiety run through my limbs, followed by a surge of protectiveness.

I will just have to be what evolution failed to provide her.

I pat her rear gently.

"We are down now, small one," I tell her, putting a comforting purr in my voice.

She scrambles off of me.

"Oh, I'm so sorry!" she says in a rush, her face red again. "I was treating you like a giant *teddy bear*."

I move closer to her and pat her rear again to calm her. "No need to be sorry, though I don't know what a *teddy bear* is."

I hope it isn't a bad thing.

She clears her throat, looking down at my hand on her rear, likely happy I have helped ease her. "Oh. it's something soft and cuddly. Meant to be held to help someone feel better. Safer."

I am glad she already knows one of my most important roles in her life now that I've found her.

"Then I'm your *teddy bear*," I say, feeling elated that I make her feel safe.

When she bares her teeth at me again I have to remind myself that she isn't contradicting herself.

"Climb on my back," I urge her, stepping to the side and pitching forward onto all fours. "We can find a better tree for me to *teddy bear* in."

She lets out a quiet version of her lovely trill and then uses my outstretched elbow to climb up, tightening her legs in readiness for me to move.

She starts vocalizing, stops, clears her throat and starts again. "Could we find water? I haven't had any for a long time."

I'm instantly annoyed with myself that I hadn't already accounted for her needs and taken her straight to a water source. She probably would also like to wash off the remnants of the noxious gas.

"Yes, I'll take you to a stream I can hear close by."

Running with Ree is quickly becoming my favorite activity.

I keep my ears swiveling for threats and make sure I leave no trail, but otherwise I simply enjoy the feel of her. The tug of her hands on my mane.

The little sounds she makes when I jump over logs or dodge around trees.

I had been content simply to evade hunters, but I might need to leave her safely in a tree and systematically kill every single one of them I can find. Until I rid this entire planet of hunters and do whatever is needed to take over their space elevator, Ree will be in danger.

Yes. They will all have to die.

I can feel the venom dripping from my whipping tail in anticipation, even as the discomfort rises from embracing such violent thoughts.

21

Ree

For someone who looks downright deadly Thivoll really is just a giant stuffed cat-bear.

I doubt he would ever hurt a fly if simply left alone. I smile thinking of him turning teddy bear into a verb. I'm eagerly awaiting being 'teddy beared' and as much as I find our headlong, rolling gallop exhilarating I hope it's over soon and we get settled into another tree so I can pet his fur again.

Then I feel incredibly guilty because I keep forgetting about Silver and letting myself get swept up in... whatever it is I'm feeling about a giant furry alien.

Discussing how to rescue her must be the first order of business.

Not nanite-fueled lust.

No, not only lust, I correct myself. *Nanites didn't change my opinion of the genali.*

Not all of my attraction to him is related.

Ugh, but his to me might be, I groan internally.

I'll have to talk to him about that, too. Just the thought of that conversation makes my face turn into an inferno.

When a stream comes into view, I let out a big huff of relieved breath.

It should be boiled and filtered, but since there's no way to do either I'm just going to risk it.

I slide off Thivoll's back when he gets close, and kneel in a rush. I never remember being this parched in my life. The water is very clear and smells clean when I sniff it.

I take a long drink, starting off with desperate gulps, then trailing off into smaller ones until my stomach feels like it might burst.

I know from experience over the past few weeks that I don't really need to bathe after the modifications they made, but the impulse to wash is too hard to resist. I cup water in my hands and use it to scrub at my face, wishing I could jump in.

I don't want to get him wet from my clothes, or of course get naked.

I'm reconsidering the getting naked plan, my libido making its own demands, when a splash next to me makes me jump.

I look over to see Thivoll holding out a wiggling version of this planet's fish. It's a muddy brown, has legs like a salamander, but with billowing membranes that look like they would function as fins.

"In case you're hungry, too," he explains.

I try not to gag at the thought of eating the slimy thing.

"Eating that raw would make me sick," I tell him instead of voicing my distaste.

He hums. "If you are as modified as you look, then your nanites would also make this safe for you."

I grimace. "Maybe, but I'm not that desperate yet. I appreciate the thought, though."

He nods at me, then tips his head back and downs the thing in one gulp.

I don't contain my reaction this time and retch. Luckily he doesn't see it and my face is schooled by the time he looks at me again.

I give him a weak smile and climb back up when he crouches down. I get my foot wrapped up in my long hair and have to flip it back behind me, but it whips around too far and then is in the way of my other leg.

I get it sorted and eventually scramble up, my face burning at the delay.

After about fifteen minutes of running, Thivoll stops under the same type of tree as before. This one with unmarked bark. I wonder how he will manage a climb with me stuck to him like a cowardly barnacle without damaging this one, too.

I don't ask, though, trusting him to know his abilities and limits.

I slide off as quietly as I can. He tips back on his back paws, his tail held out as a counterbalance. It must be difficult to maintain. I wish I could help more, but he is too tall for me to just grab.

He lifts me and I hold on tight.

He talks quietly near my ear, the feel of his warm breath on my skin raising goosebumps.

"I'll need both arms for this climb, Ree," he explains.

I gulp, then nod into his chest.

"If you start to slip, I'll grab you. I promise," he says with a purr in his chest.

It turns into a soothing rumble against my cheek as he gets closer to the tree.

His purr suddenly cuts off and his body tenses.

It's the only warning I get before the roar of a gun echoes across the forest and a searing pain blooms in my left bicep. It pulls a scream from me as another shot rings out and tree bark explodes out from the tree behind me, grazing my cheek with a stinging impact.

A moment later Thivoll has me crushed up against the tree, one arm gripping me tight as he scrambles up it.

Another shot and a deep groan from him lets me know he's also been hit, but he continues his mad scramble.

A glimpse of the forest lets me know he's moving us to the far side of the tree as he climbs it.

"Can you hold me?" I don't understand right away. "Ree! Are you too injured to hold on?"

The question knocks me out of my shock and I cling hard to him, my adrenaline helping me ride out the searing pain.

"I'm alright," I hiss out through gritted teeth.

We are high in the canopy when he lets out another pained groan and launches us away from the trunk, twisting us around so he can grab onto the branches of another tree.

Our impact is jarring and the swing of our bodies almost jolts me out of his arms. I have to clamp down hard on a chunk of his mane with my good arm to keep myself from falling before he wraps his tail around me.

It pulls me tight to him as he moves us up into the twisting thick branches of the tree.

His tail unwraps again and I let out a small mewl of panic as I frantically pull all my weight to his chest, gravity trying to pull me down and his moving limbs jostling me from where I'm clinging to his chest like a baby ape.

"I need it, sorry," he pants out.

I can't reply.

All of my focus has to be on making myself continue to grip him as I get increasingly dizzy from the pain and rapid changes of direction.

A small, agonized eternity later he slows down and wraps an arm around me.

"We should be fine now if we aren't too loud," he tells me in a whisper.

I nod against his chest as shivers of fear and agony wrack my body.

I push through them to ask about his wound. "Where'd they get you?"

"Nowhere dangerous. You?"

"I'll have to stop the bleeding quickly or I'll pass out."

"So soon?" His low voice sounds panicked.

There's no reason to risk an answer, so I focus on staying conscious and not screaming each new torturous time he bumps into me.

Eventually we stop moving and he repositions me as I hiss in a breath through my gritted teeth.

"Ask your suit to recede?"

I realize what he means after a long, dumb moment of confusion. A quick image of a sleeveless black shirt and my wound is exposed. The blood flow is sluggish, but my arm is coated in it, as is his fur.

"Is there an exit wound?" I ask him.

He tips me forward slightly as he moves his head to the side so he can look, his large body caging me against the trunk of a tree. His claws are digging into the bark and his tail is anchored on a limb above us.

"No, just the one in front."

"Shit. Can you dig it out?"

"What? I don't think I should—"

"It has to come out, Thivoll."

"Won't your body just expel it? Mine is already out."

"The fuck? No, it won't."

His eyes are wide as he looks back and forth from my face to my arm. "My fingers won't fit."

I growl and push my back against the rough bark so I can do it myself. "Hold me tight, then."

"Don't you think you should wait for... Alright. I see your point," he admits with a shaky voice as he moves a hand to grip my waist.

I wipe the blood away so I can get a better look.

It's a smaller hole than it should be.

"Nanites are working, at least. I need something to bite down on so I don't scream."

"Wait. Why? They should dull the pain as they heal you."

I snort out a breath. "The slimes wanted us to feel pain."

"Thela-cursed pieces of..." he trails off as he snaps off a branch.

"You're going to have to use a claw to cut it open anyway. Fish it out."

"I can't—"

"You will," I cut him off with steel in my voice.

"I can't have a bullet in my muscle. The scar tissue will make it harder later."

"But the pain and the blood..."

"I've had endometriosis most of my life. It's fine."

His whiskers droop. "I don't know what that is."

"It's... never mind. I can take a lot of pain."

I snatch the branch from his shaking hand.

"Just do it."

I cram it between my teeth and brace myself.

He closes his eyes for a long moment, then opens them. He raises a shaking hand as the claws extend from his fingertips. My heart is pounding and I look away.

Then I can't stand not knowing what's about to happen so I dart my eyes back to my arm. Just in time to see him fold back all but one of his fingers and make a quick slash with his claw.

After that, it's all I can do to keep myself from screeching out in agony.

Hot flares run through me as he digs around searching for the bullet, the muscles cording in my neck so hard they send another layer of pain darting down my spine. I clamp my teeth down as hard as I can on the branch as my lungs burn with their need for air I can't give them right now.

My vision is fading to black by the time he finishes, then I lose track of time.

When he speaks again, I push through the haze, though I don't know what he said.

"Ree!" He's pressing a hand hard against my arm. "There's too much blood."

I take in a ragged breath. My teeth are chattering against the stick in my mouth as my body quakes.

I spit it out so I can speak to him. "W-rap your t-tail around m-my arm."

I take another long breath in to collect myself as he unwinds his tail from the branch above us and does as I ask.

"Higher. Yes, t-there. Now squeeze."

My body arches again from the pain, and he loosens his tail in response.

"No. Keep going."

I close my eyes and focus on each breath in and out, just like we teach so many of our patients.

In. Out. Over and over.

When the pounding pulse in my fingers becomes too insistent, I open my eyes again.

"Pull your hand away," I tell him.

The bastards might have skipped the pain reduction feature, but the nanites have already started to do their work. The wound is still gaping open, but at least the blood flow is under control.

Well, at least with a tourniquet in place.

"Ok, loosen now."

My whole arm pulses and aches as blood flow returns to normal. I let out a huff of breath when there's only a small increase in the rate the blood oozes out.

"Will your skin close itself?"

"Let me guess. Yours already did?"

"I'm sure my scales already shifted, yes."

I grunt. "Will the nanites close mine up anyway?"

"Eventually. But it'll take more time and resources."

For now, I ask my suit to expand back over the wound. Hopefully it will keep it moderately clean that way.

My teeth are still chattering and now that we've done all we can the fear rises to the surface. I can't stop trembling. My heart pounds as he repositions us so I'm cradled against him.

He pets my hair and I take deep breaths to get myself back under control.

As my heart rate lowers, I realize that the pain in my arm is rapidly diminishing right along with it.

Soon all I can feel is a slight ache.

"It doesn't hurt very much now. That's weird."

He growls. "They must have programmed in a delay."

"Maybe one tied to heart rate?"

"Yes, that's possible. Seems like we should keep you calm for a while."

He purrs and I focus on the thrum for a while as he continues to run his hands through my long hair, working through tangles as he goes.

"Do you like when I touch your mane?"

"Oh, yes," I breathe out. "Do you like it when I do?"

"Most certainly," he says with emphasis.

I smile at him, then stroke his soft fur.

We stay like that for a few minutes, then I start lightly scratching at the transition between fur and black scales. He responds like any cat I've ever known by tipping his head back, pursing his lips, and extending his whiskers out.

It's even more comical and rewarding when he does it and I smile.

"I didn't think an alien would look so similar to a cat," I say aloud, then feel my face heating.

"I'm guessing that's an Earth creature?"

"Yes. Your fur, ears, whiskers, purr..." I trail off, feeling weird now.

"It's common for us to make connections to what we already know," he comments. "Plus, from what you describe, it's likely that creature originated from manticorids visiting your planet. We have several creatures with similar features to my own. As I mentioned before, we were once empire-seeking so I'm sure we surveyed your planet and we were too full of pride to hide ourselves."

"Huh," I say, my mind blown. "You do seem like something from our mythology."

He nods. "It's been thousands of standard cycles since we dismantled our empire, but the myth was probably based on an encounter with us."

I shake my head and mentally berate myself.

I'm letting my mind think of soothing distractions instead of doing what needs to be done.

"What about Silver? I think she needs more medical attention."

He scratches his chest with a scaled hand while he thinks. "I could go move her, but I don't like the idea of leaving you."

"I'm concerned she'll be recaptured if we wait. I'll be fine."

He growls, but doesn't argue with me. "I can move in haste and put her somewhere safe, then we can figure out how to get medical supplies for both of you. I'll need to stalk some hunters for those."

I gulp, my hand wanting to rise to brush against my wound at the reminder, but I know he's right. "I can stay here this time because I don't want to slow you down, but I want to help."

He hums again. "I would rather you remain in the trees, but we can talk about that soon. I'll run back to the ship and move her. First, let's get you to a tree that isn't covered in your blood."

I look down and see what he means, then nod.

It doesn't take him long to move me, but when he starts to leave I remember his own injury.

"What about your wound?"

"It was minor."

"A gunshot is minor?"

"That one was."

I'll need more time to get my mind around that one.

Time we don't have.

"Alright," I say, "please be careful."

"I'll take the utmost care of your fellow human, Ree," he vows.

I pat his mane. "Oh, I know you will. I mean be careful to not get hurt."

He purrs in response and his whiskers wiggle.

I'm pretty sure it means he really liked what I just said, but I'm too shy to ask.

He makes sure I'm firmly wedged against the tree trunk, then pulls away. He uncoils himself, runs a hand through my ridiculously long hair, and then disappears into the canopy.

I listen carefully, but can barely hear him descend.

I realize I didn't think of two important things when I agreed to this plan. For one, I'm now who knows how high in a tree by myself with an injured arm. And for another, I really should have peed.

"Dammit."

22

Ree

I have little to occupy my time aside from worrying, so for a distraction I focus on my breathing and keeping my heart rate as low as possible.

Unfortunately, eventually I can't focus on anything else but the increasingly insistent demands of my bladder.

Just when I'm desperate enough that I'm trying to figure out how to climb out on a limb for a makeshift mile high bathroom Thivoll returns.

"I—" he begins but I interrupt him.

"Is it safe?"

"Yes," he says in a confused drawl, his whiskers drooping.

"I need out of this tree," I say in a rush. "Now!"

To his credit he simply blinks at me, then grabs me and we scramble down at a dizzying speed. Once we reach the ground, I push away from him and start trotting away,

"Stay there," I order as I all but dive into a nearby bush.

Thankfully, the increase in my heart rate only results in a moderate responding increase in pain.

I try to pull my pants down with my good arm, but instead of hooking into a band, my thumbs slide off the fabric.

"Argh!"

"Are you alright?" Thivoll asks in a concerned voice.

"Yes!"

I realize my error and instead picture my pants disappearing and the weird black fabric recedes.

The relief is instant.

"Ah," Thivoll says, with a knowing tone. "Yikes!"

I smile at his not quite accurate use of the term, but one that completely fits with the definition I gave him.

"I'm not doing well at thinking of your needs."

"No, you're fine," I tell him. "I'm an adult and should think of these things myself. I'm usually very organized and cool under pressure, but it's been a hard day."

That's a serious understatement, but I don't want to sound like I'm angling for pity.

Instead, I just finish my business, wish I had access to modern amenities and so many other things I took for granted, and step back out.

I cringe when I see the damage to the tree. "I guess we'll need to move again? Sorry."

"There are thousands of trees," he says, his whiskers quivering.

It's getting dark and I would feel a lot better in a safer spot. "I'm sorry I interrupted. Let's go find a tree so we can talk."

He nods, crouches down, and just like that, we are back to running through the thick forest.

Thivoll slows down soon after and makes a whistling sound. His ears are swiveling wildly.

"What is it?" I whisper to him, leaning forward to get close.

"Something caustic on the wind. Something living." He takes another long breath. "Diseased."

That doesn't sound good. I stay still and quiet so I don't distract him.

"I don't—"

Luckily I still have a good hold on his mane because he whips around all of a sudden. I only get a glimpse of what alarmed him, but it's enough to send a spike of terror through me.

It's about the size of a bear, with leathery looking dark-red skin with black blotches. It doesn't have eyes and its head seems to mostly be composed of a large gaping maw of maroon-colored teeth. Yellow drool is dripping from it.

Then it's running on its six legs, using its pincher-type hands to dig into the forest floor to gain speed quickly.

"We aren't the enemy," I yell at it, but it just keeps charging at us.

Then there's no time to do anything but hold on as Thivoll tries to keep it at bay, twisting around in a way that is clearly meant to keep it away from me. From the way it tries to dart around him, I'm the prize snack in this raid.

I grit my teeth and squeeze as tight as I can with my legs.

Thivoll's tail whistles through the air several times as he spins us, but the creature keeps dodging out of the way, using its smaller size to its advantage. Thivoll slashes out with a hand and rakes his claws across its back.

It lets out a screech that makes my ears ring and seems to move even faster.

It darts in for its own revenge, catching Thivoll's side and my left leg with an extended pincher hand, a burning pain sparking up on the side of my knee and up onto my outer thigh.

I let out a yelp as Thivoll roars his rage and strikes back, but it darts out of the way again.

"It's too fast. Run!" I urge Thivoll.

He lets out a roar of frustration but must agree because when it comes back in to try to rip me off Thivoll's back he whips his body around, using his greater size to send it rolling into a nearby bush.

I almost slip off his back, my heart in my throat, when he starts bounding away.

I glance back when I hear another ear-piercing cry, the sight of it tearing toward us making my heart skip a beat. It launches itself toward me in a powerful leap and I scream in terror as it opens its disgusting mouth in preparation to eviscerate me.

Thivoll twists himself in the air mid stride and the thing bites into his flank instead of ripping into me. Thivoll lets out a groan of pain as the thing latches on.

His tail whips around, but it seems to be too essential in keeping our balance to be used as a weapon.

After a moment of panic, I notice the drum-like membranes on the side of the creature's head and take a risk. I let go with one hand, twist my body around and punch the one closest to me as hard as I can.

The thing lets out another scream, but also releases its hold on Thivoll.

As it falls, Thivoll kicks out with his injured back leg, sending the thing into another roll.

This time we're close enough to a tree and Thivoll bounds up just as I get my grip back on his mane. It's a blur of tree jumping after that point.

Soon after he gets us settled into the crotch of a tree as he swivels his ears and pulls in whistling breaths to test the air in between taking panting breaths.

I take a quick glance at my leg, relieved to see the blood flow is sluggish. I take a moment to order the fabric to mend, then turn my mind back to another pressing issue.

"Did it follow?"

"I don't think it can climb and I don't smell it anymore."

I let out a shuddering breath. "How's your wounds?"

"Mostly surface, but it has a diseased mouth. Nothing my biology and nanites can't handle, but we should make sure it doesn't bite you."

I let out a dark chuckle. No sense in pointing out to him that I wouldn't survive the initial chomp.

"I should have taken us straight into the trees when I smelled it. I've never heard of anything like that being here. Or anything that fast."

"Was it sapient, you think? It didn't respond to what I said and my translator didn't kick in when it screamed."

"No. Just sentient. It would have been introduced as part of the experience. When they terraformed this planet they eradicated the existing species."

My jaw drops open. "That's... I don't even have words."

"Yes, I agree. It's horrific." He huffs out a breath. "I'll remember the smell. It won't catch us off guard again. Let's move again."

I wrap myself around him in my monkey grip so he can keep moving us through the canopy.

By the time Thivoll stops it has long since been dark. He must have night vision because I would have careened right into a tree many times.

Not to mention the whole falling to my death thing.

"How is your wound?" I ask him. "Mine is just aching now."

"It's healing, but my body is having to fight the infection. That is one disgusting mouth on that thing."

When Thivoll has us settled again, he speaks. "I moved your Silver. She would have been safest in a tree, but I didn't want her to be stranded or accidentally fall if she comes out of cryo before we return. I put her in a deep thicket instead, but we should look for a better hiding place."

"How long does she have until her chamber stops working?"

"It depends on the person and relative processing efficiency. I don't have enough data on Silver to predict."

I open my mouth to ask what he means, but realize it doesn't really matter. "How did she look?"

"Her nanites should be able to heal her if she stays in stasis. It'll help remove additional stressors. If you can stabilize some of her wounds, I think it would be wise, though, since we don't know how much time we have until she wakes up."

"I wanted to before I put her back in cryo, but I can't without supplies," I say, my voice full of guilt and regret.

He wraps an arm around me. The feel of his scales sliding against the thin fabric of my odd black jumpsuit makes me shiver.

"We could get supplies from hunters," I say, the idea popping into my head and then out of my mouth before I have time to think it over.

I remember a beat later that he already came up with that plan and we discussed it, then feel stupid.

My brain needs to catch up already.

"I agree. It's the best plan overall," he says. "We can start tomorrow, but for now we should rest so we can heal."

Him saying it makes me realize just how exhausted I am.

It's just as cold as the night before, but the difference between shivering on a cold floor and lying circled by a furred body is stark.

"May I lean against you, Thivoll? My back is killing me from sitting like this."

"Of course, please do what you need in order to be comfortable."

I lean back, and the relief is instant.

As a bonus, I'm even warmer. I can't help myself from letting my hands sink into his soft fur and I enjoy the feeling of the smooth scales in between the many tufts of soft orange hair.

"How's your arm?"

"It's not bad, actually."

His purr picks up again and with the pain and adrenaline diminished, I'm even more aware of my body's reaction to him. It reminds me I need to talk to him about how my nanites are affecting him. I think of several ways to start the conversation, then shut them down.

While he continues to purr, I get more and more self-conscious and anxious.

"Is something wrong?" he asks, and I realize I'm clutching his fur, my neck is tense, and my breathing has turned shallow.

I just make myself blurt it out. "If you happen to maybe possibly be attracted to me it's because of what they did to me."

My face is on fire and my heart hurts for some inexplicable reason, but at least it's said.

Maybe not using the best grammar, but it's out there.

"Ree," he says, then starts chuffing.

Luckily he doesn't make me wait long to say what's funny. "They would never work on me, or at least only for a short time. I am attracted to you, but because of who you are, not because of the pheromone cocktail your body has been producing."

"Really?"

I'm relieved, but also embarrassed. Pleased, and also terrified of the idea of talking about attraction after just meeting. Just meeting an alien no less.

"Yes, really," he assures me. "I won't deny that the program has done an admirable job of creating an appropriate mix for my species, but it just makes you smell better, nothing more."

My body melts in relief, then I realize I haven't reciprocated and figure I might as well just get the embarrassing statements out of the way.

"I'm attracted to you, too," I say, then keep talking faster, "and not just because of this stupid nanite lust, but also because you are beautiful and funny and smart and..." I trail off, not because I don't have more to add, but because I sound like an idiot.

"Sorry," I say, once again mortified.

"No need to be," he purrs, "I like these words you say."

To underline his point, he runs a hand through my hair, then I feel his tail wrapping around me.

Once it's tightly around me he pulls me closer to him. "How do humans position themselves for sleep?"

"Ideally laying down, but we can sleep sitting up if we have too. It just usually means pain in the morning."

He responds by moving me again, this time with my back tight up against his chest and belly. I pull my knees up as I move so I don't invade his space.

When I'm fully laid out I feel his tail tighten more and then it rocks me for a moment before it stops moving.

"What was that?" I ask him, since I can't see anything in the deep cover of the leaves where moonlight can't enter.

"I wrapped my tail around a branch so you will be secure."

I get a warm feeling in my chest and it's a testament to just how upsetting things have been lately that such a minor act brings tears to my eyes.

"Oh, that's so thoughtful. I'm not sure I'll be able to sleep thinking of the height, but that makes me feel better."

He responds by pulling me closer to him, wrapping both of his arms around me.

"My limbs hold whatever position I go to sleep in. A remnant of our arboreal past," he explains.

"That's really cool."

"What part of you needs covering?"

The question confuses me, then I realize my error. "I'm very warm, thank you. That was just something lost in translation."

After that, our conversation dies out.

I have a million unanswered questions, but no energy left to ask them.

I reach one of my hands up to stroke the fur of the arm crossing my chest, especially enjoying the feel of where the fur recedes, and it's just his smooth black scales.

I love the transition of textures.

His purr deepens, and he moves one arm so he can stroke the long fall of hair draped over my hip. He reaches up and strokes the length of it in a soothing repetitive motion.

It helps lull me and I feel myself getting heavier and heavier.

I lose track of time, but then I startle back awake, convinced I'm falling, but Thivoll just squeezes me a little tighter, pats my butt, and makes a soothing sound.

I grip the arm he has around me with one hand and his tail with the other, and then drift back to sleep.

23

Thivoll

It's a long time before I'm able to sleep.

The events of the day and the remnants of my fear crowd my brain. I knew she was fragile, but the difference between raw knowledge and hard experience is stark.

That would have been a minor wound to my species, but I almost lost her today.

Terror spikes through me, trembling along my limbs, especially when I think about how determined she sounded to help find medical supplies.

I know I can't cage her in a tree. It would be just as sure of a death for her once she responded to the confinement.

I would never harm a woman. Especially not like that.

The stronger the personality, the quicker the confinement sickness sets in, and she is a formidable woman.

She is just as fierce as the best of our females.

Pride fills my chest when I think of how composed she was, especially considering she felt all the pain.

Could I have done the same?

I have no idea. I've had nanites in my system since before I was even born.

They never remove all pain, of course. That would be unwise, especially for the more adventurous kits like I was.

It means I don't know how she must have felt.

I take in a long breath. Mixed in with her exotic scent is the aroma of our blood. It sweeps away any remaining qualms I had about killing.

They will pay. All of them.

I growl, knowing just the sight of my sharp rows of black serrated teeth and extended dark claws will make most of the hunters quake in fear, regardless of how much training they bought before coming.

I'm not sure how concerned I should be that this is starting to sound like fun.

Then I imagine genali gray blood mixing with the ever-present pink mucus and a purr starts in the back of my throat.

Maybe it wasn't just my ancestors who were bloodthirsty.

Manticorids are adaptable.

Recently I was an air tech and acted like one. The genali put me on their hunting ground and gave me something to protect and so now they will become the hunted. That makes my lips rise and my teeth bare.

They will never take her from me.

Manticorid males are notorious for quickly identifying a suitable life mate. Though we all recognize there can be many good matches, we tend to pounce on the one in front of us.

There are no guarantees you'll come across another, after all.

As much as I've been trying to talk myself out of it, it explains my continual focused interest. She is just the type of woman I want.

As fierce as she is loyal, with a kind heart.

I never imagined my mate would be on a backward planet. Or that she would be from the more primitive species.

It doesn't matter.

Thela help anyone who tries to harm my little human ever again.

***

Raucous sounds from the trees around us wake me up.

I tense, expecting a hunter to have somehow slipped past my guard, then relax. The small creatures fighting over something nearby have confused whatever part of my brain that scans for threats in my sleep. It's merely a battle for food or nesting grounds.

Ancient instincts can't be right all the time, I suppose.

She must have either been exhausted or humans never move in their sleep, because she is exactly where she was the last time I pulled her close to me.

I look forward to finding out based on repeated exposure.

I'm not sure how much sleep humans need, though clearly more than I do since I remained awake for quite some time after her just listening to the forest and enjoying the sensation of her against me.

The small creatures bring their fight closer to us and it becomes more violent, or at least more vocal. She startles awake after a particularly obnoxious screech, her body instantly tense.

I stroke her hair.

"Do not fear. it's merely a disagreement among local fauna," I offer in reassurance.

She makes a humming sound in response and settles back against me. "What time is it? Nevermind, that's a dumb question. I'm still waking up, sorry."

I feel my whiskers lifting forward in amusement as she mutters and retracts her question a second time.

She must find waking up from her sleep as difficult as falling into it. It makes me want to cuddle her all the closer and be there for each transition to help ease it for her.

I don't tell her this, though. It's better to show than to tell, after all.

"When you're ready, we should discuss how to proceed."

I feel her nod. "To be honest, the only way I can likely help Silver is to stitch her wounds closed. Anything else would require equipment that wouldn't work here even if we found it."

"Hopefully that will be enough of a boost to her nanite healing so she is stable before her chamber stops functioning."

She grunts. "I assume that should be among any basic medical supplies a hunter would carry, right?"

I nod, the movement becoming more natural. "Yes. It's unfortunate the genali I killed yesterday didn't have basic kits on them. They were reckless in their attempts to recover you, it seems."

"From comments made on the ship I think losing my harem group will probably get them killed, Thivoll. I bet they were panicking, plus they probably thought they would just be dealing with a loose naked human or two. Not you."

She breaks off into a lower version of her trill, the spacing and tone suggesting a sort of dark humor I can certainly appreciate.

"Hunters won't be nearly as easy to kill," I warn her. "I behaved recklessly when I realized they were slavers. We will need to be more strategic. I cannot allow you to be hurt again."

"I know it would be safer for me to remain in a tree, Thivoll, but I would be completely trapped. That scares me more than being with you."

I growl, not liking the sound of her being in danger, but I do understand her point.

"I would never trap you. But I would feel more comfortable if you remained hidden. At least until we gather some tactical gear and weapons."

She trills. "Oh, I know I'm no fighter. I just don't want to be separated."

I feel something in my chest loosen to hear her say she doesn't plan to fight. "Let's climb down and get something to eat."

I pat her rear, and she moves away from me to give me room to rise. I shake out my mane, then grab her for a quick descent.

I don't bother hiding my marks on the tree.

There's no reason to return here and it will hopefully waste a hunter's time trying, and failing, to track us.

24

Ree

Thivoll doesn't give me any time to overthink our descent. I'm still distracted by the way his fur is flopping around from him shaking it out when he grabs me and we quickly descend.

I make my way to a nearby bush, and assume Thivoll is doing the same. I avoid thinking about how much I really miss modern conveniences so I don't end up whining.

It's never a good look.

When I come back, Thivoll is on all fours. His hands stretched out far in front of him, his butt is up in the air, his head is thrown back, and he's yawning hugely. I thought his teeth looked menacing before, but now I realize he has three of the razor sharp ebony rows that resemble shark teeth with a somewhat similar jagged triangle.

I blink at the sight of it, but the rest of his pose is so comically feline that I can't help but smile as I walk toward him. He looks over at me and slightly recoils, which makes me remember that to him I'm being threatening.

The idea of barely over five feet me making such a giant, incredibly dangerous alien recoil with my small little white teeth, sets me off laughing.

The way his whiskers droop, which I'm beginning to associate with him being confused, makes me laugh even more.

"I'm sorry, Thivoll. I keep forgetting what a smile looks like to you, but you have to admit that I'm not particularly scary, right?"

"My dam was smaller than me long before I was grown, she doesn't have venom, just like any female manticorid, but she is one of the fiercest beings I've ever known. It isn't always about might. Presence is more important and you have an intensity about you."

The way he says it makes my heart warm. "I've been in a leadership role at my emergency room for a year now. Maybe that's where it comes from."

"I know little about humans but what I did research suggests you are very young for a leadership role."

I cringe when I think of how young I must now look and how that would affect my career.

If we ever get off this planet, let alone get me back to Earth.

Plenty of people would literally kill someone to go back to looking this young but I've worked hard to get people to trust my judgment.

If I went back to the ER looking like this, I don't think anyone would listen to me.

It was hard enough to be taken seriously as a female in my thirties. I think any advocacy for my fellow nurses would just be scoffed at now that I look like I'm barely old enough to drink.

But no need to burden him with that. "I'm older than I look. How about we find some food?"

He blinks at the sudden topic change, but doesn't press the issue. "This plant can be eaten raw by many species. I'm certain your nanites will make it safe."

I look at the plant he's pointing to, then walk closer to it. It's a light lime green with a variegated white pattern.

"Do I eat the leaves?"

"Yes, and the stem if you would like. The roots are likely too hard for your blunt teeth."

Blunt teeth, huh? I raise an eyebrow at him, but he just keeps looking at me with his normal expression. So I guess there was no joke or insult intended and he also has no idea what a raised eyebrow means.

Of course.

Fancy tech swimming around in my head only gets us so far.

I look back at the plant. Good thing I like salads.

"Hmm. Raw or cooked?"

"Both."

I grab a leaf, turn it over to check for bugs and then cram it in my mouth before I can overthink it.

I'm starving and can't afford to be picky.

It has a tart, slightly bitter flavor that reminds me of lime mixed with kale except nothing quite like either.

I grab several more.

"Do you know the protein level?"

"Moderate," he explains, "but there are several other plants that in combination would provide what you need."

I nod, and finish chewing what's in my mouth. "How do you know the wild plants on a planet you've never been to?"

"These were introduced. The planet was a failed colony before the genali claimed it. The colonists broadly distributed food crops so they would naturalize."

A failed colony doesn't bode well. "Did it fail because of the technology interference or something else?"

"As far as I know the braceaaer colonists simply didn't want to make the dramatic cultural shift it would take to live with basic technology. Windmills and water generation work here, but not if you want to store the power or do anything more than simple things like milling grain. No instant communication. No power. Few are interested in such a primitive existence."

Interesting. "Braceaaer?"

"You know what they look like, actually. They've been abducting humans for hundreds of years and your journalists have provided accurate portraits."

My jaw drops open. "Little Green Men are real?"

Luckily he knows it's a rhetorical question so I don't feel like a fool.

My lips quirk up when I think about how much of that I've been doing since meeting him. Tam would give me her I-know-you-like-him eyebrow waggle as soon as he turned away.

It makes a giggle try to bubble up.

But then my thoughts turn more serious. "Do you think we will get back to Silver soon?"

"Yes, I'll do whatever I can to help your friend."

"Even after getting shot?"

"Seems to underscore the importance even more, my Ree."

I blink at the sudden possessive he uses, but push the thought aside. "You'd risk yourself for a bunch of aliens you've never met?" I ask, somewhat bewildered.

"Well, of course," he says, not elaborating further.

I feel my chest filling up with some sort of unidentified emotion.

Not long ago I was despairing over how to find my way in the woods, wracked with guilt to be leaving Silver.

The rush of appreciation I feel overtakes my good sense and before I can think better of it I take the two steps between us and throw my arms around him.

"Thank you so much, Thivoll. I had no hope of helping her without you."

I ignore my brain trying to overthink and just enjoy the sensation of his fur against my cheek and the heat from his body. One of his arms wraps around me and his rumbling purr soothes my remaining anxiety.

He pats my butt again, this time making me jump a bit in his arms.

I open my mouth to say more but he gets us moving for the day. "You gather more of that and I'll get some of the other plants."

I grab several handfuls of the leaves, careful not to fully strip the poor plant. He returns with a much larger bounty.

So much that I can't eat it all and I'm not sure how to carry it.

I hope he plans to help and hasn't just gathered a Thivoll-sized meal I can't fit in my stomach or store away.

"Are you eating some, too? Your teeth suggest you're a carnivore, not an omnivore like I am."

"We can eat almost anything, but do feel best with a mostly protein diet, you are correct."

"I can't eat all of this, Thivoll."

"Take what you can eat now," he instructs me. "I'll eat the rest."

I grab a very healthy portion. I stuff some in my mouth so I can fit more in my hands.

Thivoll's whiskers droop. "Should I hold some for you?"

I regret the giant mouthful now and shake my head. He keeps staring at me, waiting for me to finish chewing so I can more fully answer.

"This is plenty."

He blinks rapidly. "How many times a day?"

"Three, maybe four if it's only plants."

He huffs. "You will be very simple to provide for, it seems, though we will need to find more than just leaves."

He tilts his head back and simply dumps the rest of the food in his gaping mouth, his jaw hinging back much farther than my eyes are comfortable seeing.

I jump when his jaw closes with a snap.

I really like the man-cat-alien and my body is all on board with all kinds of naughty ideas, but at times like these I'm reminded just how very alien we both must seem to each other.

He falls to all fours and crouches down. "Let's find water."

25

Ree

I don't think Thivoll has caught on to the fact that I can't just gulp entire meals down.

He is looking at me expectantly and I have no clue what to do with all the leaves I'm holding.

I wish I had a pocket.

"You dummy," I grumble under my breath. "Sorry, that was directed at me."

I look down at my black suit. It's still just as embarrassingly tight, but it does indeed now have a pocket. A giant one over my belly like I'm a kangaroo, but I don't want to push my luck trying to ask for a different arrangement.

I simply stuff the vegetation in there and clamber up. Thivoll takes off at a run and I have to hold on tight, my stomach protesting that I gave it a small taste and then didn't keep feeding it.

Luckily we don't run for long and I fill it so full of water it doesn't have room to gurgle at me anymore.

I pull out leaves, chewing as Thivoll deftly grabs a half dozen aquatic creatures and throws them down his throat. Luckily one at a time so I don't gag.

His jaw doesn't have to open as wide, but I'm still not the least bit accustomed to it by the time he finishes.

I try not to think about how they must be squirming around still. I heave at a fleeting image, then shut off that line of thought and go back to chewing.

And chewing some more.

Salads are time consuming to eat, but this is even worse.

"So you are a ruminant species," he comments.

I swallow the latest round of bitter leaves, trying not to choke as I imagine myself as a sheep.

"Uh, no. We only chew and swallow once. But we do need to chew thoroughly."

"No additional set of teeth or grinders in your stomach?"

My jaw drops open and I'm instantly burning with curiosity. "No. How do they work? Is it mid-digestion or pre-digestion? Is it an additional jaw-like structure? Is it—"

He interrupts me with regret in his voice. "I wish we had time to discuss it, but we need to start stalking. It may take some time. I'll keep a slow pace while you ruminate... I mean chew."

I climb on his back, my legs tight around him and only one hand buried in his mane so I can keep eating. An image of an alpaca riding a lion pops into my head and I snort in amusement.

"Are you well?"

I get my ridiculous grin under control. "Oh, yes. Just entertaining myself with silly images."

He purrs in response.

Thivoll seems to appreciate my odd humor. We set off at a rolling pace. I keep steadily eating and then whisper to him I'm done so we can begin our run.

I'm sad I have to contain my whoop of joy as he begins his smooth gallop through the trees. Each dodge and jump causes a jolt of adrenaline. After letting myself enjoy the sensation for a few precious moments, our continually precarious situation weighs on my mind again.

I have so many questions with no answers and it seems like Thivoll has at least some of them.

I lean forward so I can talk as quietly as possible. "What can you tell me about the genali?"

He growls, the rumble of his displeasure passing up my spine. "I wish I knew less about their methods. We've tried to keep ourselves isolated, hoping they'd simply find us unappealing, but it hasn't worked."

"Have they attacked your home world?"

"No. They pick at the edges like scavengers. Mostly they attack vessels, but sometimes they make it through planetary defenses to make a raid."

"I'm sorry to hear that. For slaves?"

"Not exactly. They've been killing us for sport for many years, but generally they come to steal our technology. We don't make good slaves. Which is why we weren't prepared for the recent uptick in abductions. There are now two males to each female."

"That's terrible."

He hums in response. I suppose there isn't much you can say about losing a quarter of your population.

"It feels rude to ask, but why don't you make good slaves? You're strong and I assume your females are beautiful if they look anything like you."

My face burns once I realize how my mouth got ahead of my mind.

He chuffs. "Thank you. Our females are definitely attractive. It has to do with how we respond to captivity. Males enrage to the point of destroying everything around us, including ourselves, rather than allow ourselves to be caged. Females are also difficult to capture, but rarely enrage. They simply waste away until they die."

A pain stabs my heart and dread spiders up my spine. "So your cousins..."

I can't finish the thought. It's too horrible to contemplate.

"Yes, they are likely dead. Unless they've been stored in cryochambers. But either way, they are irretrievable once they leave our system so we mourn as soon as we find out."

"If you are advanced enough that they steal from you, why don't you strike back?"

"The short answer is politics, but that doesn't tell you much. My ancestors were once bloodthirsty. Expanding out into nearby star systems. Picking fights with other species over resources. Fighting amongst themselves. We're a species particularly suited to dominating others. We gave it up, painfully, and now we fear it returning."

"That makes sense, I guess. Was it really that bad?"

"Well, we never stooped to the level of the despotic races like the genali and braceaaer. There was a code we followed, however barbaric it might seem now, and we didn't torture, rape, or sell anyone into slavery. That said, many people died. Some planets were destroyed. It was such a difficult cultural transition for us that no one wants to lose what we gained."

"I see your point, actually. Humans don't have claws or venom and I know we couldn't be trusted if given the opportunity to take over the universe."

"Exactly. It left us vulnerable, though."

My forehead wrinkles. "But it sounds like you have some sort of defenses, so it isn't complete pacifism. The line seems drawn in a weird place. What's the harm in being more proactive?"

He chuffs. "I agree. They were still debating it last I heard, but I think this will bring us out of slumber. But not without fear and a lot of restrictions, especially ones on non-Abstainer males."

I wait, but he doesn't elaborate.

"And they are...?"

"Sorry. It's usually not a topic you discuss when you first meet someone. Being vague is a habit. It all comes down to our venom. And how using it can be addictive."

"Oh... Oh! It can lead to wars just for the opportunity to use it more."

"Excellent deduction. Abstainers remove the temptation along with the tip of the tail."

I grimace at the brutality, even as I understand the thought process. "At the risk of being culturally insensitive... I think if you're missing that many women, addiction is the lesser evil compared to extinction."

"Indeed. I hope our government realizes that before all the women we love are gone. You would think even one would have been enough, but no."

He falls silent after that. I loosen my grip with one hand and stroke along his neck.

There's nothing I could say that would help ease that pain and tears well in my eyes at the thought of it.

Then it opens the door to my own trauma and sadness is replaced with the ever-present horror of memory.

Of the women I vowed to protect.

I've done almost nothing to follow through with that promise and it feels like a lead weight on my shoulders.

My chest feels tight with each breath as each one of their faces drift into my mind.

It's been such a short time, but their features have already started to blur. Except for their vivid hair colors and my stomach clenches at the idea of that becoming their identity. I need them with me again, but this time out of their cages so they can become individuals.

Anything short of that would be losing them completely, just like I lost Navy.

My mind circles on wild plans, what-ifs, terrible memories, and the weight of responsibility in endless loops as Thivoll continues to move us through the forest.

26

Ree

We run for nearly an hour, stopping once more for more food and water. The whole time Thivoll's ears swivel in all directions, his paws and fists barely making any sound.

My body is stiff and sore from holding on for so long by the time I see his ears both swivel to the left and he stops to look that direction with an intent gaze.

I hold my breath, not wanting to interfere with his surveillance.

He speaks quietly. Almost too quiet for me to understand.

"Two genali. They sound like they're arguing. I think they're lost."

My hands grip harder onto his mane. "Suitable targets, then. Distracted."

Thivoll nods, then turns toward them, his pace slower, but still moving us through the forest at a good clip. Even I can hear them yelling at each other not long after, but Thivoll moves even slower.

I appreciate his caution.

As we move in closer, I can better make out the source of their argument. One of them thought they should be following a nearby creek to look for prey, but the other feels like they should continue to dig in and wait for prey to come to them.

Considering how loud both of them are, either they are complete idiots or maybe this is their strategy to get unsuspecting prey to come to them for what seems like an easy fight.

Or I guess an easy meal? Gross.

I take a moment to truly appreciate how lucky I am that Thivoll is the one who found me.

It could've ended very differently.

Thivoll is taking long, deep breaths as we get closer to the sound of the fighting. I hear a very gentle whistle like he is pulling air in so it moves along the roof of his mouth.

We continue to stalk closer and I'm afraid to even breathe, concerned that the aliens may suddenly stop arguing and hear us.

I still can't see them when Thivoll stops, the angle of his head suggesting that he's staring at something on the ground. I move to the side so I can see, careful to keep my balance. It would be a disaster if I tumbled off so I clutch his fur tightly.

I see what caught his interest.

A thin metal cable stretches across the path in front of us. I follow it with my eyes, every once in a while having to jump ahead past some foliage to keep following the line of it. At the end it's simply tied around a tree.

I start back in front of us and follow it the other way. It terminates in some sort of device with multiple holes pointed toward us.

It must be some sort of rudimentary trap.

Thivoll carefully steps high over it. I turn in my perch to watch him pull his back paws slowly and deliberately over and notice that his tail is held high. He must be taking no chances.

I approve.

Later I should talk to Thivoll about possibly coming back and disassembling it so we can take it with us.

We come across one more trap before Thivoll moves us into the trees.

The genali are very loud now but I still don't see them, since the foliage is extremely thick. Thivoll repositions me and then climbs and I'm impressed that I don't even hear his claws make purchase in the bark as we smoothly and rapidly ascend.

I hold on as tightly as I can to ease our passage.

As much as I want to know what's going on, the heights still bother me so I keep my eyes closed. I can tell we're making our way along branches and moving up and down tree trunks from the difference in where gravity pulls me.

Soon after, he gently rearranges me so I'm sitting on a thick tree branch, with my back against a trunk. He catches my attention with a hand wave and then points.

We are high above the arguing genali. I can just barely make out the top of their gray and pink slime-covered heads.

Thivoll lets me know with gestures that he wants me to wait here and I nod at him. He moves away, then turns back to me. His eyes soften and he reaches forward to stroke my cheek and run his hand down through the fall of my hair. I smile at him and then cover my mouth.

Maybe someday I'll remember it's a threat.

Or maybe he'll just have to deal with it as a permanent human quirk. His whiskers move forward past my shoulders, something about his face letting me know he knows what I'm thinking.

Or at least knows that I'm embarrassed.

After one last pet, he silently disappears into the thick canopy of the trees. I carefully avoid looking down, but luckily most of my thoughts are taken up by anxiety.

I hope he'll be alright.

I assume if they have traps they definitely have weapons.

He moved so quickly with the genali who were threatening me before it was mind-boggling, but they were unarmed, simply relying on that terrible choking gas that had no effect on him.

I carefully keep my breathing under control but I can't help my hands from wringing. It would be a lot better if I could see him and know where he was in relation to the shouting aliens.

A long, anxious minute later I see an orange flash above their heads. Thivoll must've decided to pounce on them from above.

Now the aliens are yelling for a very different reason.

I reach forward and pull down the branch that's blocking my view, more concerned about his safety than the heights. One of the aliens is already on the ground, jagged lines across its throat and a gray viscous liquid coming out.

The other one scrambles back while Thivoll pounces on their compatriot.

I gasp in a breath when I see them pull what looks like a gun, but before they get it fully into position Thivoll's tail whips around and knocks it from their sticky grasp. I wince when there's a loud retort, but I can't see if the bullet contacted Thivoll.

The slime continues to stumble back while Thivoll repositions himself for another strike.

The genali pulls a long serrated knife from a sheathe near his other flipper hand.

He moves toward Thivoll with a gurgling cry, raising the knife to make a stab toward his side as he dances away from them. Thivoll continues the arc of his movement and whips his tail around to drive the ovoid shaped end of it into the alien's side.

The slime tries to take a swipe at him with their blade but his tail pulls back as fast as it struck.

A moment later the genali is overtaken by violent tremors and starts screaming. Despite what I know about them and that they would absolutely kill, rape, or sell me into slavery, the sight of it's still disturbing.

I hope I get used to it, I think.

And then my mind violently reacts to how counter that is to everything I believe. All the oaths I've made to myself in relation to easing the world's suffering, not adding to it.

I'm no longer on Earth, I remind myself. These hunters are not innocent.

It's definitely an us or them situation.

I carefully suppress all those thoughts. They are luxuries from a different life in a different reality. They won't help me find or help all the missing women. In this reality, I need to feel grateful that we have such a protector.

He is absolutely magnificent.

He's scanning around him, obviously assessing if there are any additional threats. There's a raw purple score across his flank that's oozing blood. At least the bullet only grazed him, but it's yet another reminder of how dangerous even stupid hunters can be.

He stops scanning and stills, his bright eyes losing focus and his ears no longer moving.

I remember he commented that his venom made it difficult for him to think clearly. It occurs to me that this is our most dangerous moment and I'm nowhere close enough to him to help ease it or to watch out for him.

If there is another genali hiding, he could be killed.

For now there's nothing I can do. I'm not able to get myself out of this tree, which tells me just how little we actually thought this through. I have no way to help him if he's injured. If he is killed, I'll be stranded or captured.

I know both of us are smarter than this.

This certainly warrants a conversation as soon as possible.

I sigh, thinking of how few of the skills I focused on building in my life are a natural fit for this insane situation. Then I push all of those thoughts aside and focus on Thivoll. I hope he breaks out of his trance soon. I watch him closely, hoping for a sign that he is working through whatever has him locked down.

I'm pretty sure a hiding hunter would have struck by now and some of the tension leaves my body.

Now that the danger has passed and I've rerouted my overthinking brain, there is nothing to distract me from the ever-present lust. My nanites are telling me he is everything my body needs and wants.

Right. Now.

Even though the violence bothered me, I have to admit there was a beauty to his movements and the raw power is incredibly attractive. He was as poised as he was brutal and as I play the sequence of his motions back through my mind, I have to squeeze my legs together to provide some relief.

I shouldn't enjoy seeing that level of efficient violence, but I can't deny that it turns me on.

The thought of him up against me with such a graceful and powerful body makes me moan.

Thivoll whips his head toward me, his mouth open and his lips pulled back as he takes a deep breath.

Then he is on all fours and bounding in my direction.

27

Thivoll

Part of me knows it's not a good idea to be letting the euphoria make my decisions, but the sound she made and the smell of her on the wind is all the excuse the other part of me needs to tell that voice to shut up.

This lovely, heady feeling from my venom release would be all that much better if she was in my arms.

And so I make it happen.

It takes far less time to make it back to her than the slow stalk I made before that brief fight. I hadn't been sure if it was a ruse, but took a chance the genali were just as idiotic and unprepared as the shouting made them seem.

The frisson of pleasure I feel isn't just from the venom, but also from the satisfaction that two fewer hunters are a threat to my Ree.

Her smell is much stronger now that I'm at the base of her tree and I scramble up it, completely unconcerned with hiding my trail.

Anyone who looks at the genali I envenomated will know who I am, or at least what I am.

The little space left in my mind for those sorts of thoughts is overtaken completely when I finally reach her. She has a stranglehold on a nearby tree branch and her eyes are wide and wild. Her long indigo hair is draped all around her and I brush against it as I move from the enormous trunk of the tree to the thick branch I left her on.

I grab her with my right arm, the scales rubbing against the smooth fabric of her black suit, sending little jolts of pleasure up into my spine.

As I pull her into a standing position so I can feel more of her against me, I dig the claws of my left hand into the trunk of the tree and wrap my tail around the branch.

She's breathing rapidly and that musky scent that drives me wild is flooding the air all around us.

I lift her higher, wanting better access, wishing my hand was free so I could stroke it through her mane. She makes it possible by wrapping her legs tightly around me and pushing her back up against the trunk of the tree.

I'm momentarily distracted by how this pushes the heat of her core against my sheath. I keep myself from extruding by raw force of will.

I want to enjoy other parts of her first.

I snake my arm back out through the space left by her arched back. Down along her hip, up her stomach, between her breasts, and then grab onto her neck. I use my hand to tilt her head back and then pull my whiskers back and push my muzzle into the crook of her neck.

I take a long deep breath, the sensation of her silky hair against my whiskers almost too much to bear.

When I blow out a hot breath, she makes that same low, long moan that made me bound over to her. Her scent is overwhelming and I must know what she tastes like, so I take a long hard lick up her neck, the pounding feel of her pulse betraying her excitement.

She tastes salty and sweet and I think I've made a mistake because I won't ever get enough of it.

On the second hard lick, her moan turns into an inarticulate low keening and she tightens her legs in a rhythm that has me rocking against her.

So that's how she would like it.

I almost lose control thinking about her without a barrier between us, then my purr rattles between us and something about it must excite her because she writhes against me.

When I graze her lightly with my teeth she freezes, her body rigid before relaxing again as I bring my teeth away.

The natural reaction of a ruminate with a predator at its neck pulls me out of my venom-fueled frenzy.

28

Ree

"Did I scare you, sweet one?"

It takes a moment to clear my mind enough to respond. I've never been this aroused before and it short-circuited my brain.

"Oh, no. I liked it. I was just startled," I reply.

I probably should just leave it at that, but of course I also blurt out the rest of what's on my mind. "Your teeth look wicked sharp, Thivoll."

His whiskers droop, and the lilac coloring around his mouth darkens to a violet shade.

"You think me wicked?"

He moves back from me but is still supporting my weight. "I apologize. The venom euphoria overtook me, but that is no excuse for scaring you, my Ree."

I rush to reassure him. "No, no, no. That's a translation error. I just meant that they look incredibly sharp, and I just wasn't sure for a moment. But I do trust you."

I say the last in a rush of words.

He still looks unsure. "I would need to put pressure into my bite to cut you. But to my shame, I didn't ask and I hate that you were unsure, even for a moment."

I don't like the distance this is creating between us and figure it's best to address the issue straight on. "May I feel?"

I point toward his mouth with a question on my face.

He pulls his lips back and cracks open his mouth, something about his eyes letting me know he's trying to be extremely careful.

Like I'm a scared rabbit.

I smirk thinking that so far I've, just in one day, imagined myself as an alpaca, sheep, and now a rabbit.

I had best start thinking of myself as a woman or I'm going to be giving him all kinds of mixed signals.

I reach forward and cautiously test the edge of one of his teeth.

He's right, of course. Although the tooth looks intimidating with its ragged edges, I would have to press down quite hard to cut myself.

I nod at him. "Thank you, Thivoll. It's the unknown that makes someone's instincts kick in. I enjoyed what you were doing, and I hope this doesn't make you less likely to keep doing it."

His lips have returned to their normal lilac coloring, but his whiskers are still drooped. "I still feel as if I violated your trust."

"You didn't," I say firmly. It looks like under all that deadly predator vibe he has going there's a very sensitive soul.

The combination is incredibly appealing.

"May I kiss you, Thivoll?"

"I have no translation for that."

Oh this is going to be very fun, I realize.

"There are different kisses. But for now I would just like to put my lips to your cheek."

His whiskers stop drooping and push forward slightly. He now has a twinkle in his eye. "You mean like sharing scent?"

I think of my tabby cat rubbing against my legs and it doesn't quite conjure up the intimate moment I was looking for.

"Uh, no. Alright, well I guess technically yes, there would be scent transfer, but that's not the point."

This is getting far more technical than I was hoping and I can feel my face burning, but I persist anyway.

"It's more a sign of affection on the more innocent end of the scale and a very erotic act on the other end. Humans generally start on the less erotic side and work their way up."

He is focusing on me intently. "So how am I supposed to tell which one you are giving me?"

I take a breath and open my mouth to explain in detail, then think better of it. "Thivoll, I think we are both a little too prone to overanalyzing. How about I just kiss you and you see if you like it?"

He gives me an exaggerated nod and then moves his head to the side and close to me in a comical angle. I suppress my smile so we don't have a whole other layer of weirdness in our communication struggles.

I move closer to him, using the arm he has anchored to the tree to steady myself, the feel of his soft fur against my palm a pleasant invitation for more contact. I thread my other hand into the longer fur of his beautiful orange mane right below where his neck transitions from naked black scales.

His body is tense and one would think that suddenly I was the predator and he was the prey from the wide-eyed look he has.

I very much enjoy the sense of power it gives me.

It makes me want to make this an incredible experience for him.

I start by slowly roving my gaze over his strong facial features. His lilac scales, the broad nasal plate, the lovely mix of colors and textures that invite exploration.

I move my hand up from his mane to stroke it along his muzzle.

The scales around his mouth are surprisingly soft and I get distracted from my original goal by tracing the spaces around and in between his whiskers.

On the second stroke he lets out a low, gravely moan.

It must be a very sensitive area, and I confirm that by taking a long slow pass with my hand on his longest one, keeping my touch light. It feels like a quill, except much larger and with ridges running lengthwise and becoming closer and closer together until they are indistinguishable at the tip.

I do the same for another of his long whiskers.

Soon after, he looks like he's having a hard time keeping himself from melting into me.

His eyes are closed and he's no longer holding his head at the comical angle, but the best one to give me full access.

This time as I near the tip of the whisker I lean forward and kiss him on the muzzle just below the mass of whiskers.

I can see his eyes shoot open from my peripheral vision and keep putting feather-light kisses all over his muzzle.

On the fifth one his purr starts up in a steady rhythm, on the tenth I add back in stroking his whiskers and it rumbles like an avalanche. I wish I could wrap my legs back around him so I can feel that against my core again, but I keep focusing on my task.

I spend a few more moments interweaving kisses with stroking and then pause.

"Do you like it?"

"I love this kiss. I thought you would start on the innocent end, though, and so you caught me unprepared."

I laugh, delighted. "Oh, that was a pretty tame kiss, Thivoll."

He blinks, processing what that means, and his purr picks up pace again.

Then he huffs out a breath, followed by a growl. "I feel like that person who is always delivering bad news and telling us we need to stop being fun... but we've been here too long."

"Cock blocker," I blurt out.

"Pardon me?"

My face flames again. "Uh, the person who stops erotic fun. Blocks, you know... cock?"

My voice ticks up into a trill at the end, betraying my embarrassment.

Thivoll's whiskers move forward and his chuffing is deeper and more pronounced than usual. I let out a relieved laugh and then a more genuine one when he just keeps chuffing.

"I learn so many new things from you. But we do need to leave soon. I can't hear anyone, but I'd rather be cautious."

I give him one last kiss and then lean back. "Sure, let's see what supplies we can find."

He turns the tables and pulls me close to him, pushing his face close and taking another long lick near my ear, causing a deep shudder, then grabs me and descends instead of continuing.

"A cock blocker and a tease," I grumble and he chuffs the rest of the way down to the ground.

He lets me go when we're at the base of the tree.

He swivels his ears and takes a long breath, his lips curled back and the air whistling along the roof of his mouth.

"I didn't see any other traps, but stay behind me a few paces just in case and only step where I step."

29

Thivoll

There almost isn't any point in rerouting air along the glands in my mouth.

The air is so full of Ree's musk it's hard to pick out any other scents. It's the only way to ensure I'm using all the tools at my disposal to keep her safe, so I keep at it.

Unfortunately, the other dominant scent is genali blood, which gets stronger the closer we get to their disorderly camp.

From the brief glimpses I got as I fought them, I know we won't find much. These hunters truly were as stupid as they sounded and they seem to have prioritized luxury over practicality.

I turn back around to discuss it with her and catch the look of horror that flits over her face when she sees the state of the genali I envenomated.

It's an incredibly painful way to die, I admit.

Our venom quickly invades their circulatory systems, increasing the flow rate and then causing all the pathways and vessels to burst.

The genali is essentially one giant bruise with gray viscous liquid leaking from every orifice.

To her credit she simply shakes herself and then keeps moving toward me. "I don't recognize everything, but most of it looks useless, Thivoll."

I purr thinking of how intelligent and practical she is. It makes me want to go right back to licking her.

"Yes, unfortunately. Let's look for a med kit and I'll start destroying anything we can't use."

The hunters seem to have used up most of their pack space with tents and bedding. The bedding is a specialized fabric that helps keep them moist and warm.

I try not to think of how full of their pink slime it must be as I shred it with my claws.

Their packs are made of the same fabric and I know Ree won't want it against her skin any more than I would, so I simply dump out the contents and add the packs to the shredded pile.

Ree sifts through what I dumped, almost instantly locating the ribbed metal container of medical supplies. She takes a moment to figure out the clasp, which is designed for the wide webbed hands and small claws of a genali.

She pulls out the stitch clipper. "Does this use dissolving staples, you think?"

I look closer at the design. "I believe so, and your Silver's nanites will break them down once they are no longer needed."

She sits down as her black suit recedes from her arm, then calmly starts pinching the wound together and stapling it. She makes a hissing sound through her teeth as she does it, but keeps going until the task is complete.

She shakes her head when I hold my hands out in a wordless offer of help.

Then moves to the wound on her leg.

Only a slight tremor in her hands as she puts the stitch clipper away betrays her.

"I could have done that."

She looks at me, and her lips twitch up on the sides. "I know. But it made me feel more in control of how fucked up all of this is to do it myself."

"I respect that."

I spy another useful resource, and it distracts me from our conversation. "These will taste terrible, but they will sustain you more efficiently than your ruminating."

I open the foil pack of meal cubes and show her. "Oh, I'm quite familiar with those, unfortunately," she says with her tiny nose wrinkled and her tone suggesting she despises them.

I toss them aside. I don't like the thought of her eating something she hates.

"I'll search for better food."

She shakes her head. "No, we need to take them. They bring back memories of being on the ship and terror, but food is food."

I whip my head over to her, a spike of rage shooting through me, reminded that they didn't have her in cryo for her journey.

"I thought their buyers were particular about harems being untouched before delivery or auction."

"I was in an isolation chamber, but they had a camera up and needed entertainment for their viewers. Plus, they just enjoyed scaring me, I think. They didn't touch me because they didn't want to trigger the metamorphosis."

I'm confused. "I didn't know humans did that."

She shakes her head. "We don't, but they changed us. Speaking of... I've been around you long enough... Actually, that doesn't matter right now. Let's get out of here. I don't want to be anywhere near them anymore."

We've mostly sifted through their belongings, anyway.

Aside from the med kit and meal cubes there was nothing else of use. Just a lot of personal hygiene items only suited to genali, clothes, and highly questionable reading material that I quickly shred before Ree sees any of the disturbing images that only the depraved would find erotic.

She looks at the partially erected tents, then moves to pick up one of the genali knives. "Damn. I think I'd be more likely to cut myself than anything else with this design."

She drops the weapon, which I agree is not suited for anyone except genali. "Could you cut a large circle out of that tent and a few long strips so I can make a bag?"

I nod, moving to do as she asks. "That's a good idea. It's the only fabric we'll find that isn't covered in their mucus."

She shudders. "Actually, now that you mention it I can see marks all over it. I'll just imagine more pockets."

She stows items in pouches that appear on her black suit. I've seen her do it before, but haven't really thought through how responsive nanothread would react to this planet.

It's very useful, if prone to hacking, though I suppose that's impossible now and she will be the only one capable of delivering it commands.

"Be sure never to remove that nanothread or you'll permanently lose your link to it," I warn her.

She grunts in response. "Good to know. I found ammunition. Where's the gun?"

That's a good question. I think through the fight, then go to where it was likely to have landed.

The barrel is dented in.

"It's useless. I hit it too hard."

"Better a broken weapon than me digging a bullet out of your hide," she replies.

I chuff once, not liking the reminder of our time up in the tree. "On that we agree, but few would need your help."

She lets out a low groan. "You have no idea how jealous I am of that. The other gun should still work," she's pointing to the one still holstered and attached to the gruesome pile that was once a genali.

I get it and then hand it to her.

She flips it over to inspect it, careful to keep the barrel pointed down. "Their hands are so different I'm not sure if it's worth taking, but why not."

I spend a few moments tearing the tents enough to make them useless, then gather up the knives. I had hoped to use some of the weapons we found, but hadn't factored in the sizeable differences in our anatomy.

We would be better off looking for braceaaer hunters for those, I realize.

At least I can take these out of use, though. "I'll be back in a moment."

It's an awkward climb trying not to cut myself as I ascend a tree with the two knives and a broken gun without leaving evidence, but I'm tucking them away in the crook of a branch not long after.

I shouldn't have shredded the sheathes, but I got in a frenzy.

I pull the clip, then almost neglect to open the chamber to remove the bullets, but carry those back down with me.

It doesn't take much longer to take another quick sweep of their poorly made camp.

"Climb on," I urge her, ready to leave the stench of the slimes.

She nods, patting the various bulges of her black suit, repositioning some. "Should we take that trap and look for others?"

I consider it, but shake my head, the movement less natural than nodding has become. "I think I would rather move out of the area this time, since we tarried for a while in that tree."

I say the last with a purr, images flashing through my mind.

"Besides, hunters are far more likely to trip those sorts of traps than prey. These genali were clearly overconfident coming to this continent. As far as I know this is where they place the most dangerous, which means deadly, sapient, and intelligent."

She climbs up on my back as I finish speaking.

"Wait. So all the prey are people?"

Her voice is full of horror and disgust.

I growl, agreeing with her assessment. "Yes. Genali decided that the beasts of the northern continent were no longer suitably entertaining, so they started gathering people."

She tries out her own growl and my whiskers move forward at how adorable she sounds for a moment before the weight of our topic makes me serious again.

It isn't safe to keep her at this camp.

I make sure she has a good grip with her hands and legs and then start loping out the same way we came in.

30

Thivoll

I bound over the poorly hidden trap, briefly considering hiding it better, but wanting to put as much distance as possible between us and the smell of genali blood.

Ree makes a drawn out high-pitched sound that doesn't translate, then a moment later she speaks.

"I overheard the genali talking about this place before we crashed. That they put blocks in the prey so they can't attack each other. They haven't placed more than one of each of you on the continent it sounded like. But they never accounted for someone like me being here, Thivoll. They made us translators as a harem package upgrade."

I instantly see her point. "You mean we could try to become allies with the prey?"

I can feel her wiggling in her excitement and it's heavy in her tone when she speaks again. "Yes! We need to speak to one of them."

I think it over for a moment. "They might have a block against hurting me, but they won't have one against hurting you."

She makes a lower-pitched version of the sound from before. "One of the genali hinted the block wouldn't work on you, though."

"Yes, you are correct," I concede.

She loosens her grip with one hand and strokes my mane before holding on again.

"I trust you to keep me safe, Thivoll. We need to try."

I take a moment to check my bearings to ensure I'm headed back toward Silver, then respond.

"I don't like the danger they would pose to you, but I know you're right. We will just have to proceed with caution and figure out a way to get you close enough to speak, but far enough away they cannot hurt you. I've heard several sounds that are likely other prey and it would be easy enough to find someone."

The sun is setting, and I change the subject to more immediate concerns. "Now that you are rested I think we should move to a nocturnal schedule. It will give us a greater advantage. I propose we keep running as long as we can tonight."

Ree groans. "I can't argue with your reasoning, but I did always hate the late night parts of my day-long work shifts."

I'm caught by surprise. "You worked entire days? I thought slavery was already outlawed on your planet?"

She lets out her trill and I can't help but chuff in response, even though I don't know what she finds funny.

"Oh, Thivoll, I wasn't a slave, though you could make a strong case for wage slavery."

I'm still confused, but I'm glad to hear the levity in her voice after how grim she was in the genali camp.

"I always knew I wanted to help people and the long hours aren't really that bad. What about you? You said you were a cleaner?"

"Essentially, yes. But actually an air technician, so cleaning is a large part of it, but also maintaining equipment and keeping all the biologics healthy."

"That sounds a lot more important than just cleaning. Do you talk about it like that because you don't like it? Seems like a pretty critical role."

It doesn't surprise me she picked up on my discontent. "I actually wanted to join the Thorisian Sentinels, which patrol our home sector."

"Thorisian?"

"Yes, named after an ancient regime. An underfunded amalgamation of non-conformists and aging vessels is all that remains of it. Nothing like the Thoris of long ago, but still important."

"Ah. What kept you from it?"

"Partly my dam, but only because it's considered shameful. It's a career everyone knows people have to go into, but no one talks about. People pretend only reprobates join, if they think about it at all."

"What the fuck? That's messed up. No wonder the slimes have been winning. Shit. Sorry, that was rude."

I chuff. "Hard truths aren't always polite."

Our conversation dies down naturally, both of us realizing we should be as quiet as possible now that we've left the camp far behind.

We continue through the night, stopping periodically for water and food. I can tell she is exhausted, but she doesn't complain, just clambers back on me each time we set off again, though her movements slow as the night wears on.

I'm also tired by the time I feel her almost slip off of me.

It's a while yet before morning and we have longer to go before reaching her Silver, but I know we are at our limit. I find a suitable tree and come to a stop.

"I know you are exhausted, but I need you to hold tight as I climb."

She nods sleepily, but pulls herself firmly against me when I lift her into my arms.

I'm getting better at climbing like this and it isn't long before I have her pulled up against my stomach and chest, tail and arms wrapped around her so she remains safe as we sleep.

I pat her rear lightly after I have her suitably arranged. "We aren't far from your Silver so we can sleep until the latter part of the day and still have enough light for you to close her wounds."

Ree shivers. "That sounds good, but I'm not sure if I'll be able to sleep during the day when I can't pretend there isn't a drop right next to us."

I enfold her more securely with my tail and one of my arms, then use the other to massage her hair at the base of her neck. She takes a deep breath and then lets it out slowly, her hands gripping me tight.

I keep petting her mane and she becomes more and more limp in my arms.

I can tell my Ree is asleep when she makes little nasal sounds and starts randomly twitching.

I wouldn't expect anything less than this level of charm, even in her sleep, but it makes my whiskers move forward just thinking about how utterly delightful she is.

I love the sensation of her in my arms and the pride that fills my chest that I make her feel safe enough to sleep despite her fears.

She has the same alluring mix of vulnerability and tenacity common among manticorid females, just in a very exotic package.

My hand is still stroking down her long mane, even though she is now asleep. Its texture is fascinating. It's so slick it almost feels cold, though I have her thoroughly warmed in my embrace.

I didn't lie to her when I said her nanites don't affect me, but I didn't say just how much her smell excites me. I suppose it has a lot to do with how the little robots are unnaturally fueling her arousal, but it just makes me incredibly eager to do what I can so it's of my own making.

The idea of finding out what is under that tight body suit and licking it all makes me harden against my sheathe.

A growl mixes in with my purr as I think about letting my thick purple member slide out with her positioned to take all of me. I'll have to delve her with my fingers and tongue first to ensure it would be safe for her.

If not, we will figure something out.

I know I won't be able to get enough of her taste, so if that is all we can do, I'll still be a thrilled manticorid.

Her grip on my tail earlier was almost enough to make me lose my composure and attempt an advance, but luckily my good sense reminded me she has just suffered a horrible amount of shock.

I'm also sure she doesn't know just how blatantly sexual her grip and my decision to wrap her around the waist was, even if it's very practical.

My tail is my deadliest weapon, but it's also used to hold our mates as we rut.

I desperately want to feel her clutch it again, but while I'm finding out what sounds she makes when I'm pleasing her, not just because I want her secured safely in a tree. After that, I'll find out if she would like it wrapped around her neck. And other places.

The way her body structure works is fascinating and I can't help but think of the possibilities it opens up.

When I imagine her kneeling in front of me, my tail pulling her head back, her back arched, and me taking her from behind I almost lose control and extrude.

I make myself abandon such delectable thoughts after that near miss.

I doubt she would like to wake up to a hot, sticky pressure against her sex. When I pulled her into my arms the past two rest periods, it hasn't escaped my notice that the difference in our torso lengths means she is positioned perfectly for me.

I growl at myself, annoyed with my lack of control over errant thoughts.

I need to just let the woman sleep and get some myself. We need to ensure her Silver is healed and safe, but I'll also need plenty of energy so I can stalk my Ree and convince her to let me touch her in more places than just her lovely mane.

To lick her places besides her neck.

And for her to *kiss* me in other places besides my muzzle.

31

Ree

I wake up to the feeling of something hot and hard suddenly moving between my legs and pressing against my core.

It's the long length of him, I realize, angled so he is laying against me, but not positioned to penetrate. It's startling, but then makes me groan in relief.

The constant arousal has been hard to ignore and sleep does nothing to tame it.

Then my next thought is that he should have asked and I stiffen. Just when I take a breath to object I hear light snoring, much deeper than a human could ever make, but still recognizable.

"Ohhhh," I say, realizing that this is the equivalent of a wet dream for him.

My hand really, really wants to stray down to feel the tip of him where I'm sure it's extending past the juncture of my thighs. I'm incredibly curious about his shape and texture, but it's one thing for him to do this in his sleep and quite another for me to grope him.

It's still tempting, but I instead move my hand to where his tail is wrapped around my waist.

I hold on tight, then unsuccessfully try to keep my thighs from squeezing him tighter against me when he makes small hip thrusts.

I'm so aroused I already feel myself cresting higher with just that small amount of stimulation. I moan again, squeezing him harder against me, then chide myself and try to stop.

Just when I've decided I really should wake him up, his snoring transitions to a purr, and he moves his scaled hand up to grab lightly onto my throat.

Soon after I feel the slight prickle of claws against my skin and it makes me moan.

Suddenly his grip loosens, and his hips stop moving. His purring stops abruptly and I hear him take a sudden breath.

"I'm so very sorry," he says in a rush, his voice even rougher than usual. "That was completely unacceptable."

I don't tell him that what I find unacceptable is that he has removed his hand from my throat. When I feel his cock retreat I have to hold in a disappointed whimper.

"Well, I could have woken you up, Thivoll," I confess. "I got lost in the moment and it wasn't like I was complaining."

"It was wrong," he says with conviction.

"I don't agree," I shoot back, my hand still gripping his tail and my voice colored with my sexual frustration. "As soon as you realized what was happening you stopped. And I was really enjoying it before you did, so if I can be frank, I'm more annoyed you didn't keep going."

I want to slap myself after I let the words escape, but I've always been too blunt for my own good.

I'm relieved when he purrs again. "In my culture, clasping a tail is a sexual advance, my Ree."

I make a little yelp and let go of him, suddenly getting a sense of how he probably feels right now.

"I'm so sorry!"

"Well, as you said, I didn't tell you and I was enjoying it," he purrs out, putting a pin in reversing our roles.

Something about his tone lets me know he knows exactly what he's doing.

I laugh, and he joins me with his chuffing. It feels good to be sharing a moment of levity with him and even better to be doing it in the warm cocoon of his fur.

Then I realize the light filtering through the trees suggests it's evening.

"As much as I would love to talk over all of our relevant erogenous zones, and possibly touch them if that sounds good to you, I need a bathroom break, water, some food, and then to get Silver in a place I'm not having to worry about her," I tell him.

"I want to touch all of your places and for you to touch mine," he says, his breath hot against my neck. "But I also agree that your Silver needs to be our priority."

Thivoll loosens his grip on me so I can sit up. My hair is wrapped around my limbs in ways that make repositioning difficult.

I have a long strand of it caught under my armpit and my temper flares. "Could you use your claws to cut off all this ridiculous hair? Ugh!"

Thivoll takes a gasping breath. "I love your mane, my Ree. Please don't ask me to do such a thing."

I grumble internally, but must admit it also feels nice that he likes it. "It just grows right back, anyway. I already tried to be rid of it."

He growls, but doesn't comment and simply moves us into a better position so we can climb down. When he sets me down on the forest floor he tilts back onto his haunches so he can run his hands through the offending length of it.

His purr builds and then stops shortly after. "It has changed."

I look down and stiffen at the sight of it. "Is it orange?"

It's a stupid question, but it pops out anyway.

"Yes, you have large orange streaks among the indigo. It's beautiful, but why has it changed?"

I huff out a breath. "Apparently each of us will start to take on the traits, and I assume somehow some of the genetics, of whoever we are around. At least for a certain period until the changes halt. Or something like that. They didn't really explain it."

He's silent for several long moments. "So you are becoming partly manticorid? I've not heard of this technology. I wouldn't think it would be possible and that I would be immune."

"Well, I guess since I'm not immune that it can make me more like you? Or maybe I'll only partially change because at some point I'll be immune? I wish I knew."

I gulp, the realization that everything has or will change suddenly crashing down on me. I can't even rely on my body being the same and just want to find a corner to hide in.

Preferably with ice cream and potato chips.

Thivoll pulls in a breath along the roof of his mouth. "I see. You are afraid."

He pulls me close to him, one hand on the back of my head and the other stroking down my back, over my butt and down my legs. He pulls his hand back up and pats my ass and then starts again.

On the second repetition, it brings a small smile that lightens the heavy weight of panic, if only slightly.

It's been interesting interacting with each other with no good sense of where it's socially acceptable to touch each other.

No need to explain, thankfully, since it's quite pleasant.

I sigh. "All the change has been hard and you're right. I'm a little scared, but mostly I just feel overwhelmed and like there's nothing I can rely on anymore."

A comforting purr radiates from his chest. "You can rely on me. I might not have a lot of control over what's happening to either of us, but I promise I'll do everything I can to keep you safe and as comfortable as I can."

I swallow a lump in my throat and tears spring to my eyes.

I believe him.

In just a matter of days, he's made me feel more cherished than any of my previous relationships had managed to over years. That it took traveling light years and meeting an alien to find it seems pretty much how things would go for me.

Not that what we have could be defined as a relationship in such a short period, but it feels like there is at the very least a mutual draw to one another.

"Thanks, Thivoll. I appreciate that. Right now we need to get back to Silver, but I look forward to more of this later."

I pull back from him, looking into his earnest eyes. "I'll teddy bear you better than ever before, my Ree."

I laugh, the tightness in my chest loosening. "I would love that."

I step to the side, and he tilts forward onto all fours. I like to think that I'm getting a bit more graceful and hopefully pulling less fur each time I climb up. I prefer to keep my delusions, though, so I don't ask.

Thivoll runs just as quietly as ever, stopping for a break at a stream soon after, then we continue loping along.

My arms aren't aching anymore like they were last night and I feel stronger than I ever have. Better able to respond as he dodges trees and leaps over fallen logs.

At one point he slows his pace considerably, his ears mostly pointed toward our right as he angles us left. I assume he hears someone, though I can't ask him who he thinks it might be. Did someone find Silver?

Could she have died in stasis?

My heart's in my throat as I think of all of the possibilities.

Thivoll continues to move away and his ears change directions to let me know the sound is behind us.

When he picks up his pace again shortly after, I let out some of the tension I was holding in my shoulders.

32

Ree

We run at speed for a while before he slows us and crouches down, a clear signal for me to slide off.

He looks at me and then cuts his eyes over to a small hole in a thick patch of the brambles like the one I fell in after my first time leaving the ship.

I wrinkle my nose, then crawl through.

I mostly avoid the thorns, keeping my curses under wraps the few times one hooks through my clothing and into my skin. After extracting myself, I keep on crawling.

I'm not paying enough attention and bump right into Silver's chamber with my head. I had expected the light to still be on, though I realize it was a stupid assumption.

Thivoll would never leave her with a beacon announcing her presence.

There isn't much space, but I move out of Thivoll's way enough so he can come through. Considering how much smaller I am, I don't know how he made it unscathed and then realize that he is simply pushing against the bush like it's no barrier.

His scales must be protecting him and I'm jealous.

He moves to where he can work the touch screen controls, then speaks in a whisper.

"Prepare your tools and I'll open the chamber to rouse her."

I hope she doesn't wake up screaming, but if she does, I'm sure Thivoll could quickly take us all out of the area.

I remove the stitch stapler and nod to Thivoll to let him know I'm ready. It kills me to be doing this without proper sanitary procedures, but I'll just have to hope her nanites will protect her.

The chamber snicks open and Silver's breathing picks up pace, but she doesn't wake up. That's a blessing in one way, but very concerning.

Of course, I have no idea what's normal.

"Do people usually wake up instantly? It seemed to happen quickly on the ship."

He shakes his head. "It will take a short while if she isn't jarred awake, but I would work fast to take advantage of the transition."

I get right to work, no need to cut off clothing like we would in the ER because she is still naked.

As I rapidly close the wound up, the tool incredibly awkward in my hand and my work not nearly as neat as I would like, I try to ignore my rage over what's been done to her.

Thivoll must sense it because he purrs and nothing about this is pleasant so it can only be meant to soothe me.

I finish up in just a few minutes, my hands sticky with blood and nothing to wipe it on. I end up smearing it on the interior of the chamber, hoping it seals off the scent.

I move up to feel her head. There are several large bumps under her thick mass of silver curls. I grunt as I try to wrangle her hair out of the way so I can feel better. Thivoll reaches forward to help me.

"No," I blurt out and he snatches his hand back. "Sorry. I just would prefer to give her a choice in her transformation. If we can."

He nods. "I hadn't thought. That's a good idea."

I don't like what I find on her head. "Could you turn the chamber light on for just a moment?"

He complies, and I waste no time in peeling her eyelids back. As I suspected, her sclera and iris are the same light green that sometimes shows in her hair, just like my aquamarine eyes.

But the pupils are far too large. "Are my pupils, the inner black part I mean, as big as hers?"

I look up to Thivoll so he can better compare. "No, yours are much smaller."

I groan. Not good.

"I can't say for certain with her still unconscious, but considering how dilated her pupils are she at the very least has a concussion. I'd guess that since she won't wake up, it's severe. I'm afraid she might have brain damage, Thivoll."

"You're probably correct. She should have come out of stasis by now."

I frown, feeling helpless again. Nothing we will ever find in a hunter's camp could solve this issue.

He pats my shoulder, careful to keep his distance from Silver. "We have done for her what we can. Getting her back in stasis so it can keep her stable while her nanites work is her best hope."

I nod and move out of the way so he can close it. As the gas puffs back over her, I feel sick at heart.

"I wish we could have at least dressed her. It isn't right, Thivoll."

His purr starts up again. "What we can do is find a safer place for her and move her there. Then keep returning to her with supplies as we wait until the chamber stops functioning."

I know he's right but I have a hard time accepting that I have to keep leaving her. "What if I stay?"

He doesn't speak for a moment. "This may sound heartless, but the smell of her chamber and blood will attract prey. Not all of them will be peaceful and I would rather you stay away from her unless I'm with you."

I don't think he's heartless, but there is a layer of brutality among the practicality. "I don't know, Thivoll. It doesn't feel right."

He huffs out a breath. "I want to respect your freedom, but I'll not hesitate to carry you out of here by force. I'll help you find and protect your fellow humans, but never at the risk of losing you. Never."

His voice is firm and part of me wants to argue, but I also know he's right. Risking myself doesn't help Silver.

My shoulders slump.

"Alright. I'll leave, but I won't feel better until we have her in a less exposed area and have enough supplies so I can nurse her back to health. We need a place you can defend in that scenario. Is that a reasonable compromise?"

He growls low in his throat.

"Yes, though I don't like it and would prefer you safely moved every day to a new tree. We can't risk her waking up and falling from a tree and so our options are more limited."

My brow furrows. "There can't be many options nearby or you would have found something when you came here the first time."

"I can hear far and we can continually move back within range to check on her. We have much we can explore."

It seems like evolution handed me a very short stick.

"Of course you can, Superkitty," I grumble good-naturedly.

"I'll assume that means something amazing."

"Only the best nickname anyone could ever get!"

He blinks at me, intelligent enough to know I'm pulling his tail.

Our banter helps me put things in better perspective. My arm is healing rapidly after having a bullet lodged in it. It should have taken weeks to heal this much. Silver has the added benefit of the chamber keeping her still as the nanites work.

Things aren't perfect, but I've kept my promise to her.

We'll get her to a safer place soon and I'm sure we'll keep finding more women and doing the same for them. I feel lighter, my breath coming easier and muscles I didn't even know I was clenching start to loosen.

Hope never felt so good.

Thivoll is still looking at me with his cat in the cream look. When I give him a cheeky grin in response, he chuffs and then snaps his teeth at me. He chuffs even more when I jump in alarm.

"I really should pull your tail," I grumble at him.

He stops chuffing. "Is that meant to be some sort of punishment?"

"Oh yeah, you're right. I should not, not, not pull your tail, you wicked Superkitty."

He snaps his teeth again. "You are in danger of losing teddy bearing privileges."

I chuckle at him. "You are on permanent teddy bear duty, regardless of tail-pulling, Thivoll. Get used to it."

He purrs. "They aren't mutually exclusive. But I'm glad you agree I won this argument."

I don't have a ready reply. He got me.

My expression must let him know it because he cuts his eyes at me, blinks slowly, and then pushes back out.

I'm still chuckling as I crawl my way back out of the brambles he pushed through like they were tickly feathers.

33

Thivoll

I love that I've made her laugh, but then it abruptly cuts off and I hear thrashing.

"Are you alright, sweet one?"

I hear more squirming and muttering. "Mostly, I guess. My stupid hair is stuck."

When she lets out a muted yelp, I push my way back in.

She is properly tangled up. Long indigo and orange tresses are wrapped up in a branch on one side. The braid she attempted to contain it with unraveling as I watch.

She must have tried to backtrack and turn to address it and stickers are embedded in the fabric of her rear. I can't even pat it to help her feel better without making it worse.

Instead I reach out, extend my claws to slice through the offending branches, and then gently remove the barbed ends.

She puffs out a breath. "Tell me you'll cut the damn hair and not just the branches."

I lightly snap my teeth just at the thought of doing such a thing, then go back to removing stickers.

Once I have them all removed from the fabric I rub all over the globes of her rear to comfort her with one hand while my other extends to do the same to the branches holding onto her hair.

The movement makes me less aware of where my other hand is and it strays to the heat of her core, which was made more readily available by her kneeling position.

My hand freezes when I feel moisture.

Is she bleeding from her battle with the plant? It seems like the wrong location.

"Are you wet? Is that normal for a human?"

She yelps again, when I make another pass to assess if she might be bleeding from the brambles. It occurs to me that it's not a sound of pain.

"Uh... yes..."

Then she suddenly growls at me, the sound of it making me twitch under my sheath.

"I'm wet all the fucking time right now, Thivoll. All. Of. The. Time. My body is no longer my own. No, that isn't exactly normal."

She says it all quietly, but vehemently.

"But, yes, it's apparently exactly what happens if a human woman is abducted, jacked up to be perma-aroused, and then isn't having any freaking sex."

From her tone I would expect her to be baring her teeth at me and for me to be scared she might extend her claws and take a swipe, but my cock is pushing against its confines.

Then my mind catches up to the fact that human women of course don't have claws... and provide lubrication.

I'm struck dumb by the possibilities as she scrambles past me.

I follow her out, then shake my mane to help center my errant thoughts. I panic when I see she is trying to break off a section of her hair and surge forward so I can wrap her with one of my arms, the other three limbs providing stability as she tries to push me off.

"Dammit, Thivoll. I am really pissed off right now. Just let me fucking breaking it off," she growls at me, her voice still low so we don't attract attention.

I hold her tight to me, then shift my back legs under me so I can start rubbing and patting her rear again.

"I love your mane. Maybe there's another option besides destroying it?"

She wriggles in my arms, silent and enraged, but I don't let her go. "We also cannot leave a large amount of your fur or it might attract someone to your Silver."

She goes limp. "Fine."

There are a few moments of stony silence.

I purr to help ease her, continually rubbing her rear.

I move the arm that had been caging her up to the base of her hair and massage her neck. All the while I'm throbbing and wishing this was a very different sort of struggle.

One without her clothing and me no longer having to keep myself contained.

She lets out a long breath. "I have an idea. Could you let me go now?"

I put a growl in with my purr. "There is no mane destruction as part of this plan?"

"No, *Superkitty*."

My whiskers move forward at the sound of her special name for me and at just how fierce she is, even when so easily thwarted.

I hope we can revisit this in a warm nest.

She steps back from me and then gathers her hair at her nape, her shoulders lifted back at an angle a manticorid could never manage and my mind shies away from even thinking about it.

She then moves her arms so they can reach to her lower back. A moment later she turns around to show me. Her nanothread has her hair trapped, but loosely enough she can still move her head.

I growl, hating it.

"It won't brush against me anymore as we run," I grumble.

She snorts. "You want tail pulling privileges and my hair always at your disposal. You are one greedy *cat*."

I purr. "Who says we can't have everything we want in life?"

She snaps her adorable little blunt teeth at me, using one of my own favorite gestures.

"You are lucky I not only like you but that you are usually extremely charming, you giant fur ball."

I chuff, crouch down so she can climb back up and we run again.

My whiskers are still pushed forward as we move away from the thicket. My Ree is clever and now she has me thinking of tail pulling.

And her *kiss*.

And the feel of her legs squeezing my cock as she moaned before we left our warm nest.

I also want to figure out why my purr made her so excited when she was against me in the tree. It hasn't affected her like that at other times.

It's all one giant, delicious mystery begging me to unravel it.

Preferably I will have her begging me very, very soon.

I want to know how different she tastes between her legs. It's thrilling that she's wet there. Males of my species are the ones who provide the lubrication.

The thought of our juices mingling and easing my passage as I slide into her as many times as it takes for her to flower for me makes me want to scale a tree and see if her nanothread will let me tear through it.

As much as I love a good chase, I might die if I don't find out soon if she can accommodate my size.

My mind is running different scenarios when I hear a branch break. A long draw of air lets me know it's a hunter.

She leans forward so she's closer to my ear. "What's wrong?"

"Genali," I whisper back.

I move the opposite direction.

"Wait. They're too close to Silver."

"She's hidden well. I'll get you safe first."

I gather myself to run, but she slides off of me.

"No," I hiss out. "They're too close"

"I won't leave her," she tells me as she pulls the gun out of one of her many suit pockets.

It flops awkwardly in her hands while she tries to figure out a way to hold it steady and get her finger near the oddly angled trigger.

She crouches down behind a bush. It will never hide my bulk, but I try one last time to convince her before seeking better cover.

"Please get back on."

Her eyes are wild, like something is haunting them. More than just the danger of an approaching slime, something far more terrifying.

Part of me is screaming to grab her and run, just like I threatened. The other part knows that it would skirt far too close to true confinement, nothing like our playful interaction near the thicket. I don't know how to proceed if both options could harm her.

I let out a low growl and scramble to the other side of a tree.

The slime keeps coming our direction, the squeaking and squelching of their wet limbs very distinct.

I consider trying to climb a tree, but I'm uncertain of their exact trajectory and I can't risk being too far away from Ree if they see her first.

If I was alone, this would probably be fun, but I'm panting and blood is pounding in my ears as I imagine all the ways Ree could get hurt. I'm feeling lightheaded by the time they come close enough to see.

As I suspected, it is a solo hunter, but he is well-equipped and holding a rifle in both flipper hands.

His bulging eyes are scanning as he walks.

He won't be able to miss Ree if he keeps walking that way, even in the fading light.

If I show myself now as a distraction there's no way I could get in range before he shoots me between the eyes.

Tremors pass through me as I make myself lie in wait.

My legs are twitching with the need for action by the time he gets within ten sticky paces of her. Bile rises to the back of my throat as I make myself wait for three more.

My haunches are wiggling in preparation when Ree bursts up out of her bush.

I spring forward the moment I see her.

The genali has just enough time to yell out as she swings her handgun up and fires. She misses and the only thing that saves her from his answering shot is the kickback of the gun making her fall backwards.

I roar out a challenge as he takes a lower aim, relieved when he moves the gun my way instead.

Another shot from Ree's bush makes him duck, which gives me just long enough to close in on him.

My claws tear into the turf, letting me gain speed quickly, then help me swing my body in an arc.

My tail sings as it whips toward him, but he raises the rifle to block me. The spike shatters against the metal, splashing venom across his oozing flippers. He shrieks when it makes contact, but it isn't deadly in those concentrations.

I'm still repositioning myself when he abandons the rifle and slashes across my side with a long knife.

I roar and strike out with the claws of one hand. He twists to the side and I only rake long scores into his non-dominant limb. As he screams he stabs forward into the meat of my shoulder. I pivot away, and it rips the knife out of his flipper.

From there it only takes one more swipe to his throat to end it.

I'm still standing there panting when Ree moves over to me. She's clutching her side and dread makes me harsh.

"Were you shot? We should've left!"

She's shaking and her face is twisted in an expression I've never seen. "No. I fell back on a sharp stick. It's just a puncture. It'll be fine."

My shoulders slump in relief, but I'm still angry. "You could have died. You nearly did."

"I know. I'm sorry. Actually... No. I would do it again. I'm sorry I scared you and I feel terrible that you're hurt, but I needed to stay."

My whiskers droop and I tremble. She would do it again.

She will do it again.

I'm still lost to the roaring in my ears when I feel her hand on my shoulder, near where the knife is still protruding.

"Lay down," she orders me.

I'm too shaken by her revelation to do anything but comply.

I barely feel it when she yanks it out. The sound of a staple clipper pulling into position tugs me out of my haze.

"No. That will just interfere with my scales shifting."

"But there's a lot of blood."

"It's as you said, just a puncture."

Her face screws up again into another unidentified expression, but she doesn't comment.

"Should we open his bag? There might—"

"Yes, that's fine."

I stalk over and slash open the pack, then quickly snatch up anything of use and push it into her hands.

They're shaking. "Will it heal alright? I'm so, so sorry, Thivoll."

I take a deep breath and push down my anger. "I'm not worried about the wound. I'm afraid I won't be able to protect you."

Her eyes are glimmering more than usual as she looks me in the eyes.

"But who will protect her? All of them? It must be me, but I understand it isn't your responsibility."

I growl out in frustration. "It's mine, too. It just can't be at your expense, Ree. I can't help you if you're dead."

An image of her laying behind that bush, broken, rises and my throat feels tight. The next breath sears my lungs and my chest aches.

She nods, but says nothing to help assuage my fear. It feels lonely to have it trembling through me, unacknowledged.

She glances down at the dead slime. "Should we move him? Will he attract people to her?"

"It would be more suspicious than leaving him. He isn't all that close to her."

I can't help the barb, though it does nothing to make me feel better. From the look that flits across her face, it hits home.

"We need to leave," I say instead of apologizing.

One of those would get stuck in my throat right now.

She bites her lip, her eyes glimmering again, but she simply climbs on.

Running soundlessly through the glow of trees in dusk helps slowly ease my racing thoughts, but the ache remains.

The light is almost gone when I hear a rasping sound. Like something soft is dragging against the ground. I pause and pivot my ears toward it to better hear.

Something chirps out, then continues into a melody, the structure suggesting language and not just a song.

34

Ree

"What do you hear?" I whisper to him.

"A melodious language. One I don't recognize. Or their scent."

"An ally, maybe?"

"It's likely prey. But they could be hostile."

He doesn't sound pleased to be sharing the news.

It's a worthwhile risk. I know it in my bones.

"Let's go find out."

He doesn't move and another spike of guilt clenches my stomach painfully. He's angry with me and while I don't blame him, I also can't tell him I won't do it again.

Lies don't help anyone.

"We can't do this alone, Thivoll."

He huffs out a long breath, turns, and picks up his pace. His long strides devour the distance, then he slows down, stalking closer.

Not long after, I hear a series of beautiful sounds.

I break my silence to translate for him. "They said they can hear us coming close and request we leave them alone. What a beautiful language, Thivoll. It sounds like singing, but in no way I ever could."

I'm excited, which helps ease the pain when my throat shifts so I can start singing, instantly contradicting myself.

Another painful shift and I translate for Thivoll. "I told them we aren't hunters but they don't believe me."

I grunt in pain and then sing again. My song is intricate and beautiful, then I hear a reply.

I tense, then translate. "I told them I was taken as a slave and given a translator, then crash landed here. That you helped me. And that we hope to gain allies."

"Just keep speaking with them and only let me know what you must. I don't like you being in pain. I can wait."

I pat him and then go back to singing.

This language is otherworldly and I'm making and hearing sounds I never knew existed.

I don't know what instinct lets me know it, but from the sound of the person's singing they are incredibly sad. And I know they are male by their melodic structure.

They were sorry to hear I was taken as a slave, and that I was changed. The wind carried their empathy in the quality of their tones, the harmonics letting me know the depth of it.

I don't know if my reply has the same tonality, but I hope I give them the same sort of emotional support. "Are you from here?"

The lilting sadness of their response makes tears spring to my eyes. "No. Stolen from my aerie. I was changed. Something taken, not gained."

For a language of so few words, it takes a lot of note changes to communicate.

It's little wonder the sentences are short.

I sing back. "I am sad. What was taken?"

"Part of me," he replies. "All of me."

My heart aches from the pain communicated in the undercurrents and harmonics. "May we come?"

"You may," he sings.

The shifting in my throat sends a spike of pain and then I'm back to speaking Thivoll's gravely language.

"He said we can go to him. He sounds like he's lost hope, Thivoll. We need to help him, though I don't know how."

He hums. "We'll go closer, but if he seems dangerous, I'll retreat if I'm able to or kill if I must. You should be ready for fast movements and keep holding tight to me."

I don't think it'll be necessary, but I can appreciate his caution. "Alright."

My throat painfully changes and I let the male know we're coming closer.

"I await," he sings back.

Thivoll lopes forward, then pulls up when we can make out a figure among the trees. The light is rapidly fading, but I can still see him clearly.

I'm instantly struck by the beauty of his coloring.

His skin is mostly a canary yellow, but with beautiful cobalt spots. His skin looks leathery, but soft, with intermittent thin feathers along it, then much thicker and longer feathers around his head, sweeping back from a triangular forehead.

His mouth is broad, and it reminds me more of a salamander's face than a bird's, despite what the feathers would suggest he should have.

He's easily ten feet tall, with two sets of arms that are much longer than his legs. Each one has long, thin fingers with white claws on the ends.

His eyes are on the side of his face and are a brilliant green with horizontal irises. The same green shows up in mesmerizing patterns along his feathers, mixed in with yellow spots.

He holds all four of his hands together, clasping onto the set not directly aligned and tilts his head. "My greetings."

I try to mimic his gesture, but assume a lot of the meaning is lost with only two arms. Thivoll shifts under me, I assume so he can somehow return the greeting.

"Greetings. I am Ree. Your name?"

"I am—"

What follows is a long string of sounds that don't translate. My mind is busy trying to make associations and I think I pick out the *chicka-dee-dee-dee* sound I used to hear outside my window as a child growing up in the suburbs.

"My regrets. Do not understand."

He sings it again, but the nanites don't help clear up the mystery.

"May I name you Szhe'ka-day-day-day?"

The sounds take on a new meaning and nuance when sung in his tonalities. When I sing it back to him it sounds flat.

"If short you like, then Szhe'ka."

"My regrets."

He holds out two of his hands and makes a small circle with his fingers. "No need for regret."

With that settled, the male deflates.

He crouches down, a feathered structure that isn't quite like wings shifts behind him. He wraps both sets of arms around his comparatively short legs, as if hugging himself.

Or trying to hold himself together.

His feet are bloodied and bruised. I'm itching to ask him if I can treat him, but I only have enough to clean and stitch a few wounds.

What if we find another woman and she needs treatment? Prickles of unease rise as I decide to withhold treatment.

The clenching sickness in my stomach is a fitting punishment for such a betrayal of my base principles.

But maybe I can help in another way. I need to know why he sounds so depressed and try to fix it if we can.

I'm just as blunt as ever, speaking or singing. "What taken, brother? Can we find?"

He makes a long, keening cry and spreads the mass of feathers at his back.

What looks like it was once an incredible wingspan is hacked off in two different places on each side, one shorter than the other. The longest one stretches out as long as my own arm and yet doesn't reach where I assume the first joint should be.

They must have spanned over twenty feet.

The stumps of his ravaged wings are burned and raw, with the beautiful feathers sheared off in places and mangled in others.

Thivoll makes a vicious snarling sound, then joins the male's mournful cry with a low yowl of his own. Tears are streaming down my face at the brutality of it.

They took the sky from him, the monsters.

I don't have words that would convey my sadness or anger, but I find my own lilting cry when I reach for it. Both of us run out of breath before he does.

He stops a few moments later, then speaks again. "I thank you for shared song. You seek allies, but I am broken. I will sing death soon."

I can't accept that.

I've worked with enough people with devastating wounds and illnesses to recognize when someone needs something to help them look beyond themselves.

"You not fight? You let them win?"

He makes a hacking noise. "I not give them pleasure of kill. No joy left. No shelter for fledglings. None will be mine. All die if grounded. May be best you kill."

I narrow my eyes. The bird-man needs something to live for and the empathy he sang to me earlier gives me an idea.

"Will help my sisters?"

I blink at the term, but it's what the translator provides instead of 'friend.'

He stares back at me. "They taken?"

I chose my next words carefully. "Yes. Changed and caged."

His long-fingered hands clench when I say caged.

"Broken if found. Forced and touched. Need help."

His gaze is sharper. "Look like you?"

I think I have him. "Yes, but different colors."

I tell the jumpsuit to release my hair, pulling it forward. "Bright long threads. In silver cages. Fell from sky."

He rocks forward into his haunches. "I saw cage. Land in tree."

I gasp, excited. "Which color thread?"

"Not see," he says. "I go get and bring. Keep sister safe. Monsters will not break. Not force or touch."

His singing is fuller, richer, and his body is no longer trying to fold in on itself.

This next part will be tricky. "Must keep in cage."

He hacks at me again. "Thought it was monster's weapon. Hopped away. Ashamed I left sister. Will not keep in cage. No."

Well, shit, I think to myself.

I feel bad I'm essentially guaranteeing a woman takes on his traits, but I don't think I'm going to dissuade him now. Thivoll and I need to help Silver.

I feel torn, and shift my language to ask Thivoll for advice.

"He knows where one of the women is but now that he knows she's in a cage he won't leave her in it. He says he'll keep her safe. What do I do? She should get to choose."

"We don't know where she is. Even if we did, we can't protect all of them without help. Wouldn't you choose to be protected over being raped and enslaved?"

I huff. "This place sucks, Thivoll."

"I don't think that translated correctly. Just tell him to go protect her."

My throat hurts again, but then I'm back to singing. "We save other sister. We thank your help."

He pushes up to his feet with a pained low cry. "Walk is long. I go. I bring. I die to keep not broken."

I really dislike all the death talk.

If he pulls her out of that chamber I doubt she won't get attached. I've known him for less than half an hour and I want to give him the absolute biggest hug. That doesn't mean she'll be attracted, of course.

They can sort that out.

I feel bad to keep meddling, but I do it anyway.

"She will imprint. Like hatchling, but woman. Not fledgling, but changed by monsters. She need you if you open cage. Forever. Yours to protect. Be sure you know and choose."

My song was complex, but worth it.

He looks down, thinking. Then looks back up and the change in his bearing is immediate.

"I choose. I go. I bring back here."

He wastes no time after his announcement and simply moves his clawed feet in a shuffle across the clearing. His gait is awkward, with intermittent little hops, like he hasn't quite figured out how to keep moving along the ground in a steady rhythm.

His enormous hands are clenched, and he looks like a new person.

Someone with purpose.

I sigh. Conflicted. I don't know which woman he's headed for, but I hope she forgives me.

Maybe right after I forgive myself for using him.

35

Thivoll

The sound of her singing was beautiful, but I'm ready to converse with her again and relieved when I see the male leave the clearing.

He seemed harmless, but I doubt the genali would've brought him here if his species wasn't capable of violence.

I feel better with him away from her.

I walk away from the clearing as I ask her to update me. The novelty of the interaction and the beauty of the language was just what I needed to help shake off the last of my dread and anger from earlier.

"Did he agree to go look for your friend or did he simply leave?"

I barely contain a growl when I hear her take another gasping breath from the pain caused by the nanites.

"Yes, he will protect her, and I hope she doesn't hate me for it but I told him he would be stuck with her forever."

I chuff. Leave it to my Ree to not only convince the male to do what she wants, but to make sure her friend has a dedicated protector.

"You did well. He looked in far better spirits when he left."

"Thanks, Thivoll. I was afraid he would kill himself and I just felt bad for him, but I will admit I also used him and his grief toward my own ends."

She has a good heart, but spends too much time questioning her actions. Not to mention too much time putting herself in danger.

I veer away from that thought and back to the topic at hand.

"Did you lie to him?"

"No. But I didn't tell the whole truth."

I push my whiskers forward.

She never wants to concede and I love it. "Can anyone ever tell the whole truth?"

She growls at me. "Stop being so reasonable, Fluff Face."

"We both know my face is distinctly lacking in fluff."

"Fine. How about Fluff Ass? Fluff Tail? Fluff Brain? Oh, I like that one."

I chuff in response.

"I can keep going," she tells me in a needling tone.

Her tone turns serious again. "Are we alright, Thivoll? Are you still angry?"

"No, I'm not. But I'm still scared."

"I know. I regret that. I'm scared, too."

"I'd prefer if some of that fear translated into caution."

"I'll try," she tells me in a small voice.

I know it's the best I'll get from her, so I break the tension by returning to our conversation.

From the look of that male, I think he could use his own little human to scare the life right back into him, but I know better than to tell her that.

"So he knows how to use the chamber controls?"

"Dammit," she bites out. "I didn't explain it. But, wait... that could be a good thing."

I almost don't want to break her out of her delusions, but I have too much fun prodding her so I do it anyway.

"He looked pretty determined. You were too successful convincing him. Maybe next time make the secret prize inside the package seem less tantalizing."

I can't help but let out a quickly cut off chuff that ruins the serious tone I had maintained.

She lets out a growl of frustration, but with an edge to it let me know it's directed at me not the situation. I think I like that sound just as much as her trill.

My whiskers move forward and a purr starts in my chest.

"You really are a Fluff Brain. Thivoll... are you pulling my tail now?"

I growl at myself for getting us back to that again, but know I completely deserve her bringing it up.

"That's enough of that. We need to move your Silver as soon as possible. Far too many tail-pulling teases. One more and I'm going to climb you straight up a tree, use my claws to take off that inconvenient suit and use my tail to punish you on your... Where would humans normally be punished?"

She sounds out of breath when she responds. "On my ass. You hit me with your tail on my ass."

Not what I would've expected.

Human parents must be especially harsh if they hit the area you should be comforting.

I shake my mane, focusing back on the important point I was trying to make. "Right. I will hit you on your rear with my tail."

I feel her squeeze her legs and grind into my back. After a few moments of silence, she speaks.

"What? That's it?"

Her voice sounds accusatory.

I purr, her impertinence and movements exciting me. "What else should I do?"

"I don't know," she draws out in a long moan of frustration.

"I just want you to touch me and for us to stop dancing around this. You're killing me, Thivoll!"

A thrill passes through me as I realize she wants me to decide.

Manticorid women are notoriously demanding and prescriptive in rut. The idea of flipping that role makes me want to tear the bark off the nearest tree in my haste and push myself between her legs.

The ones that keep right on squeezing me as she rolls her hips against my back.

Now I'm the one growling in frustration and it's not lost on me I was the one that led us here with my poking.

"Hold on tight. It's time we dealt with our responsibilities so I can wrap my tail around your neck and find out how you taste."

36

Ree

I dig my hands into his fur, thankful for my newfound strength as he springs forward.

I realize I forgot to pull back my hair when it cracks like a whip behind me. He's no longer running silently, and instead is moving us in great leaps.

After about fifteen minutes of heart stopping running and bounding over obstacles he stops abruptly, shifts me into his arms and rapidly ascends a tree.

For a moment, I'm hopeful he plans to do what he threatened, but he instead plops me on a thick branch again.

"Hunter," is all he says before he disappears.

"But— " I whisper before stopping myself.

Then I realize we never talked about how much I hate being left where I can't get down or help. I guess lust has completely hijacked my brain.

Considering how dangerous it is here, that seems like a great way to get killed.

I'm not even sure I can really fully blame the nanites, either. We keep putting our attraction off because of a sense of duty, but I think it's clouding our judgment.

That alone is a tremendous risk here. Or I'm just trying to justify taking time away from helping Silver to scratch an itch.

A very demanding, persistent, desperate itch.

I can't see Thivoll. He is too far away, and it's too dark, but I hear the muffled sounds of some sort of altercation.

I dig my fingernails into the branch I'm clenching so hard my fingers hurt, holding my breath so I don't miss any nuance or small sound. I don't hear any screaming, so I assume he hasn't used his venom and then the sounds stop.

My heart beats faster, since I have no way to tell who won.

I have a hard time making out anything over the pounding in my ears, but I listen as closely as I can for any clue. Any sign that Thivoll is still alive.

As the minutes drag on, the pain in my heart grows and I panic. Not because I can't get out of this tree although that's not exactly a pleasant thought, but because the thought of losing him so soon after meeting is wrenching.

When I hear his claws digging into the bark below me I let out a giant breath.

By the time his face pops up next to my perch, my panic has turned into anger. And I lash out, even while knowing it's not fair.

I bare my teeth at him so he knows I'm serious. "I hate when you leave me like that. Hate it!"

His whiskers droop. "I thought your smile meant you were happy?"

That makes me even more upset, even though I know his confusion is valid. "Ugh! I am mad, Thivoll, not happy. Mad! What if you were hurt? How would I have known? Or climbed down to even find out? You left me trapped here!"

The skin around his mouth goes from lilac to violet. "I'm safe."

"But I couldn't see. Couldn't know. I was scared!"

He finishes climbing up to the branch and instead of replying he pulls me up and against his chest with one of his arms, the other anchoring us.

He simply squeezes me against him and purrs.

I stay rigid for a few moments and then I huff out a breath, letting my anger out with it. The aftermath of fear rushes in, with its telltale chest ache, and tears spring to my eyes.

I reposition myself so my arms are around his chest, the once odd shape of it feeling just right.

He takes a pause in his purring. "I'm sorry."

I swallow a lump in my throat. "I am too. You didn't deserve my anger."

He squeezes me a little tighter. "Most anger comes from fear, my Ree. And you are right, I shouldn't leave you in a place you can't escape. I was reckless and overconfident."

The tightness in my chest eases, not only because of the apology, but from a flood of relief. I hope we won't be revisiting this issue.

"Was it another genali?"

He lets out a breath. "Yes. I have another med kit and some rations stowed away in some tree roots. The rest wasn't suited for us and so I destroyed it."

I nod, feeling self-conscious now and stiff. "Let's keep looking for a good hiding spot."

He moves away from me, but doesn't descend. "Will you kiss me, sweet one?"

The corners of my mouth lift, the invitation helping ease the tension between us. "Gladly."

I grab onto his wide muzzle on each side as he lowers his face. I look deep into his gold and orange eyes, the sight of them no longer feeling strange. The rough skin around his eyes loses some of the tension it was holding as I sweep my hands up and intertwine my fingers in the spaces left between his whiskers.

My eyes fill again when I think of how fast his face has become so precious to me.

I picture how his whiskers move forward, and his golden eyes sparkle when he's teasing me. The hooded side-eyed looks he gives me when he's talking about something erotic. The violet flush he gets around his lips when he's embarrassed.

I lean forward, gently pulling his head lower, and press my lips midway up his broad, flat, blue nasal plate. I make sure all of those thoughts are plain on my face as I do it. My hands are gentle, but firm.

Then I rest my forehead against where I kissed, and close my eyes.

We share several breaths before he speaks. "Now I know what you mean by there being different kisses."

I lightly scratch him with my nails in response, the corners of my mouth twitching when I feel a shiver pass over him at the sensation it causes.

"I look forward to experiencing all of them," he tells me in a near whisper.

I give him a quick peck on his rough cheek to add another to his list and then hold him in my usual cowardly monkey pose.

He's purring as we make our way down.

We take a quick detour and I add more pockets to my suit and stuff the supplies he found in them.

Then we set off again. He runs at a more sedate pace, so I'm no longer in danger of having a heart attack each time he shifts and leaps.

Nevertheless, it's so dark I don't have a way of predicting how his body will shift next so I just have to keep my muscles clenched tight.

After the fifth jump in as many minutes, I risk speaking. "Has the terrain changed?"

He slows us to a fast walk. "We are on an escarpment. I can't see a mountain, so it might be the base of a plateau."

I take a breath to speak but he interrupts me. "I hear a hunter. I'm going to put you on a ledge you can get down from as needed."

My heart pounds. "Alright."

Now that we aren't running so fast, I can make out the vague shapes of a sheer rock face in the muted moonlight. Between the intermittent cloud cover and thick canopy of trees I was all but blind and so the reflective light-colored rocks are a relief.

The lichen and moss create beautiful contrasting patterns.

Thivoll comes to a stop at the base. "Lean forward and hold me around the neck."

I move to comply, likely strangling him in my dread.

I'm glad for the tight hold when he rears up onto his back legs and then leaps through the air. I nearly let out a screech, but we quickly land on a ledge I couldn't see from the base.

He crouches down and I get off him shakily. I push my back against the rock as far from the ledge as I can get.

I assume we can't be up all that high, but my body is still trembling at the mere thought of the drop.

Thivoll squeezes my shoulder, then disappears over the ledge.

Ree

I can't hear which way he goes and my heart is in my throat for many long minutes. I keep my breathing shallow to hear as much as possible.

I startle when I hear a scream. He must have envenomated the hunter.

It seems like it's at least a mile off and behind me, possibly on the back side of this rock face on the other end of a plateau. Then it sounds like the scream is rapidly moving farther away.

My brow is furrowed, trying to work it out and then it occurs to me.

The hunter must have fallen off a cliff.

I have a sudden image of Thivoll tumbling over the edge with them and then I shut down that line of thought. I know I can't get any farther away from the ledge, but I try anyway.

Long moments pass with me trying to think of anything else but cliffs and falling.

I'm still actively pressing my body against the rock behind me when a dark shape is suddenly flying at me.

I let out a screech and barely dodge to the side as a clawed pincher scrapes along the rock beside me. Then I can smell the caustic scent of the creature that bit Thivoll.

Was it just waiting for me to be left alone? It must have been stalking us.

I kick out at it, catching it square on its powerful chest and causing it to slide backwards off the ledge.

As it scrabbles to regain its footing I have just enough time to pull out the gun. There is a long, thin band across its face that expands and contracts. I assume it's a nose and I aim straight for it and squeeze the trigger.

There's no missing at this distance and a hole blooms on one side of its face, propelling it backwards.

I hear a thud and its horrifying scream that rattles around in my skull.

I can't believe it's still alive.

Thivoll's roar from below is a relief, as is the sound of his tail singing through the air and the long, keening cry of the creature as his venom takes effect.

A moment later another dark form is in front of me, and even though I know it's Thivoll I can't contain a scream.

He gathers me to him, crushing me against him as he moves his hands over me, checking for injuries.

"I'm alright. It didn't get me."

I go limp in his arms, relieved he's safe and very glad to have him holding onto me again.

"Did you..." I trail off, completely losing my train of thought when he pulls me close to him, and takes a long lick up the side of my neck.

Thankfully, his tongue doesn't have hooks like a feline, but it's far rougher than a human tongue.

It's an exhilarating combination of smooth glide and scraping sensation that leaves a path of fired up neurons in its wake.

The lust that had died down in his absence—pushed back by my fear—comes rushing back and I moan.

I tilt my head back, ensuring he has better access, and thread my hands into his mane at the sides of his neck.

Each time he starts a new lick at the base of my throat I feel a zing race from the spot down to my core. On the third repetition I'm clenching my legs, trying to gain some relief.

On the fifth I get lightheaded from the overstimulation and my ragged breathing.

He moves one hand down, sweeping it across my hip, then around to my ass, pulling me up and into him.

When I feel his teeth scrape against my neck, this time I don't freeze or panic and instead focus on the sensation of them gliding against me.

He squeezes one of my ass cheeks, then pulls his head back. "Is this where I should hit you with my tail?"

I let out a long groan. "Get us off this ledge and somewhere with more room."

He starts his growly purr, squeezing one cheek, then the other, moving farther down.

"You are wet again, my Ree. I want to taste you, then see how we fit together."

He might kill me. "Now, Fluff Brain! More moving, less talking!"

He growls, pulling me close to his chest and speaks in a rough voice. "Hold on tight."

I do what he says, expecting him to drop us back down to the base of the rocks, but he instead starts climbing the cliff face.

It's too dark to see much of anything, but I still squeeze my eyes shut as hard as I can and press my face into his fur. It's a few long minutes of terror before I feel the change in gravity.

He crouches down and my back presses against the cool, smooth stone. "Where are we?"

I can't see anything at all, not a trace of moonlight left.

He settles down onto his lower elbows and haunches, the feel of him pressing against me making me forget my question altogether and I wriggle underneath him.

He rocks his weight onto one arm and then starts rearranging my hair. "In a cave."

I tense, not liking the idea of being in a place something else might live in without being able to see. "Nothing else is in here with us, right?"

He pulls a long fall of my hair over my chest and then strokes it from my collarbone down to where our bodies are pressed together. I gasp when he moves over my breast.

"Do you like being touched there?"

He moves his hand back up, cupping me, the thin nanothread warming between us. The reaction of my body is answer enough, but I remember I had another pressing question.

"Thivoll. Are there creatures in the dark?"

"Of course there are. This is a biodiverse planet."

I freeze, then realize I might need to be more specific.

"Are there any creatures likely to attack, bite, crawl over, be—"

He breaks in. "There is nothing of concern here and if that changes I will take care of it. Relax."

He purrs, then he squeezes my breast. "Tell your nanothread to recede."

His usual easygoing tone is gone, and in its place is an authoritative growl that sends a thrill through me.

I imagine my suit baring my breasts and from the sudden chill that makes my nipples instantly pebble, I can tell it receded.

His purr deepens as he shifts his body down.

I spread my legs, hoping he makes enough contact when he settles back down to give me some relief from the throbbing between them.

He doesn't disappoint, pushing his upper chest down against my core right before he licks the breast he had just been squeezing.

The rough nubs of his tongue send a zap of pleasure each time one makes contact.

I let out a long, low moan and push myself harder against him. "Purr harder," I demand in a clipped tone.

He obliges, the vibrations making my back arch. "Like that?"

I make an inarticulate sound and grind myself against him.

He changes breasts, pushing down even harder with his long tongue. One stroke of it seems to last a small, blissful eternity. On the third I feel my orgasm building.

When I feel him shift again, I move my hands from their limp sprawl next to us and grab onto his mane on each side.

"Don't you dare move."

His purr is interrupted by a few chuffs, but then he is back pressed against me, this time alternating between breasts.

I'm cresting higher in undulating waves with each transition. When he scrapes his teeth against a nipple, my orgasm explodes through me, my body rigid with the force of it, a cry making it through my lips before I cut it off.

He abruptly stops purring. "Did I hurt you?"

It's a struggle to get my scattered mind together to respond.

"Oh, no. You made me feel very, very good."

38

Thivoll

Humans are confusing, with all of their mixed signaling and facial expressions that mean different things at different times.

I shake my mane and push those thoughts aside so I can get back to making sure I am the one who gets to be demanding.

Ree said I could decide and my mind has been obsessed with the idea ever since the venom bliss hit again.

I didn't even bother climbing down the cliff to see if any of the hunter's supplies survived the drop.

I remind myself of my goal. I am going to taste her. I shift farther down her body, sad to be leaving her breasts, which are so delightfully malleable. The salt of her skin and her sweet musk inviting me to linger, but I move on.

She is still covering her legs with nanoweave and it simply will not do. "Make it recede everywhere but your back," I growl at her.

My cock is partially extruded, no longer willing to be contained now that she is under me, but I ignore it for now.

I pull in a deep breath as the black fabric recedes, her musk making my cock jump and my mouth water. I settle between her legs, then use my hands to push them farther apart.

I love the feel of her soft skin, but leave the wonder of such large expanses of it available for licking for future exploration.

Right now I'm fascinated by the sight of her core.

It's wet and smooth, with folds that invite me to delve into them to find out their secrets.

And so I do, gently exploring her with the tips of my fingers, taking careful note of the response of her body. She especially likes when I glide over the semi-rigid structure right above her opening, so I decide to focus my efforts there.

I lean forward, taking one last breath to savor the anticipation and then lick her gently and slowly. She writhes under me, making more of her pain sounds that she says mean pleasure.

Her taste is indescribable.

Complex, sweet, tangy, and I want more.

I move her folds to the side and take another long lick. Then another. I get lost in the taste, only vaguely hearing her make another one of her long pain sounds, her body tensing up again.

Right after a flood of her juices move over my tongue and I feel like I've found a delectable secret.

It leaves me greedy for more and I pull my tongue from its flat positioning and in on itself so I can start gently prodding it against her opening.

"Oh. Yes, Thivoll."

She breaks back off into moaning as I delve increasingly deeper inside her, my cock throbbing now and fully extruded.

My tongue reaches a terminus and I'm distracted for a moment by the disappointment that she won't be able to fully take me, but push the thought aside so I can keep lapping her up.

I get lost in the experience for a while, though I move my hands at one point to keep her writhing under control enough so I can keep roving my tongue along the smooth walls of her channel. Suddenly it occurs to me that my tongue is deeper than it was before.

I almost spill my seed just thinking about how malleable she must be inside.

My cock is thicker than my tongue, and so I pull it back out of her and test how much she can accommodate by lapping at her bud as I push a finger inside her, very careful to keep my claws sheathed.

"Holy shit, Thivoll. Your scales."

I pull back out, concerned I've hurt her.

She growls at me. "No! Back in."

This time I push two of my big fingers inside, her juices easing the passage and her walls quickly stretching for me.

I keep licking her, pumping those two fingers in and out until she shudders again. I pull my hand away and lap greedily at the gush, then try to push three of my fingers back in.

A moment of disappointment is followed by the realization that she has muscles that clench and then release when my fingers suddenly glide into her.

I growl, needing to know how that feels with my cock deep inside her.

I wait a moment then ease those three fingers farther inside, waiting between the contractions of her muscles to keep gaining ground.

When she stretches again my cock twitches, knowing it's possible and no longer wanting to wait to feel how her slick heat will feel mixed in with my own juices.

"I want to mount you, my Ree."

She pulls her head up from the nest of her hair, which is fanned around her and mussed by her moving her head back and forth.

"Good. I want you inside of me. Right now."

I push back from her. "On your knees."

She scrambles upright, flipping over and then pushing up and rocking back so I have a full view of her. I'm momentarily distracted by seeing her juices flow out again, wanting to lap them up, but I simply enjoy the view.

It's a shame she doesn't have a tail to wrap around me and anchor me to her, but there is also nothing creating a barrier between us.

Nothing to stop me from burying myself fully inside her, hopefully stretching her little by little until she can take every bit of my throbbing cock.

I take a moment to explore her ass, delighting in how it is just as malleable as her breasts.

And that I can pull each cheek away and see her opening, even more mysterious and inviting than when she was spread out before me.

I focus on willfully pulling my cock back into my sheathe, wanting the pleasure of grinding against her and then extruding into that wet heat bit by delicious bit.

39

Ree

I've never had so many orgasms so close together.

Each more intense than the last.

The feel of his scales inside me was just on the very edge of too intense. Just on that knife's edge of pain in a way that drove me up and crested me over in no time.

Now I'm waiting in anticipation, not knowing what to expect from an alien cock. Trusting him to know if he would hurt me and so just making myself stay kneeling as he teases me with his hands.

I get impatient and growl at him.

A moment later comes the stinging whip of his tail against my ass, pulling a high-pitched moan from me, then again when it is repeated on the other side.

He goes back to rubbing me where he made contact, the light tugs of his scales even more noticeable on the extra sensitive skin.

I'm ready to growl at him again and take the punishment when I finally feel his fur tickling against my thighs and back.

It sends a shiver through me. He tips his weight forward, one arm caging me on the left. He uses his other arm to pull back on my hip, moving me into position and pressing against me.

I'm not sure what to expect, since he has so much fur and even though I've tried to take surreptitious looks, I've seen nothing that looked like external genitalia. Nothing that would have swelled into the hard member I felt between my legs in the tree.

When he rocks into me, causing my legs to part wider, I don't feel fur up against me, but what feels like the same rough skin he has around his mouth and whiskers.

He rocks into me, the roughness of his skin getting covered by my wetness and creating a delightful friction.

His arm is still holding his weight to the side of me, his other one pulling me back into him with a tight grip, both of the thumbs of that hand digging into the flesh of my hip.

Then I feel the slow glide of scales followed by fur snaking along my lower ribs, circling around my waist, then between my breasts, before moving up and around my throat.

He moves his other arm to the opposite side, caging and covering me. At the same time, his tail constricts around me, holding me tight around all but my neck, although with enough pressure on the latter that it makes my heart gallop.

Then he mostly holds us still, except for small rolls of his hips that continue to rub him against my core.

It's beyond anything I've ever experienced with a lover.

I just let all thoughts of what might be—or what could be different—dissipate and focus on the sensation of him grinding into me. I'm enjoying the beginning of an orgasm starting in my belly and then hyper focus when I feel an increased pressure against me and the glide of skin moving in opposite directions toward the outside of each ass cheek.

It pulls them apart as a wet heat moves against my opening.

His tail tightens even more, locking me to him as he penetrates me a millimeter at a time.

He's enormous. Much larger than I realized when he was trapped between my thighs when he was dreaming.

Had he moved this slowly with his tongue I would have been growling at him by now, but I'm thankful he's allowing my body to adjust slowly.

I feel fuller than I ever have, but he just keeps coming.

He presses against the opening of my womb, still pushing in, some of the pleasure giving way to pain, but my body just keeps adjusting.

My medical brain can't help but rise to the surface when he can keep slowly sliding into me far longer than should be possible.

This must have been what the genali meant when they said I would change in order to be more desirable.

I'm stuck between awe and a rising panic when he stops. He rocks into me with his hips in small little movements, groaning.

Now that he is fully seated I can't decide if I'm relieved or disappointed.

When he slightly loosens his tail's grip on me and moves gently in and out, pausing to grind against me each time he fully seats inside me, I stop thinking about it.

By the time he is pulling his huge girth back out to the point of almost coming out of me and then gliding all the way back in, my world has narrowed to just that one thing.

His ever-present purr is mixed with a growl now. "You are so wet, sweet one."

He pushes back into me, his movements becoming more forceful and bringing a low moan each time he hits against my body's limit.

He pounds into me harder, continuing to talk but with each word said in the rhythm of our bodies slapping together. "So. Hot. So. Wet. So. Tight."

Considering the differences in our heights I'm not even sure how he does it, but I suddenly feel his teeth pressing against my right shoulder. All three rows are digging in just enough to make my heart pound, but not enough to cut me.

Then his hips pinion his giant cock into me, his tail holding me in place so each rapid pounding comes with maximum impact.

Only my breasts are bouncing. His tight hold not letting any of the force of his impact be lost.

My orgasm crashes over me without warning, sending a shock wave across my body and leaving me incapable of thought for a few moments.

When I come back to myself, his tail is holding my weight and he is pumping into me so hard and fast there is almost no time between the slapping sounds of our wet bodies colliding.

Then his thrusts become more erratic and he is clamping down harder on my shoulder as it absorbs the sound of his roar.

The increased pressure helps tip me over the edge again.

This time we both sink to the ground, neither of us capable of staying upright.

He shifts forward with me, keeping himself locked inside of me as I rest my chest on the cool stone, my ass still raised. The feel of it is welcome against my heated body.

Thivoll holds enough of his weight off of me to avoid crushing me, but otherwise drapes over me, panting.

I'm twitching around him still and he is just as full and erect within me after several minutes.

Then he takes a deep breath, licks the back of the shoulder he recently had caged in his teeth, and starts to pull back out of me.

He is still locked tight against me, the hold incredibly intimate. He's still licking my shoulders and the back of my neck as I feel the skin of his sheath close, no longer pushing my ass cheeks open.

He shifts to the side, then uses his tail to spin me and pull me up on top of him. I let out a contented sigh and bury my face into his fur.

He tightens his arms around me and his purr starts up again as I drift to sleep.

40

Thivoll

I wake long before my little human, her weight on me a pleasant welcome to consciousness.

She is still naked, her nanothread reduced to a thin band around her waist. I don't want to disturb her, so I resist the urge to stroke my hand across her back or gather up her long mane.

To distract myself, I inspect the surrounding cave.

There is just enough ambient light from the opening that I can make out details. The ground is smooth, but not naturally, and there are shelving nooks carved out in the walls of the cave.

There are also a couple of receded chambers leading off of this main one that show tool marks and doorways with carved-in hooks at the top clearly meant to hold fabric drapes.

I'm relieved to see that there are two exits.

I highly doubt colonists would have bothered with the years of tedious carving It would have taken to do all this work without modern technology.

That means there was, or still is, in the unlikely chance the braceaaer didn't exterminate them, a sapient species here.

As far as I know this was one of the many planets that hadn't evolved to that point, but we have suspected for years that many of those situations were simply secret cases of genocide.

I suppose looking for native inhabitants will have to be added to our already too full task list. In the meantime, I can tell by the smell of it that this cave hasn't been occupied in many years.

Whoever they were, they must have either had a system of ropes or they were also arboreal because very few species could reach this cave. Or even know that it existed.

I'm not sure I would have even found it if I hadn't let the primitive part of me that wants to take over after using my venom have control.

Before I knew it, we were in a cave and I was covering my Ree.

My hands pull her tighter to me at the memory, and then I inwardly curse myself when the movement causes her to stir.

Then she is suddenly twitching in my arms. A moment later she slides off of me, sits bolt upright, and then has her arms folded behind her scratching at her back.

"Agh! Is your skin itching, Thivoll?'

"No. Are you well?"

She continues scratching, moving her hands all over her upper body. "I must've gotten into something. My neck and back are burning, but it isn't too bad."

Her movements suggest otherwise, and I shift my body so I can help her. After a few minutes, she speaks again.

"Alright, that feels better, thanks."

"Of course."

She looks around the cave, though in a way that suggests she can't actually see anything. "Are you sure something didn't bite me while we were sleeping?"

I take a closer look around. "It's possible, but there aren't many creatures in here and they don't seem interested in us."

She shudders, then leans back against me. "I don't like not being able to see."

I can't reach her bottom to pat it so I settle for running a hand through her mane.

"I'm sorry. Though I was just thinking that this is an excellent spot for your Silver. It looks like some sort of ancient dwelling and would be very difficult, if not impossible, for hunters to reach."

She hums, considering. "I'll trust your judgment. But I swear you scaled up the rock forever to get here last night. How would we get her chamber up the cliff?"

She makes a valid point.

"We'll need to come across a hunter with a long rope."

She nods then turns, so she's facing me. "May I lay on you again?"

I tip back on my side, and then reposition us so she is draped over me. She twitches again and so I use my scaled hands to help relieve her itching.

She lets out a relieved sigh. "I fell asleep before I could tell you how wonderful that was, Thivoll."

I purr. "It was lovely beyond words, my Ree. And I hope we can touch each other again soon, but for now I think we should do what we can to get your Silver here as soon as possible."

She groans. "I agree, though I admit I'm sick of constantly being on the move and terrified. I would rather stay in bed... not that we have one of those."

I pat her rear. "Let's find a stream to bathe in."

She nods and then stretches, making the most adorable squeaking sound. "You'll have to help me recover all the supplies. I wasn't thinking about them last night."

There are indeed packets and items scattered all around us.

My whiskers move forward at the sight of it, a clear sign of how wrapped up we were in each other.

"I was far more interested in being inside of you than doing inventory. "

She lets out her beautiful trill and I join her with my chuffing.

It doesn't take us long to gather up the items. I set some to the side but help her place the more essential items in the pouches she creates on her suit.

Then I grab her, taking a moment to squeeze her rear, hoping to be positioned behind it again soon, and we make our descent.

I run us a respectful distance away before we relieve ourselves, since it's best to be cautious. I will point out to her exactly how to get there just in case I'm not around.

I still feel ashamed at how reckless I have been. All caught up in the heady experience of pursuing her.

Not that I plan to ever leave her side long enough for her to tread out alone, but there's no need to make stupid mistakes because I feel over-confident.

41

Ree

Thivoll throws far more aquatic creatures in his mouth than usual and I think it might be because of our rigorous activities the night before.

I feel a throb between my legs just thinking about it, then notice that my raging lust has subsided.

What a relief.

Especially since now I'll know each time he makes me wet that it's all about us and nothing to do with the genali.

I'm almost jealous of his ability to swallow creatures whole. Almost. My jaw hurts from all the chewing it takes to get enough nutrients from these plants, but almost anything is better than the genali rations.

Though I'm quite certain I will eat them before joining Thivoll noshing on salamander fish, regardless of jaw pain.

Thinking of jaws gives me a flash of the creature's mouth as it tried to bite me last night. I won't forget that any time soon.

It was about the size of a black bear, though it moved nothing like one. It had a diseased mouth. Hmm. A Komodo Bear, for sure.

"Do you think there are more of those scary creatures? The Komodo Bear?"

"I don't know." He growls, then shakes out his mane. "I doubt they introduced many or we'd all be dead. Including the hunters."

I shudder. "I'd rather deal with genali."

"I agree. But, wait... a bear? As in teddy bearing? I've had that very wrong in my mind if..."

"No. No. Well, somewhat related... But it's very different. There are bears, the animal. Then there are teddy bears, the stuffed animal."

"That sounds even worse!"

"What? Why?"

"Stuffed? That's barbaric."

"It's not a real animal. It's... You know what? This isn't important right now."

"It is! I'll never be able to teddy bear you the same again."

"Thivoll! It means what you think it means. No animals are harmed if you cuddle me."

He starts chuffing and I realize he's been messing with me, though at the start he seemed genuinely horrified.

I growl at him. "Fluff Brain."

"Animal stuffer."

"I've never..."

Damn. He got me.

I don't let him know that, of course, and simply scowl at him and then take the offer of his outstretched arm to help me climb onto his back.

After that, we spend many hours searching for hunters.

Each time Thivoll leaves me to fight is just as terrifying as the last, especially when I periodically hear gunshots.

I've yet to see any other species aside from the genali, and by some unspoken agreement we avoid talking about exactly what happens when he is away.

When he brings a pack and bedding that isn't covered in their slime I know he must've been fighting an array of species.

It makes me sick to think that there's that many people evil enough to want to come here.

The items he brings are from radically different cultures and manufacturing methods. We have to take several trips back to the cave to stash the bedding, rations, knives, handguns, medical supplies, and other items.

We even find some sort of lighting that Thivoll says is a type of bioluminescence in stasis.

My curiosity is still burning over that one, but mostly, aside from some whispered words here and there, we've been as silent as possible.

What we don't find is a rope.

By the time the sun is coming up we are both at our limit, possibly me more than him which is embarrassing considering he's been doing almost all the work.

We agree it's time to rest, but our body language betrays how disappointed we are and guilty we feel that we haven't put Silver in a safe place.

As we head back to the cave, I'm running through alternate plans, each one less impressive than the next. The latest one involves cutting our newfound bedding into strips and continually cutting off my hair until we have enough to braid a rope.

A glimpse at the rock face and a quick calculation lets me know it would take weeks of hair growth and many, many more blankets.

When we make it into the cave, it's lit with the muted light of the bioluminescent lamp.

The nurse in me is itching to reorganize and store the supplies we've been dumping unceremoniously in small piles. I'm too tired to complete a full inventory, but I grab the lamp and go around pulling out medical supplies.

While I do that, Thivoll grabs bedding and moves it into one of the two smaller rooms.

From the way he's purring as he makes a nest, I have a good idea of what he might have in mind.

I'm smiling at the thought when he turns to speak to me. "I think we should... What's that on your neck?"

I almost drop the lamp in my panic, but make myself put down what I'm holding before shooting my hands up to check for creatures.

A quick, frantic round of swiping reveals nothing.

"What?"

He walks over to me, his gait awkward on his back paws. He uses a hand to tip back my head and turns it to the side.

"Make your nanothread recede."

I raise an eyebrow at him, but do as he asks. It goes back to just being a black band around my waist.

His eyes rove over me, then he moves around to my back, pulling my hair off my neck and to the side. "Beautiful."

"What is it?"

He purrs. "You have black scales."

My heart leaps in my chest, and I hold a hand to my throat.

I can feel them now. They are more subtle than Thivoll's, closer to my skin, but the same shape. They start just under my jaw, sweep back into my hair, down to my collarbone and over my shoulders.

I look down.

They come to a point between my breasts, but don't cover them. They don't descend my arms, but I can't feel how far they extend behind me.

"Where do they end on my back?"

"Similar to my mane shape. They come to a point a few inches above your rear. Like they are pointing the way to bliss."

His last word ends in a purr, which intensifies when he takes a step closer to me.

He wraps one hand around my neck from behind, covering my new scales and keeping me in place as he runs the other hand along where my scales transition to smooth skin, teasing but not touching my breasts before he sweeps his hands over my shoulders and slowly glides his hand down my spine.

He keeps moving down, rubbing the globes of my ass, then dipping a finger into my already wet core. "Yes, it does in fact lead to bliss."

Instead of moving me to the nest he made, he keeps me in a chokehold as he continually runs his other hand up and down my back, occasionally rubbing on my clit or slowly pumping a finger in and out of me.

I'm panting by the time I feel his tail snaking up from my thigh, tickling across my belly and then reaching up to cup my breasts.

Its prehensile grip is like nothing I've felt before. The furred length of it wraps around one breast, squeezing it, and then I gasp as the scaled ovoid at the tip of it brushes against my taut nipple.

"Ready for me already, my Ree," he says as he pushes a second finger into me.

He pulls on my neck, making me bend forward. "Spread your legs."

I do as he says, and he picks up the pace of his finger thrusts. He also rubs the fur of his tail in a long glide across both of my nipples. He begins by simply gliding it across, but then pulls it in the other direction, running opposite of how the fur lies so it increases the friction.

The feel of it on both breasts simultaneously is almost too much and I can't contain my moans.

He adds a third finger and increases the pressure of his tail pushing up against my breasts. The cave is full of my mewling cries and the wet sounds of him pumping into me.

His tail shifts away and I growl at the loss of it.

"So greedy."

I don't have time to think of a pithy response. His tail smacks first one, then the other nipple, the sting followed by another smooth glide of fur.

His grip is too tight to let me move much, but I try to squirm away.

It's his turn to growl, and he pulls his fingers out of me and smacks me hard on one ass cheek, my juices on his hand making it a sharp impact, but the sting is quickly overtaken when he pushes his fingers back inside me.

His tail continues to smack and glide against me in a random order, making me more and more excited.

When he crooks his fingers slightly just as he's roughly running his tail against my nipples, my orgasm suddenly explodes through me and I have to bite off a cry.

I'm still processing the sensation when he spins and lifts me, then drops me on my back on the nest he made.

He pushes my legs apart and starts greedily licking at me, purring deeply as he laps me up.

The combination of his purr, the roughness of his tongue, and my recent pleasure brings another release hard on the heels of the other.

My back arches with the strength of it.

As I come back to myself, he is repositioning me again, this time so we are both on our sides, with my ass pulled tight against his sheathe.

This time it doesn't slowly move into me, but pushes in rapidly all at once. I have to put a hand to my mouth to contain my squeal, excited to be so full.

Thivoll grinds against me, growling and snarling as his hands roughly move across my belly, up over my breasts and then back down to hold my hips tight so he can keep pushing hard against me.

His tail replaces his hand around my neck and he moves one arm underneath my side and up to squeeze my breast as the other digs into my hip.

With each rocking grind, I feel a building warmth deep inside me. It grows and grows until it blossoms across my belly and up into my spine.

My channel contracts around him in waves, milking him.

"Dear Thela," he says, and then he lets out a muffled roar into my hair as his hips twitch.

Pulling that sound from him is immensely satisfying, and I feel a purr build in my chest.

It cuts off abruptly when I realize what I'm doing.

"Holy shit."

42

Thivoll

"What's wrong?"

I'm twitching inside her and my mind is fuzzy with the aftermath of my release, but I force myself to focus.

"Stop purring for a moment."

I do as she asks, then feel her own purr vibrate against me.

"You have a kit purr," I blurt out.

I chuff and can't seem to stop. She uses her elbow to deliver blows to me several times, grumbling the whole time, but I just keep right on chuffing.

Soon after, she relents and joins me with a low version of her trill.

I pull her close to me. "You are perfect. Including your dainty purr."

It starts back up again and I add my own deeper rumble to it.

We fall asleep wrapped up in each other's arms.

***

I wake us both up well before dark.

The wind was howling for most of the morning, but it has improved now.

I'd rather hunt at night, but I feel like we would fail her Silver to not keep moving. She groans, but grabs on to me without complaint.

We continue our practice of me leaving her in a nearby hiding spot, but I decide to be more choosy today. There are several newly downed trees, presumably from the wind storm.

There are more and more hunters each day.

If I took the time to kill them all, it not only increases the risk when my Ree wouldn't be able to get in and out of our nest alone, but it also lengthens the time before we can help her Silver.

I've already checked several camps with no sign of the equipment we need when I come across one with a small cache of supplies covered with a heat-reflective material.

It piques my interest and I spend some time observing the mixed camp of genali and braceaaer.

They aren't getting along well, as usual.

I only know a few words of the clicking braceaaer language, but from the insults being hurled by the genali it seems like they are on the brink of pulling weapons on each other.

I suppress my purr, mentally urging them on.

After a few more minutes of observation without violence, I decide to help inflame the situation.

Some careful creeping is all it takes to position myself above them. I carefully detach a branch, then carve it into a sharp point.

It would be more helpful to have one of the knives we've pilfered, but it's not worth the discomfort of carrying a pack when I have plenty of sharp claws.

The small spear works just fine when I drop it from a height onto the exposed neck of a bending over braceaaer. They dart their long-fingered hands up to their neck, whipping around to berate the innocent genali behind them.

I sharpen another projectile, but it isn't needed. It seems like all it took was a little nudge.

Bullets and knives are flying not long after. One of the two braceaaer simply picks up one of the three genali and hurls him into the trunk of a tree.

They are far stronger than they look. They're one of those species where size and strength don't align with expectations.

It stuns the slime just long enough for the other braceaaer to run in and slash his blade across its quivering body, spilling entrails before they reverse the trajectory and stab forward through one of the screaming blob's eyes.

Several bullet wounds open up on the torso of the triumphant killer, and he lets out a series of high-pitched clicks as he crashes to the ground, green blood pumping out of his blown open chest cavity.

There's plenty of competing noise now, so I let out my suppressed purr, its rumble increasing my satisfaction.

This is the most entertainment I've had in a very long time.

The remaining braceaaer learns from the blind rage of his companion and dives behind a tree for cover, still peppering the two remaining genali with blasts from his handgun.

One catches a retreating genali in the head, pitching it forward as it instantly spreads out into a boneless puddle.

The remaining two hunters fire a few more shots from cover before the genali wetly calls for a truce.

"You destroyed the dried-up whiner. What's the point of killing each other?"

I don't understand the braceaaer's reply, but it must signal some sort of agreement because the genali lets out a gurgling sigh.

"Of course I can moisten the deal. You can have your pick of any of my slaves in stasis on the moon."

As certain as I am that these two will eventually be back to blows, I don't want to bother waiting. I'm sure my Ree is wondering what's keeping me.

Knowing her, she might even try to climb down from her perch.

They've provided me with plenty of cover. I creep through the canopy as they continue to haggle out an agreement. Of the two, I'm most concerned with the braceaaer, so I head for him first.

He's still busy berating the genali as I creep down the trunk of the tree he's hiding behind.

I've never enjoyed descending headfirst.

If he hears me, it will take him a mere moment to train his gun on me.

My progress is slow, since I need to be quiet and also keep my body from showing to the genali, but it isn't long before I let go of the tree and fall, my claws extended in front of me.

His body buckles under my weight, the sound of his spine snapping bringing my purr back in force. Just in case, I slice my claws across his thin throat, severing his oversized head from his body.

The genali gets a glimpse of me and he's filling the opposite side of the tree with gunshots as I climb back up.

He must have seen enough of my fur to know what I am, and now he's panicking.

Not long after, I hear the telltale click of an empty chamber and I leap from tree to tree to close the distance between us. He's still shakily trying to attach another clip when I pounce on him.

I let out a roar as I shred his disgusting body with my claws.

The desire to bite into him is strong, but I stop myself midway when I think of the *kisses* I would like to get from my Ree once I return to her.

No sense in being overly dramatic, anyway.

I suppress a roar of triumph, but not the surging satisfaction that I could spark such pandemonium with a little stick.

I'm still chuffing about it as I use their water to rinse blood out of my fur.

The mysterious covered cache ends up being a disappointment. It's bottles of moisturizing spray and a pile of illicit substances genali are fond of, which don't even have the added benefit of any sort of medical use.

I take a few moments to create a makeshift bag to sling over my neck and grab rations, medical supplies, and the braceaaer weapons.

Everything else I destroy.

I'm sure Ree will appreciate the supplies, but I put even more care into not running into any more dangers afterwards. Unless I see a rope lying around or more hunters about to kill each other for us, it's best to just leave them be.

I make haste to get to her, relieved when she is still waiting, though impatiently.

We have roamed far from the cave when I scent a new species. It smells like exotic spices, musk, and anger. The caustic tang of the latter I can certainly appreciate, but as always, it makes me cautious.

I pause for a long moment trying to decide if I should even tell her about it. If I do, she will insist we go see them.

For all I know, she will offer to *teddy bear* it while it tries to snap her neck.

"Why are you growling?"

My face flushes to be caught out and I realize I don't want to keep things from her, anyway.

Even if I might not like what comes next.

"I think there's a prey species nearby. But they smell angry."

"Well, I'm feeling that too right about now, so how about we go greet them?"

I growl again, but start moving that way.

A few more steps and a shift in the wind and I smell a genali as well. I place my fists and paws more carefully and keep my ears swiveling.

"A slime, too," I tell her.

"Good thing I reloaded this *god*-awful gun."

Fear skitters down my spine right along with a flash of memory that takes me back to that Thela-cursed bush. I doubt I will ever be able to forget that day or the panic sizzling through me as the genali raised his gun in response.

I shouldn't have said anything.

I should likely just let them battle it out, but as much as I would like to keep Ree completely out of all of this, I can't just stand by while they attack another victim, regardless of how dangerous they may be.

The best thing to do now is to creep in and take a look, so that's what I do.

I move slowly and carefully, keeping my rounded ears perked in front of me, with the occasional sweep backwards to check my full surroundings.

It doesn't take long before I hear the squelching sound of the genali. I learned from my mistake last time. This time I pull Ree into my arms and move to scale a tree.

She gives me a narrowed-eye look, but doesn't protest.

43

Thivoll

I settle us on the branch of a tree to wait. Not long after, a slime comes into view, though just barely.

They aren't coming this way and we can only make out intermittent glimpses of gray flesh through the underbrush.

Ree pokes me to get my attention and then points at the hunter. I shake my head. She points at her gun. I shake my head harder.

She holds her arms wide and looks up. I don't know what the gesture means. Well, except that she probably doesn't enjoy being told no, but she can't do anything about it and I am feeling like a genius for trapping her up here.

I realize what that means with a jolt.

I look close for signs of listlessness, but she is just staring intently over toward the genali. A quick glance lets me know they've paused to look around. Thankfully, not in our direction.

She must not feel trapped. I let out a long breath, then quickly suck it back in when something springs from a bush near the genali with an undulating cry.

I only glimpse long black mane and dark gray skin before they both disappear.

The sounds of a quick, but brutal struggle follow. The slime's scream is easy to recognize after so many times of hearing it and purr rumbles in my chest in response.

One less hunter. One less threat.

From the sawing sounds, I assume the prey is cutting through the slime's pack.

Low muttering in a foreign language follows it.

A small gasp from Ree is the only warning I get before she speaks to it. There's not nearly enough time to shift around and throw a hand over her mouth, unfortunately.

I don't know what she yells to him, her voice sounding like an odd mix of breathy whistles across the roof of her mouth and intermittent deep clicks.

Like most languages, it has its own beauty.

Here it could prove to be a deadly call and so I cage her against the trunk of the tree and tuck in all of my more vulnerable parts.

She grunts and tries to push me away, but I don't move.

I avoid speaking with her so she won't be tempted to switch between languages, but a low growl lets her know anything that needs to be said.

She snaps her teeth at me, but stops trying to wriggle out.

The forest is completely silent.

Ree waits a few more moments and then calls out again, this time speaking for much longer.

While she does, I consider how short-sighted it was for me to never get my own translation nanites. Aside from there being no reason to, of course, since I never joined the Thorisian Sentinels.

It doesn't surprise me when we eventually hear a muted response, though from a different location. I adjust my body to compensate for the different angle.

My Ree could probably talk anyone into anything. I move a hand to pat her hip, hopefully communicating some of my pride.

They speak back and forth for several long minutes, then she talks with me again.

"His name is Kuret. He agreed we could come closer, but not too close. And if we try anything he said he'll kill us."

"Let's just leave. Or you can speak to him from here."

"I need to see him and interact for a while, Thivoll. I can't just tell him about the other women without at least checking if he will be civil with us."

"He just said he'd kill us."

"Wouldn't you say the same thing?"

I growl at her and her Thela-cursed point. "Alright, but you stay behind me. Will you do that?"

Her lips twitch to the side.

It's nothing like her *smile*, so I don't know what it means.

Who knew lips could move so many directions and communicate so many things? It would be far more interesting if we were settled at a resort with a giant nest and all the time we wanted to figure out what every twitch meant.

Right now it just heightens my anxiety wondering if it means she is about to do something inadvisable.

"I'll stay behind you."

Some of the tension eases.

"At least until it seems safe."

And comes right back.

I'm growling as we descend and make our way closer, but I do as I'm asked. The male... Kuret, rather, has some fear mixed in with his caustic anger. That alone makes me feel better.

Whatever she told him it was more than verbal *teddy bearing*.

I glance back to ensure the bulk of my body blocks her and pad closer to where he is crouched behind the trunk of a tree, just the crown of his head and one eye peeking out. It's bright green and currently narrowed to a small slit.

Long black braids of coarse mane dangle down from a broad skull and I can make out one vaguely humanlike ear, but with three sharp points rising in an arc along the top and back of it.

I decide we are close enough and sit back on my haunches so I most effectively create a barrier between them. Only the underbrush serves as cover for me, but I'd rather him think I don't need it than huddle behind a trunk like he's doing.

To complete the look, I put a bored expression on my face and start running a hand through my mane.

Worst case, he's from a culture where personal grooming is an insult, but I'll take the risk. It has the added benefit of making me seem unarmed.

If I don't know about his species, I bet his doesn't know about mine.

Ree keeps talking as I keep grooming. After removing the many tens of tangles, I'm glad I thought of it.

I hope the dark violet I know my muzzle is showing right now as I think of how unkempt I have been for my little human doesn't destroy the entire show.

She's as effective as usual and I still have plenty of tangles left when he steps out from behind the tree.

I tense up when I see a genali rifle in his hand, but he props it up against the tree and keeps talking. His face bears a passing resemblance to a human male, except with broader features, much bigger eyes with a horizontal pupil, and ears that come to three points that jut out from his head between black braids.

His braids are thick and elaborate with rough beads, bones, feathers, and even small wooden carvings mixed into them. His skin is dark gray with a bright green, glowing pattern across his face and down his arms.

It pulses like it's a type of fluid pumping across the surface of his flesh.

It may continue under his clothes, which are made from the skin of some alien creature and stitched together with sinew. It's thicker in some areas, like armor was built into its design and is scored and pitted in enough places that I know he's seen a lot of violence.

From the patina, only some of it since being abducted.

He's muscular, with a broad chest and narrow hips. The more I look at him, the more I can see the overlap in human physiology.

Two arms. Two legs, though they are much longer than a human, adding to his greater height. His hands work similarly, but he only has three wide fingers instead of four.

Almost human, at least in shape.

Judging by the dark green liquid oozing from a wound to his lower abdomen there are some very significant differences in internal makeup.

He lets out a sharp hissing bark that makes me dart my eyes back to his face. Multiple bright white teeth are showing now, all of them sharp.

I move forward at the sight of such a threat but Ree yanks on the mane at the back of my neck. I grunt, then pay closer attention to his body language.

I guess more than one species is confused about what showing teeth means. He's *smiling*.

Although I suppose I am getting used to seeing her *smile* and I'm starting to associate it with happy times.

I realize my mind had been wandering when she speaks my language. "He's injured. I'd like to go over and help him."

I shake my mane in self-reproach for not staying focused.

"No. He can do it himself. I assume he took the medical kit from the genali."

"That's harsh, Thivoll. I need to solidify his trust so I can ask him the giant favor of searching for and protecting a woman. The least we can do is stitch the man. This time we have plenty of supplies and the guilt from not treating Szhe'ka still haunts me."

If he only knew what it was like to have a human pulling him around by his tail, he would run the opposite direction. With whatever sound his species makes that is the opposite of that war cry he made earlier.

Then I concede he doesn't have a tail. And also that I enjoy having my tail pulled. I huff out a breath.

"Only if he agrees to have me within tail range. But of course, don't tell him what my tail does," I add hastily.

She trills, pats me, and then goes back to speaking to the male. She comes out from around me and stands at my side. I feel better when she shows some caution by not immediately walking over to him.

My fur stands on end at the way he looks at her.

His eyes are widened, and they rove over her body in a way that suggests appreciation and interest.

"Tell him if he keeps looking at you like that I'll rip his head off."

44

Ree

I smack Thivoll on the shoulder, but I can't really disagree with him.

"I don't appreciate it when people look at me like that, Kuret. And Thivoll is thinking violent thoughts."

He looks over to Thivoll, runs his hands along the glowing patterns on each cheek, causing them to ripple a lighter green, and then wipes both hands down his chest.

From the look on his face, I assume it's an apologetic gesture.

"Is he your chosen donor? I assumed you were not compatible. Aren't you too young?"

He shakes himself and keeps talking, not allowing me to answer his questions. "It is my error and a wound to my honor."

Donor? What an odd way to talk about being with someone.

We haven't exactly defined our odd relationship, but Kuret doesn't need to know that.

"He is my, uh... donor? But no honor has been wounded. How about we take care of that one to your stomach? I will show you how to use the genali tools so you can heal any later wounds."

He flicks one of his fingers across the top of his other hand, then sits back against the tree.

From the context, I assume it signals agreement. I hope so, at least. I move forward, keeping my hands well away from my body to decrease any misunderstandings.

I highly doubt he hasn't hidden weapons somewhere in all of that armor.

As I kneel in front of him, he pulls at hooks of sinew at his sides, releasing the front part of his breastplate. From the way the skin is pulled tight over the sharp planes of his face, it must be very painful.

"May I help?"

He stills, the skin on his brow lowering. He doesn't have eyebrows, but the movement is human enough that I think I've insulted him somehow.

Thivoll settles in close, his fur puffed out so much he looks like he's been electrocuted. I glance back to Kuret.

"Was that a violent question?"

I blink at 'violent' coming out of my mouth instead of 'rude.' I wonder what that says about his culture.

"It is an insult."

"My honor is lowered. I am a healer. I meant no insult."

"As you said, no honor is lost. We are different, but you are not offering violence. You may help."

I smile at him before I can think better of it, but he simply smiles back at me, the sharp points of his many teeth pushing little divots down into a thick bottom lip that's so dark gray it's almost black.

His mouth is much wider than a human's. His jaw doesn't come to a point, but arcs forward in a half circle. His cheek bones jut out and run under his large eyes at a sharp angle from his almost nonexistent nose up into his thick black hair.

There is a ribbed structure where a nose would be, but from movement rustling his braids in the same rhythm his chest falls, I would guess his nostrils are near the spiked structures that are in a similar location as human ears.

I move my hands slowly toward the other side of his breastplate. My hands are trembling despite my bravado.

He's huge. Not as bulky as Thivoll, but still nearly twice my height. He looks like he could break me in half and judging by his language and armor; he is well-versed in using force.

I unhook the loops despite my fear.

In a few brief moments, he can pull away the breastplate. When he pulls up a rough spun shirt, my medical brain takes over and pushes any doubts out of my mind.

His muscles clearly show through his skin, but instead of the bumps of human abdominal muscles they run in long thick ridges in a repeated V pattern that meets in the middle of his chest and stomach. Swirling patterns of the same green illumination flow along them.

I shake myself out of my burning curiosity and narrow in on the stab wound leaking dark green blood.

"I am grabbing a tool," I warn him so he doesn't stab me in alarm.

I pull out the stitch clipper and hold it out to show him. "This will tie your wound together. The ties will melt when your body no longer needs them. It will hurt when I use it. Did you get one from the genali?"

"I did. But I left it under a bush."

"That is good. Watch how I use it and ask questions as needed. May I touch you?"

"You may touch me."

"This will hurt."

He smiles at me again. I'm pretty sure he's amused. Hopefully not because I've trampled all over social decorum.

I mean, Thivoll still doesn't know what it means when he rubs my butt. I wouldn't have guessed his tail was erogenous. I might be about to get very personal.

Nurses do what needs to be done, so it doesn't matter, anyway.

I reach forward to assess the depth of the stab. It goes in at least a couple inches. For a human that is all it would take to be very dangerous.

"Did it hit anything vital? Can I just close it up?"

"It is only on the surface."

"Good. I am grabbing another thing."

More of his sharp teeth are showing when I look back up at him. Yes, I'm definitely being entertaining.

I grin back. Entertaining is far better than dead because I did something stupid.

"This will clean your wound," I explain and then I focus on my task.

He doesn't seem very concerned about the blood loss, but I don't like it. I make quick work out of spraying some of the disinfectant and closing it up. I use a few more stitches than I think are necessary, the clicks of each staple the only sound for a short while.

"That looks good, my Ree," Thivoll comments.

I turn to Thivoll with a smile, then Kuret's voice pulls my attention back to him.

"I thought you looked too young for a donor, but your teeth are worn. Are you actually old?" Kuret asks as he pulls his shirt back down.

I'm not sure why he seems so focused on my age, but I can understand why he's confused about my teeth.

It seems like sharp teeth are the norm around here and I'm just another harmless human with our 'ruminant' chompers.

I laugh, and it makes his eyes widen. "No. Humans just don't have many natural defenses."

He makes a deep clicking sound. "But those black scales look thick."

I'm still getting used to having those. "Those are new. I got them from Thivoll."

He shrinks back into the tree and a hand strays down to his thigh.

"Wait! I didn't take them. I was captured by the same aliens you just killed. It's because of them I can look more like him."

"Why would they do that?"

"I was supposed to be a pleasure slave."

The patterns along his body flare. "They truly have no honor, then."

"No, I don't think they do."

"Then they will get no mercy."

I think Thivoll will like this one.

They share a penchant for violence, though Thivoll still doesn't seem to have caught on yet to how bloodthirsty he is and Kuret has no qualms.

It seems like as good a time as any to ask him if he wants to help us. "Would you join us? We would be stronger together."

"You seem like you have honor."

"Well, yes, but maybe not like you think of it. I need to find other women like me and protect them."

He sits forward, his eyes pinning me with new intensity. "Where?"

"We don't know. Well, except for one. Maybe two. We met another person—Szhe'ka, he looks like a very large bird man, except they cut off his wings–who is going to protect the one he saw. There are six more out there."

"They would be found faster if I look where you do not."

I let out a long breath, the ever-present tightness in my chest loosening just that little more now that I have more help.

"That's true, but we are also safer together. This will be a risk for you."

I wish I had said the same to Szhe'ka. It leaves a sick taste in my mouth to think of the poor male.

"Danger is where the most honor is found."

I smile, and he smiles back.

Just like I did with Szhe'ka, I ask my suit to free my hair and then pull it forward to where he can see it.

His patterns flicker as he looks down the length of it. "Beautiful."

"Thank you. I hate it... but that doesn't matter. Each of us has different colored long hair like this. It isn't normal for us, so if you find them outside of a cryogenic chamber, they might have cut it off. I mean... they might be in a silver container or maybe already out of it. It would be best if they stay in it and you carry them back to where we can protect them."

My face burns from my ineffectual rambling. "Does that make sense?"

"Yes."

I open my mouth to tell him about the other changes they made, like the arousal and the metamorphosis, but then I remember that long once-over he gave me. Some instinct tells me that the information would make him more likely to open the chamber.

I vacillate for a long moment, not liking the idea of withholding information from a woman by extension, but it feels right.

"I will start looking," he tells me with a wide smile.

He starts rapidly reattaching his leather breastplate.

His eagerness lets me know I made the right choice. I just have to hope he shows restraint so I can give whoever he finds more choices than I had. So they can come home safe and unchanged.

A nagging voice points out that all I have is a dingy cave and I haven't even gotten Silver into it. My throat feels tight and my lips tingle.

The weight of this task might crush me under it.

I stand up and back away to give Kuret room. Thivoll's fur has relaxed some, but he stays where he's at. He's still running his hands through his fur even though it looks perfect, the light catching it in a fiery halo.

"Did he agree to help?" he asks me. I nod at him. "There was no doubt in my mind. You had him enthralled."

"What is he saying?" Kuret asks me.

A direct translation would be embarrassing, so I don't bother. "He appreciates your help."

It hurts to transition to Thivoll's language, but I need him to orient me. "Which way is our cave?"

"We aren't telling him that."

"Dammit, Thivoll. Help me out here."

"He can go to a nearby ridgeline or we could simply meet back here. The ridgeline is that way."

I turn back to Kuret. He looks amused again. "Thivoll says there is a ridgeline that direction you could look for us at. Or we could meet back here."

"I know where he means. That is a better place than this." He stands, his face twisting in pain from the movement. "I hope to see you again soon, Ree."

"I hope so, too. Please be careful."

"There is very little honor to be found that way," he tells me.

I pull a face and he smiles. "I will be careful with your women if I find them."

"Thank you."

There isn't anything left to say after that.

Kuret runs a hand slowly down one arm, his patterns flaring behind the stroke. I give him a smile and a wave. Then he disappears into the undergrowth.

I turn to Thivoll, who's body still looks like a cat trying to seem like it doesn't care and failing miserably at it.

Despite his nonchalant bearing, he's still glaring at Kuret like he wants to separate his head from his body. His face clears as soon as he notices me looking.

It pulls a chuckle from me and helps ease some of the tightness fear and guilt keep causing every time I let myself think about how impossible this all seems.

45

Thivoll

"That was surreal, Thivoll. He looked like a gray *ninja turtle* without a shell and an *orc* had a baby and then threw glowing radioactive slime all over it."

My whiskers drop so low they brush my chest. "A what and a what? And why would radioactive slime glow?"

She trills. "Nevermind. He just sort of looked like a couple creatures from Earth mythology. Except as far as I know, they weren't bioluminescent."

"It's a fairly common trait."

"Have you seen his species before?"

"No, but the genali are always looking for something novel."

Conversation dies down at that point and we continue our original mission to find rope.

I take quick peeks at tens of hunter camps, none of them look like they would have what we need. As darkness closes In, I think maybe we are wasting our time.

I take us to a stream for a drink and meal, my body slumped.

Ree looks closely at me after she climbs down. "You're frustrated? Me too."

"I'm not sure it would be a standard item to bring."

She wrinkles her forehead, and it feels like good progress that I know it means she's puzzled or thinking.

"Right! We need to look for people who need rope. That means we're probably wasting our time in the forest and need to look for people on top of or near cliffs."

I have a sudden realization. "You mean like that hunter who fell off one, and I never investigated?"

She makes a pursed lips face, her eyes widening. "Uh, yes. Just like them."

We both groan in unison and move back into position to keep running. A quick up and down scramble interrupted by a brief run and we have our answer.

I spare Ree the gruesome view and rummage through their packs, but I can't save either of us from the chagrin when I bring back their climbing gear, complete with rope, some sort of buckled strapping, and metal shapes I assume are related because they are in the same bag.

She groans at the sight of it. "As you were running off toward that hunter I was thinking about how lust was clouding our judgment. Seems I was right."

I huff out a breath. "Well, the only cure is more sex."

She bares her teeth at me and once I'm sure it's not a precursor to violence, I chuff.

The levity fizzles out when I picture Silver surrounded by an ever-increasing number of hunters. "Let's make haste to help right our oversight."

We quickly make our way back to the cave.

I have never spent a single moment thinking about climbing gear, aside from a vague sense of what to look for, since no manticorid would ever need it, but luckily Ree can make sense of it all.

Or at least most of it.

She sets a few pieces aside, rubbing at her hands with a grimace on her face.

"I can't figure out what those do, but I think I know how to rig a pulley system. I won't have the strength to hoist her up or to pull her in so we are going to have to tie her off at the bottom and then scale up. That part makes me nervous, since I have no idea how much weight this rope can hold."

I only have a rudimentary understanding of what's going on, but I hold Ree in place as she uses various parts of the gear just above our cave entrance and then runs the rope through it. She pulls until there are two roughly equal coiled piles.

She asks me to dangle from it and seems pleased when it holds me.

She rubs her hand on the back of her neck, then looks over to me. "I assume I need to stay here."

I nod. "Yes. Do you feel confident you can use this to get down if needed?"

She gulps. "Not really, but I know I'd figure it out if I had to."

She embraces me, pulling me tight. "Please be careful."

I stroke her hair, then pat her rear. "I will, sweet one."

46

Ree

Waiting for him is one of the hardest things I've ever done.

I continually have to push what if scenarios out of my head, and finally resort to pulling up the professional in me.

Compartmentalization is essential in my field.

No one can practice more than a few months without seeing terrible things happen to good people. Worrying does nothing, though it's hard not to when it's someone you love.

The thought catches me off guard and it only makes my worry double. I chide myself for another brief lapse of focus and then get to work on organizing supplies.

My fingers are aching from all the tight gripping I've been doing on our runs, but I just shake my hands out and dive in. I'm deep into it when Thivoll silently walks back into the cave, causing me to jump when his shadow moves into my periphery.

I drop the oddly designed tunic I'm holding and rush over to him, wrapping him in my arms and breathing in his wild scent.

"Was she still there?"

"Yes, thankfully. I'll need your help securing her chamber to the rope. It's all still a jumble to me."

I nod at him, then go over to the rope. I work through it all again in my mind and am glad I did when I think to add a thick knot to each end.

That way it won't ever completely slip out.

With Thivoll here it doesn't matter, but I'll need to keep working through all of it to improve my approach.

I had friends interested in climbing, but with my fear of heights I didn't pay close attention to what they said. A lot of it was acronyms and terminology that didn't help in this context, but I hope what I know is enough.

"Could you hold the rope near the top? No, both sides. Perfect." I toss the first pile down.

"Does it reach the bottom?"

Thivoll leans out to look. "Yes, with spare."

"Great." I toss over the other one and turn to Thivoll so he can pull me into his arms and take us down.

Silver is indeed at the base of the rock face, the chamber catching the moonlight. I start making a sling for it, not pleased with the shape and how much rope we have to provide a suitable lattice.

I measure it out and feel dumb all over again when I see a button on one end. As suspected, it engages a mechanism that flips out an eye hook. After rolling my eyes at myself it takes only a few minutes to tie the rope to it.

"You can start pulling. Actually, I guess you should prop her up against the rock so we don't make drag marks."

He does so, then pauses. "I think I will have to pull as I climb."

I blink. The strength that would require is crazy.

I start to say that, then get his point. "Right. Otherwise she scrapes all along the rock."

I feel useless, but he manages it like it's no giant feat.

I crane my neck up to watch him as he keeps his tail wrapped around her chamber with just enough pressure to pull her away from the rocks while he slowly moves himself higher.

He has to pull on the rope until his tail can't stretch anymore, then climb while holding it taut, then repeat the process.

I'm in awe of him by the time he reaches the top. I mean, he had already impressed me and made me feel like I was completely ripped off by evolution, but this is next level.

He doesn't even seem out of breath when he comes back to get me.

It's almost disgusting, actually.

A ridiculous joke of the cosmos that I got blunt teeth, puny strength, no venom, no... best to stop myself there.

When we get to the top, I waste no time in moving over to where he tucked Silver just inside the main area. I engage the light on her chamber so I can see her better, then gasp.

"Yes, I thought you might not like seeing that," Thivoll comments.

He's right.

Despite my best efforts, it looks like Silver has already started changing. She has silver scales on her skin in the same places I have black ones, except hers also expand up to her face.

It makes little sense.

"But I was the only one who touched her and only briefly compared to how much contact the two of us had before my changes started. Not to mention your scales are black."

"I don't know enough about what causes it to say."

I huff out a breath. "There must have been enough of your DNA on me already to transfer over to her. Or I already had mixed DNA, I dunno. But why did her metamorphosis happen so fast?"

He thinks for a moment. "I suspect it's because of the constant cycling of nanites to keep the chamber running."

I sigh. "I'm sorry, Silver. So many changes and you haven't even woken up yet."

She might have many more changes ahead of her if we can't find a way to isolate her before her chamber stops working.

I really have no sense of just how much my own body will change. I'm glad at least she'll have someone else to talk to about it. I'd like that too.

Not that I can't talk about it with Thivoll, but it would be nice to be able to commiserate with another human.

"Well, the damage is already done. I want to check her eyes to see if her concussion has improved."

He nods at me, then opens the chamber while I hold my hands at the ready. After it snicks open I quickly pull back on her eyelids.

Her eyes are less dilated, which is an enormous relief, but she also now has silver irises to compliment her light green sclera.

I pull my hands back, rubbing at them to relieve the ache. "Ok, go ahead and close it."

"You don't want to see if she will wake up?"

I consider it. "No. I would rather let the chamber keep working and her nanites have more time to heal her."

Thivoll nods and engages the controls, his face betraying his own conflicted feelings about that decision.

I let out a big sigh after it closes. None of this is ideal, which is of course fucking obvious, but I'd really like to feel like I'm using my experience and skills instead of hoping tiny robots keep doing all the important work on a planet that destroys technology.

Or power sources, I suppose, though the distinction doesn't make me feel any better.

All I've done since arriving here is convince other people to do the work I should be doing.

An image of Szhe'ka floats up, his mangled wings twitching behind him. His feet crisscrossed with so many wounds no amount of treatment I could give him would have helped as he bravely walked away from us and the relative safety of numbers.

And yet I let him just disappear into the forest by himself because I needed him.

A sharp pain makes me double over and rest my hands on the top of Silver's chamber.

Staring at her face doesn't give me the same sense of peace it did on the ship. Maybe because then I was the clear victim and now I've blurred the line with my own actions.

Who am I becoming on this god-forsaken planet?

47

Thivoll

I can tell she still feels the heavy weight of responsibility for her Silver, even after all we have done to protect the female.

She looks lost and depressed and I know I need to help distract her from whatever it is floating around in her overly-protective mind.

I doubt she would agree to any naps in the sun or laying under our covers.

Even I would be too distracted thinking of the other women we need to help, and they are only a vicarious responsibility.

Now that we have a way for her to exit our cave, I no longer want to risk her being with me when I kill hunters. There are safer outings we could take, but it's worth finding out if she would consider staying.

"We have a couple of traps we could set up near the entrance, but how about I go looking for more tonight?"

"Sure, but let's get her in the other small room first. I don't like how she's sitting out here like she's part of the supplies."

I move Silver as she goes into the room with our nest in it.

As I'm setting the chamber down in the back of the room, she comes in with a blanket. She drapes it over the chamber so only Silver's neck and head are showing.

I haven't really thought about how troubling it would be for a nearly hairless species to be without clothing.

"Should we dress her?"

Ree shakes her head. "I would really like to, but everything will be contaminated and we've already done enough to her in that regard."

I see her point. When I look over to her, she is absentmindedly scratching at the back of her hands and forearms.

A thrill passes up my chest and quivers along my whiskers thinking of how beautiful they will be if those portend coming changes.

"I assume you are going to have scales there soon?"

She looks down at what she's doing and pulls a face. "Likely so."

"I'm sure they will look just as beautiful as your others, my Ree."

She sniffs. "We'll know soon enough. Let's get this cave better protected."

I growl. "I would rather you remain here."

She ignores me and grabs an empty pack, then rechecks her pockets to ensure she has a medkit and rations before moving over to me and extending her arms.

I huff out a breath.

This is one of those moments where I realize that one of her most attractive traits is also one of her most annoying ones. I love all the ways she is exotic, but she is just as willful as a manticorid female.

Which is of course why I can't trap her here.

The pang of fear that thought brings urges me over to her, but not to lift her just yet. I push my muzzle into the base of her neck, loving the feel of her new scales against me, and take a deep breath of her intoxicating scent.

I want to move her back to our soft bedding, but we go out into the night.

We spend some time ensuring we didn't leave any scrapes or other evidence of our habitation on the rock face or at the base, then lope off into the thick forest.

With Silver ensconced in our nest my heart is much lighter. In fact, I've never felt so alive or hopeful, although there are dozens, if not hundreds of hunters on the continent.

Space station work was reliable, but I'd trade it without another thought for the exhilaration of leaping rock to rock with her legs holding me tight.

I had the occasional encounter with a manticorid female who was passing through the station, but never once imagined the utter delight I would find here with my precious Ree.

Her thoughts must have been far heavier while I was pondering this because she lets out a long sigh.

"What's bothering you?"

She hums. "Do you think the genali will just keep taking women from my planet until we're all gone? You have Sentinels and have lost half of yours."

I wish I could assuage her fears, but I doubt she wants lies.

"You're barely past primitive. Humans have no natural defenses and are easily captured. You weren't popular until recently despite all of that and I never knew why, but your metamorphosis explains it. I assume you died too easily before to make it a worthwhile investment."

She makes a pained keening sound. "Is that why they started taking your women, too? Would your people help us?"

My breath catches.

Maybe she's right and they found a way around the confinement sickness, but there's no way of knowing.

It would surprise me if they figured out our biology. We don't really understand it ourselves and most of our technological advancements for many generations have been toward that goal.

I hate delivering more bad news, but I never see Session agreeing to assist her species.

"I doubt it. It seems like it's only a matter of time before we move away from our sleepy, peaceful pursuits to revisiting the might of a lost era, but I think it might drive us into extinction to protect even our own system. We waited too long, I'm afraid."

"Well, maybe they will change you in ways that work to your advantage. I know I'm nowhere near as fragile as I once was," she comments.

It's hard to imagine a species being more breakable than she is, but I know better than to voice that thought as she continues.

"They said we were the most durable of harem options. With testing data to back it up. From what I gathered, we are some sort of sport package for more rigorous use, but with the shiny packaging a discerning buyer has come to expect."

Hot rage fizzles along my spine and I have to stop running in case I slam us into a tree.

"They told you that?"

She snorts out a breath. "Thivoll. They showed videos and everything."

Her voice sounds flippant but she's trembling.

I crouch down so she can get down but she doesn't budge. She's making sniffing noises and her trembling gets worse.

"I'd like to hold you," I tell her.

"No. I'm fine. I want to get back to Silver and get better protections in place."

So stubborn.

I do as she asks, though, and pick up my pace. The sooner we're done, the sooner I can comfort her.

The first place I take us is back to where I killed the two idiotic fighting genali. I smell numerous other prey species around the area, but as I suspected, none of them were fooled by the amateur trap laying of the hunters.

Ree helps me disassemble two traps before we return to the one that worked by a trip trigger.

It ends up being useless.

I had assumed the genali blood in the air was from the two hunters in the camp we have been avoiding, but another hapless genali squelched right into the trip wire.

I hear Ree retching and decide not to get any closer. From the way the slime is laying, their pack and weapons are completely bathed in their gray blood.

I've had to wash enough of that out of my fur in streams over the last few days that I'm not inclined to investigate.

All the careful stalking, listening for threats, and communicating with gestures gives a sense of nostalgia for our early, much more awkward interactions. I push my whiskers forward just thinking about it, then shake my head when I think of how much has changed over such a short period.

Not to mention just how odd it is that those are going to be our early relationship memories.

No matter; as long as she's mine then those are unimportant details.

We spend most of the night adding a few more items to the pack on Ree's back, but not nearly as much as I would like. Few hunters are using traps, unfortunately.

When they do, it makes them more reckless and easy to sneak up on.

I avoid engaging except for a few times. Not only because she is with me, but also because most of the hunters seem far more capable and aware of their surroundings.

While I would have liked to have the opportunity to take more risks and as a result, clear the field of threats and increase our supplies, it is still a night well spent.

Ree looks more relaxed as we near our nest and I'm glad we took the time away. The fresh air is healing, especially when it isn't punctuated by venom-induced screams and gunshots like it has recently.

It's entering the first stages of pre-daylight and we are on the opposite side of the plateau from our cave.

I'm taking a bit of a detour toward what smells like a large body of water. From the scent I can tell we are getting very close.

There isn't enough rotting vegetation in the mix to suggest a bog and a reliable water source is always worth investigating. It's rocky and although I'm still enjoying our outing, I'm tiring from all the leaping.

The forest abruptly parts to reveal a cove, with the moon reflecting off of the water of the larger lake behind it. Ree makes a small sound of appreciation.

I agree with her. It's beautiful.

Something about moonlight glinting off of water must be universally appreciated. I walk us closer to the edge of the water, pulling in the complex smells of aquatic life and vegetation over the roof of my mouth.

Ree talks to me in a hushed whisper. "I can feel the scales now, Thivoll."

"How extensive are they?"

"On the back of my hands, but not my palms. My fingers are oddly thick on the top now. Then the scales go around my wrists and end halfway up my forearm."

I purr. "I look forward to exploring them."

"I'm glad you like them, but it's really strange for me."

I empathize, but I also love the look of them against her lovely white-pink skin and they make the indigo and orange of her mane look so much richer.

I hear a small sound out in the water, something about it pulling all of my attention. I stare out over the lake, but don't hear it again.

"This place feels really *creepy* all of a sudden, Thivoll. I don't like it."

I'm not sure what she means exactly, but get the general idea and agree with her. I can't hear or smell anything, but it feels like we're being watched.

"Let's go home."

It's almost light by the time we get back to our nest. I come to it from the top side and as I break over the ridge, I smell a strong male musk.

A growl starts up in my throat and I can feel Ree tense. I'm not sure if I should leave her up here while I go investigate, then decide it's best for her to just stay with me.

We climb down silently and I position Ree behind me as I stalk into the cave, my claws unsheathed and ready.

The smell of the male is much stronger and I'm on high alert.

A few steps in and it's clear they aren't in the main chamber. Nor in our nest room. I check the other exit, but it is empty.

That leaves Silver's room.

48

Ree

I'm not sure what Thivoll senses, but I trust his instincts.

Nothing looks or smells any different to me. At least not until we move into Silver's room.

She isn't there anymore.

I rush forward with a cry, but being inside only confirms that her entire cryochamber is missing.

I whip back toward Thivoll. "What do you smell?"

He takes in one of his long, whistling breaths. "Not a hunter. Some sort of prey, but not one I've ever encountered. I would guess male from the pheromones."

My heart drops. "Is she alive, you think?"

"I don't smell any blood. If they wanted to eat her, they would have just smashed open her chamber, not taken it. There aren't any drag marks, just a few disturbances in the dust on the floor."

"Oh, Silver," I breathe out.

No other words come to me. I can't seem to keep the woman safe, no matter what I do.

We continue searching, this time taking a much closer look for clues.

I'm not sure how we missed it as we came in, but there is a message written in what looks and smells like a ration pack on the wall of the main cave.

The writing is in fluid whorls and loops that the rough cave wall does nothing to diminish the beauty of, but the message is a chilling counterpoint.

I'm still staring at it with dread skittering along my skin and raising the hair on the back of my neck as Thivoll comes up beside me.

"Can you read it?"

"Yes. 'You hid what is meant for light. Moon daughter is mine."

He lets out a big huff of air. "That's excellent news."

"What? How is that good news?"

"He claimed ownership. That doesn't sound like someone planning to harm someone."

"The fuck, Thivoll? We aren't property!"

He holds out his hands toward me, palms out, his face flashing to violet. "I didn't say that, Ree."

"I've completely failed her if she traded one type of slavery for another. This is not fucking good news."

His whiskers droop and I feel like I've just kicked a puppy, but there's no room left amid the burning in my mind for apologies.

There's a weight in my chest that extends beyond the severity of the situation.

One my mind doesn't want to face just yet, even though it whispers that this is more about me than it's about Silver.

She can't be gone.

My lungs seize and my breath hitches. It was one thing to be away from her in pursuit of improving her health and environment.

I feel completely unmoored to no longer have her with me.

Thivoll is gazing at me, his whiskers lower than I've ever seen them before. I know I should comfort him, but there isn't space inside my roiling mind.

He hums and walks away, taking more long breaths. He does another sweep of the cave and then returns to embrace me.

I'm stiff in his arms, but I don't pull away. He repositions me so the glow of the bioluminescent lamp illuminates his open palm.

On top of it is a dark red scale with an oil-slick rainbow of colors on it where the light hits it.

"That's huge, Thivoll. If that's to scale based on snakes..."

I can't finish my thought because a giant red cobra big enough to eat me in one gulp with glinting red eyes flits into my head.

"I don't know what those are, but yes. He would have to be large. I would guess he doesn't have any legs and moves himself by bunching up and releasing a long body."

I shudder, a lump rising in my throat. "Yes. A snake."

"He took nothing else," he says in a low rumbling voice. "He wanted her, yes, but not for food or he would have eaten our rations. From the rate the smell is diminishing I think he likely came not long after we left and hasn't returned since. She was the prize in this raid, I think, and I'd like to believe that he wouldn't just destroy or harm his prize."

I let out a breath.

Oddly enough, he's starting to convince me, even while effectively scaring the tar out of me.

"I'm not sure if that makes me feel better or not, Thivoll. What if he returns?"

"Well, if I'm right that he didn't kill her, which seems likely, he's going to have his hands too full to bother with us. One human is more than enough to keep him busy. She'll be intelligent, of course, but I'm also sure she'll be sassy and willful, if my experience is a good indicator."

I'm wondering why he knows she'll be intelligent when his last comment and the side-eyed look he gives me catches my attention.

And of course my ire.

I grab onto his tail and pull it, finally doing what I keep threatening.

"Say that again?"

I know what he's trying to do and play along. The sick feeling weighing me down isn't helping anyone right now.

"Willful," he says, drawing out the word. "Unwilling to remain in safe places. Resistant to pampering. Frequently bossy. Shall I go on?"

I yank harder on his tail, but then he draws in a sharp breath, his eyes darting down to where I have a hold of it. I look down, too.

There's purple liquid seeping from his fur near my hand.

I instantly drop his tail, appalled. "Is that blood? What happened?"

My voice rises in pitch as I speak. "I'm so sorry! I didn't think your skin would just tear."

He pats my shoulder, his voice calm. "Let me see your hands."

I hold them up, gasping when I see long, pointed black nails. They are thick and come to a sharp point. "What the hell?"

Now I understand why the backs of my fingers have been getting thicker and more heavily scaled. The claws weren't there just a moment ago when we stopped at the top of the cave and I was scratching at the base of my nails.

"They are so precious. So tiny, yet fierce. Just like you."

I growl at him. At no point did I ever think I would be annoyed with someone for being incredibly accepting of my oddities... but that was before I turned into some sort of weird caterpillar that was turning into a clawed lizard instead of a damn butterfly.

"Fuck my life," I grumble.

"Of course, I will fuck you for life, my Ree."

I can't help the laugh that bubbles up at the complete sincerity in his voice.

It's our most entertaining lost in translation moment yet and it helps jar me out of my self-pity. Considering how much bitching

I've been doing about not having any natural protections, I should be pretty damn pleased right now.

How much I want to curse in a giant string doesn't help me appreciate the example of 'be careful what you wish for' though.

"How do I retract them, Thivoll? I don't want to go around stabbing you. Not on accident, anyway," I add with a growl in my voice.

He takes another few moments to stop chuffing, but then helps me out. "Most of us learn that as very young kits. But I've overheard mothers telling their young to have polite fingers."

He chuffs again and I want to slash him, or flip him off even though he likely wouldn't even understand.

"I really feel like giving you impolite fingers right now, Fluff Brain."

"Alright. Alright. Don't maul me. For me it feels like I'm taking a breath, but in my hands. Inhale, retract. Exhale, extend. Most of my friends only really talked about extension, comparing it to an orgasm or a sneeze."

I hadn't been paying attention to my hands when I cut him. Now I look at them, taking a breath in, then out and imagining they are moving with me.

Nothing happens. I think of sneezes, orgasms, yawns, even farts and still nothing happens.

After a few minutes, I look back up at him. "Am I stuck with these out like this forever? How am I going to touch you?"

He glances down at my hands. "Look."

I do and see that my normal nails are showing now.

I pull them up for a closer look. A short distance from the base of each nail I can see where the scales would part to let through my claws.

I assume they must glide over my existing nail base. The thicker additions to the backs of my fingers are now a second nail base for my black claws.

On a whim, I picture swiping at Thivoll with my impolite fingers, and they extend. I grunt, then think of polite fingers and touching him gently near his whiskers like he enjoys and they pull back in.

No way in hell am I going to admit that his nonsense about what mothers tell toddlers worked.

Never.

Then I think about Silver again. And the unknown woman that Szhe'ka went to go find. Two people I have no proper control over helping right now, but who I still feel like I need to be doing more to protect.

At least they have someone looking out for them, even if I don't really know their protectors' true intentions. I need to do better for the others.

My claws are out again and I need to do something with them.

"We need to do more than just survive, Thivoll. We need to find more women. Gather more allies than just Szhe'ka and Kuret. The hunters can't win. I feel like tearing into something. Anything."

He purrs and pulls me close to him. "We will. And that is a normal feeling, though more common in manticorid males than females."

I growl, the thirst for violence taking up so much room in my chest I'm not sure what to do with it.

Is this how all the violent offenders who frequented the ER felt? I suddenly have more empathy for them, even while rejecting their choices to act like they did.

What do I do to let it out? I really don't know.

I desperately need some sense of normalcy.

I push his chest. "Let me clean your wound."

He growls. "It's just a little kit scratch."

I narrow my eyes. "Unless you want more of them, you'll let me sanitize it."

He huffs, but sits back on his haunches and pulls his tail around and up to a comfortable working height.

"What a good Superkitty," I say in a singsong voice, then poke him in the ribs.

My heart still feels like someone is squeezing it in a death grip, and I know I really should apologize to Thivoll for snapping at him, but right now I just want to avoid it all.

I can't think about what it means that the one person who helped keep my mind in one piece for all of those long days of terror is gone.

I just can't.

Luckily there is a big, furry distraction in front of me. He shows me his teeth. It's the first time I've seen his alien Cheshire Cat routine since his initial attempt at a smile and it pulls a laugh from me.

I give him one of my crazy grins in response.

I make quick work of cleaning his wound, which it turns out is already closing up. I don't tell him that, though. After that, neither one of us seems to have the heart to say much more.

There's a tension between us that hasn't been there before as we lay down to rest.

I don't sleep for a long time.

49

Ree

When I wake up, I'm laying across him. He must have moved me in the night and I was too exhausted to remember.

There's even a puddle of drool that's soaked into his mane near my mouth as further evidence. I wonder how long he'll spend trying to make the fur lay right with his fingers.

I should feel bad about the smirk that thought causes, but I don't. I assume we've been asleep all or most of the day.

It was a long night finding traps to protect Silver, and we were too late.

Thivoll distracts me before I can spiral down into regrets. "Did you sleep well?"

I roll off of him so I can stretch. "Oh yes. Like a log. You?"

"What an odd expression. I am quite refreshed."

"Take me to the stream?"

"Of course."

We are watered, washed, and fed in short order, then without having to further discuss our plans, we are loping through moonlit trees.

I appreciate his impressive sense of direction. With the exception of giant landmarks like our cave's cliff face and that immense lake, everything looks the same to me in this thickly forested planet.

One can hope that's another one of my future changes, but I bet they just focused on aesthetics when they designed whatever caused the metamorphosis.

Although I suppose giving me claws doesn't seem to fit well with the whole slavery plan, so it must be an imperfect process.

I hope there's a genali out there right now finding out just how bad their idea was. My lips quirk at the idea before I chide myself for wishing anything like that on anyone. Except...

I roll my eyes, forcing myself to reroute my errant thoughts.

The night sounds of the forest and the loamy smell are so pleasant it's easy to forget how much danger lurks out here.

At least easy for me.

I have that luxury because Thivoll is constantly on alert, his rounded ears forever swiveling. I'm sure he's setting our course so we avoid sounds and smells he doesn't like.

The rumble of his speech startles me. "Tell me some more about your family. We've gone from one emergency to another."

"We still found time to scratch an itch."

"Itches get annoying."

I can tell by his voice that he doesn't understand my meaning. Damnable idioms.

"I mean we took time to have sex."

He chuffs. "Time well spent," he says with a purr, and I feel an answering ping down low.

It makes me realize I still haven't had the perma-arousal return since the cave.

Small fucking mercies, assholes, I grumble to myself, imagining myself flipping off the genali from the ship.

That would be a nice revisionist history, though I guess at least some of them Thivoll already killed in one of the most painful ways possible.

"Your family?" he prompts me again, breaking me out of my fantasies.

I think for a moment, then share.

"My parents drove me hard to succeed. They both grew up poor and didn't want me to have the same struggles. Time spent together was precious because they worked a lot. So I could go to good schools and I wanted to make that sacrifice worthwhile. I didn't have much of a social life. I just focused on being a student, until they both died in a wreck when I was twenty. After that I lost my way for a while."

He growls lightly and his tail whips around to pat my ass. "I remember that. Just a kit. That's terrible."

"Well, a bit more than a kit, but yes. I miss them so much. Sometimes a song plays and I can hear my dad singing it. Terribly. His voice was terrible."

A tear escapes, along with a chuckle.

"My mom would dance around to whatever he sang, but she was graceful and creative. It made it into a beautiful show, despite the caterwauling... er, bad singing. I look a lot like her."

"She must have been beautiful. I'm shocked you didn't have a mate. I apologize. That was rude."

"Well, I did, but it didn't work out. Unfortunately, all of that social isolation to be a successful student meant I didn't recognize a predator. I married young. To a horrible person, though it took me a long time to realize he was the problem, not me. Or mostly the problem. I'm not perfect."

I suppose it wasn't something my parents felt like they needed to mention, but I wish I had known there were people who could seem like they loved you while slowly eroding everything about you until your confidence was completely gone.

It would have avoided a lot of heartache.

I shake off the memories that try to surge up and continue. "It took the limits of my body, and realizing how sick it was for him to be angry with me about that, for me to realize I should leave."

"How so?"

"I couldn't have kits. Uh, children, because of endometriosis."

I let out a grunt of frustration at how little of that translated. "Let me rephrase. I have scarring in my uterus that makes pregnancy impossible."

"The scarring is still there. Nanites only minimize them slightly on fresh wounds and do very little for old ones. There would be ways around it, though. With the right technology."

I blink, gobsmacked.

The thought never occurred to me that there would be other options. Even after healing like some sort of freak from a fucking gunshot.

I shake my head, shelving that life-changing possibility for much later.

"Anyway..." I clear my throat, still reeling. "He had a way of twisting things around. Isolating me. Blaming me. It took an extended, nasty argument about my condition for me to finally see him for who he was."

He growls in earnest now. "He sounds like he needed a few claw marks on his hide. At minimum."

I smile at him, though he can't see it.

"Well, sometimes we need those sorts of people to find ourselves. His frequent, illogical anger meant I learned how to read people. That I know how to convince people of something based on limited information my brain just puts together into an intuition without conscious thought."

He lets out a chuff. "I can attest to that. It's awe inspiring... and terrifying all at the same time."

I let out a mock growl and poke him hard on his right shoulder. Which really just earns me a throbbing finger and he doesn't even flinch.

Scales are annoying.

I let out a huff, then make the connection between the topic and our current quest to find missing women.

"I think the genali picked me to be the leader because I seem timid. It's a mask I had to wear to survive my marriage. I was strong enough to leave him. I was too strong for them to break me. Deplorable people, just making me tougher."

"They all underestimated you," he says with confidence in his voice.

"They certainly did."

He shudders. "Even I get scared when I hear that tone in your voice and I still have my tail."

A laugh bubbles up. "Thivoll... You could kill me with a single paw. Maybe even with just one claw."

"Well, sure. Lots of things can kill us, but I'm not sleeping beside them."

I let out a cackle, and he joins me with his chuffing. I shush myself quickly, but laughing feels good.

It's official, though...

Our humor is getting worse and worse by the day.

We fall back into silence after that.

I realize with a start that I was able to talk about my ex without my heart racing. Is it because he is so far away? Or have I changed?

Either way, it feels like a significant improvement. Something else life-changing, but this one doesn't need any analysis.

My heart feels lighter than I ever remember it.

After a while I realize his ears keep coming back to the same cardinal direction, and he's making more of his whistling breaths to better sense smells, so I assume we're headed toward something.

Not long after, I hear a roar of water, then shortly after that we come to a river.

It's moving fast, with numerous rapids pounding against giant rocks. He pulls in another long breath and then runs up stream.

I'm finally getting curious enough to risk breaking our silence when I see what he's after. There's a cryochamber stuck among a logjam, the water breaking over one side of it in a fan of rushing current.

I can't make out who it is from this far away. Thivoll crouches down so I can climb down and then repositions himself so he can talk near my ear.

"I don't like what I smell here. I think I should take you back and return for her."

I don't like the idea of leaving her alone.

"What if that suddenly breaks through and she hits a rock so hard it breaks her chamber? She'd drown before she even woke up. I can't lose another one, Thivoll."

My chest constricts and my heart is pounding in my ears as I think of everything that could go wrong for this woman.

He growls. "You are my priority. I smell hunters everywhere."

I thread my hands in his fur. "I want to take the risk. I would never forgive myself. Unless you think you'd be hurt trying to get to her?"

"That isn't my concern. I don't want you here while I do it."

"How about a tree? I could—"

I break off my thought when I see another log headed toward the cryochamber.

There's no way it will miss her.

"Look!"

I point at it, expecting him to start toward her right away, just like I would.

When he doesn't move tug on his mane. "Go! Now!"

"No," he says as he moves forward to grab me.

I dodge him, which makes me trip over a rock and land on several jagged edges.

"I'm not going," I tell him in a tight voice.

I can't betray how much pain I'm in or he won't budge.

"There's no time. Go!"

He snarls, but starts running.

"Hide," he growls back at me as his claws scrabble for purchase on the rocks.

I look around and see an overhung boulder with a small cubby. It looks slimy but I move over to it, ignoring the squish of water and the wetness seeping through my suit.

I haven't been able to convince myself to wear any of the clothing we've pilfered, but I'm regretting it now.

Luckily the moon is bright out here without the tree cover and I can see him clearly. My heart's in my throat as I watch Thivoll leaping rocks upstream, then making his way in a sharp arc back downstream to get to her.

He isn't going to make it in time. I hold my breath as it hits her. Her chamber spins but doesn't dislodge and I let out my pent-up breath.

Thivoll carefully tests his weight on the surrounding logs as he makes his way out to her. I'm pretty sure he's wrapping his tail around the chamber soon after, but it's hard to tell with the spray of water between us.

I don't hear the hunter before they move to block my view, a
pistol in their green hand.

50

Ree

"No screaming for your manticorid friend, female. Move out of there."

Thivoll was right about the danger. And about the Little Green Men.

Braceaaer really have been accurately portrayed in tabloids. Giant heads compared to their body size, enormous eyes, gray-green skin with a silver sheen, and pitifully weak looking.

Guns have a way of making that not matter.

I slowly raise my hands, then stand up in controlled movements.

I had a gun pulled on me a few months ago when treating a young child's broken arm and I asked one too many pointed questions about how it happened. It's not pleasant, but people who don't shoot you right away are usually after something.

Which means it's best to find out what that is right away.

My throat shifts painfully so I can do just that. "What do you want?"

"A whore with a translator. How inconvenient. Just move."

Well, that answers that question. Typical.

Hopefully he likes his 'whores' alive, so it gains me more time.

I make my way back up the rocks, hiding a glance over to Thivoll with the fall of my long hair. He would have normally heard all of that, but the roaring water must be drowning us out because he's still heaving the chamber across the logs, mostly blocked from my view by the spray of water.

I just need to live long enough for him to look over to my empty hiding spot.

Easy.

"So how do you like to be serviced?"

Their language is an odd combination of clicks and whistles.

"Silently, or I cut out tongues."

What a keeper.

Clearly I need a new strategy. I take one step into the woods and have an overwhelming feeling like going farther is a terrible idea.

I turn to the disgusting hunter.

His giant eyes are glued to my ass, which gives me an idea. I take a step closer to him, telling my suit to recede to its small band. His mouth parts, revealing a green tongue.

"The genali outdid themselves on you."

I put a bit of a bounce in my step and his eyes are transfixed by the movement of my breasts.

His gun is slowly lowering during his distraction. It comes up again as I get close and so I dip one hand down to the juncture of my thighs as I take the last step toward him.

He's letting out a whistling sound and his own hand is straying to his belt when I slash my other hand forward. My claws sweep across the fingers holding the gun, hitting it down and away.

It goes off to the side in a loud retort, but I don't let it distract me.

I slash my other claws toward his neck, but he moves back just enough that I slice across his chest instead. His camo suit parts and green blood flows.

He tries to bring the gun up again but I attack his extending arm.

It gives him an opening to punch me in the face from the other side. My vision blacks out for a moment, his blow much harder than I would expect for someone over a foot shorter than me.

I swipe wildly with my claws, making contact in multiple places.

Then he screams. One I've heard enough times now to know Thivoll found us. The braceaaer drops to the ground, bleeding from multiple wounds.

Thivoll is snarling behind him.

I've seen many thousands of wounds just as bad or worse, but never ones I inflicted on a person.

I throw up all the leaves in my stomach. Then scramble back down to the water, desperate to get the green blood off of me.

I start by plunging my hands into the water, but it's not enough. I wade out into the bitter cold flow and completely immerse myself, bracing myself against a rock, my hands rubbing all over.

Frantically working to remove all the splatter traces.

I hear a splash next to me and open my eyes in the water. My long indigo and orange hair is whipping along the current and Thivoll is wading toward me, then diving under to join me.

Instead of pulling me out, he rubs his hands over my skin and scales rigorously, then massages my scalp.

I can't hold my breath anymore so I get my feet under me and rocket out of the water. Thivoll comes up, but his movements are slow and precise.

His voice is incredibly gentle. "You did so well, my Ree. I know that hurt your heart. It's alright."

Shivers are racking my body as he runs his hands up and down my shoulders and arms, still speaking to me like I'm a wounded animal.

"It's alright. It's alright."

I take a long, ragged breath, then let it out.

He's right. I just focus on what he's saying. It's alright. I shake off my shock and then crash into him, holding him tight.

"Thank you, Thivoll. Thank you."

He chuffs. "No thanks are necessary. You had that well handled."

"I don't want to think about that."

"I'm taking you home."

"But—"

He cuts me off. "We're leaving."

He crouches down in the water and I climb up, the feel of his wet fur against me a reminder that I'm naked. The black suit covers me again, but the thin fabric does nothing to stop the shivers making my teeth rattle together.

I hold on tight as he leaps from rock to rock, then we are back in the forest.

"Did you stash her somewhere?"

He doesn't answer right away and my heart leaps into my throat.

"Thivoll! Is she safe?"

"I let her go when I saw the braceaaer."

My lips feel numb, but I make them work anyway. "You what? W-Where is she?"

"Somewhere down the river, Ree."

I'm shaking violently as I hurl myself off of him.

I ignore the sting of the sticker bush I tumble against and scramble back up, desperate to get back to the river.

I know she must be well out of sight but I have to look. I don't make it another step before one of his arms cage me.

He lifts me and completely ignores my kicks of protest. I just barely keep down my screams of rage, though I don't know how much longer I can manage it if he doesn't let me go.

Something in me is breaking and unless I find her, it won't ever be pieced back together again.

"Stop! You aren't well, Ree. We need to go," he hisses in my ear, his hot breath fanning the still dripping locks of my hair.

"I'm fine. Let me go! I can't leave her."

"I hope it doesn't kill you, but I can't let you."

His voice sounds gutted, but there's no room in my mind for sympathy as long as he's keeping me from what I need to do.

His tail replaces his arm and then I'm shifting around and along his fur.

Before I realize what he's doing he has me pinned against his back, my face buried in the back of his mane and then he's running.

I struggle against the unyielding grip of his tail, just to have it trap my legs against him in addition to my chest.

I sob. "Please, Thivoll..."

Nothing.

"Alright. I won't go. Just put me in a tree."

He doesn't respond, and I keep begging him. "I can't leave her. Please!"

He runs faster and faster the more I plead. The more broken sobs that wrack through me.

Eventually I settle down to a sort of trance of trembling, empty numbness.

Images of each of the women keep swimming through me. Being killed. Being raped. Telling me they trusted me and I failed them.

Each nightmare tearing deeper and deeper wounds.

I barely notice when his movements slow, though it's hard to miss when he repositions me so he can scale the cliff to our cave. When he sets me down I glance up at him.

His eyes are wild, his face is pale, and his fur is standing on end. There is something rigid and unyielding about him.

I've never seen him like this.

It jolts me out of my trance, pain surging right back in. This time of a different sort because I know I've harmed something between us.

I'm heartsick just thinking about something destroying our easy companionship.

I'm afraid to look at him any closer, so I screw my eyes tight, but he won't allow it.

51

Thivoll

"Look at me."

After a long trembling moment, she does. Her eyes are leaking, the surrounding skin bright red and her blue eyes shot through with it.

"I thought I lost you."

Both of us are shaking, but the space between us seems like it shouldn't be crossed.

I know something is wrong with her, of course, but at no point have I more keenly felt the impact of my ignorance about her species.

"What does the leaking from your eyes mean? It's scaring me."

She's holding herself tight, arms clenched around her elbows. I want to embrace her, but everything about her posture is telling me she doesn't want to be touched.

Considering I forcibly moved her here, I can't blame her.

"I'm *crying*. It's a result of big emotions. Sometimes humans *cry* when they're happy or even angry, but most of the time it's because we're sad. Or scared."

"Which one this time, besides scared?"

"I don't know. So many things. Right at this moment because I feel like I destroyed something between us."

A pang stabs through me. I reach forward to stroke her cheek but she dodges away.

I pull my trembling hand back.

"No. You did nothing wrong. I did. I can't ever risk you like that again."

She moves her hands up higher on her shoulders, bending them even farther in, her grip so tight her usually pink skin is white.

"I need to be alone," she tells me, then shuffles back to our nest.

So few words... to cause so much pain. I push down the guttural groan that wants to rise to give it voice. She is too folded in on herself as it is.

She doesn't need my feelings as an additional burden.

I shake myself from head to tail, flinging off remnant sand from the river right along with thoughts that lead nowhere good.

After a careful check of the rest of our cave, I lay down in the middle of the main room, my ears alert, my legs tucked under my chest, arms outstretched in front of me so I can be ready to spring up.

Even if she wanted me with her, I might not be able to be anywhere but out here.

Where I can stop any threat long before it gets to her.

Now I know genuine fear.

It's highly unpleasant, to say the least.

As much as I love the idea of personal freedom, and as much as I don't want to put her at risk of falling ill, I had an important realization today. In one of the worst ways possible.

She is far too protective for her own good. It's highly attractive, but it also has to stop.

I'm going to have to relive my glory days as a recalcitrant kit in order to tell her no. And keep telling her no. Or even simply ignore things I don't agree with, just like I did with my poor dam. Except this time for a far better cause than simple hijinks.

I'll have to stand firm, no matter how many wide-eyed beautiful aqua pleading looks she gives me.

She's the one who needs a protector, especially from her own helping impulse. Any time I need to stand firm I'll only need to think of that terrible moment I looked across the river to see her disappearing into the trees at gunpoint.

Or remember her absolute horror after she defended herself.

That male didn't deserve a single one of her thoughts, and yet I know the blows she dealt to him will haunt her. No one plunges into an icy river to wash off blood in such a frenzy if they aren't also trying to wash it off their soul.

It doesn't affect me like that, but anyone with eyes can tell she isn't someone who can hurt another without high cost.

If those aren't already plenty to help me hold on to my resolve, I can remember my terror.

Or the lost look in her eyes.

Yes, there's no danger of me changing my mind. The only thing left to do is to ensure the growing trust we have isn't damaged beyond repair.

Hopefully she will forgive me for today.

Then another thought occurs to me, and I feel like a dolt. It's been staring me right in my ugly face and I still haven't thought outside the confines of my species.

She's human.
I could lock her in this cave for years and she might hate me, but it wouldn't kill her.
No. That wouldn't be right.
Would it?

52

Ree

I walked away like a coward, the feelings too big, with a deep need to be away from him.

And yet I'm surrounded by his wild scent.

Orange fur of varying lengths, along with a few strands of bright green, puff into the air when I plop my butt down on the layered blankets.

My stomach is tight, pulling me forward, like it needs my shoulders as close as possible.

Instead of trying to mend what I broke, I left. I was overwhelmed, but part of me wished he had followed. Or insisted more.

But then he would go against what I said I needed. I groan and raise a shaking hand to my aching eyes.

I can't decide what I want, so how could he know?

I was very clear about not wanting to leave the river, though. My heart clenches when I picture the cryochamber hitting a rock and one of the women drowning. And then I'm angry instead of heartsick.

I know I was being unreasonable.

I still know it. Yet I don't see why he couldn't have spent a few minutes getting me to the top of a tree and then chased the chamber.

Then I picture a big red bullseye on his orange hide as he raced along the river and guilt replaces anger. He could have been shot going out the first time and I'm in here pissed off that a person he doesn't even know—hell, I don't even know—wasn't a priority for him.

I'm putting everyone I meet in danger. For the sake of women I don't know.

It isn't right.

And yet, what else am I supposed to do?

"Fuck. What have I even really done to help?"

Nothing.

Not a single woman is safe. Anyone but me would have been better at keeping them safe. They needed a different champion.

They still do.

I move my tight grip from my arms to my knees, pulling them against my chest. It reminds me of Szhe'ka.

Is he dead? Kuret too? Why don't I feel driven to protect them?

What if I get Thivoll killed?

Another sob rises. I need Silver with me. I close my eyes to picture her face but only get a fuzzy image of her and a sharp one of a cryochamber.

That's fucked up.

My eyes pop back open and go back to staring at the dimly lit walls. Why couldn't that stupid snake alien have simply stayed with us?

He left a message, so it's not like he thought we couldn't communicate.

"Motherfucker."

I yelp when multiple scores of pain drag me out of my mental spiral.

There's blood soaking down the outside of both knees. I guess it's a bad idea to imagine hurting random aliens while digging your fingers into your legs.

Well, if you happen to be a fucking alien experiment.

"Why do I smell blood?" Thivoll's gravely voice inquires.

I groan.

Of course I couldn't hide it. "Poor hand placement and claw control."

"We've all done that."

Part of me wants to laugh, but there's too much disbelief stuck in my throat.

Maybe all of his species has, but not mine.

That thought sends ice racing along my skin. How have I not realized this yet?

I'm not human. Not really.

I'm going to have to relearn my body or I'm going to keep hurting myself. And others.

I'm going to have to help a bunch of women as they make similar transitions, though who knows what their specific burdens will be. Finding them and keeping them safe feels impossible and it's just the first step to what I need to do.

I don't even know how to figure out my own changes.

That thought makes me realize the ache at the roof of my mouth is probably another incoming metamorphosis.

Fuck.

I don't want another change in my life.

My heart's pounding and my head's spinning just thinking about all that needs to be done. All the things I can't control.

I don't even notice Thivoll's in front of me until he speaks.

"Being in here isn't helping you."

I'm not sure what to say, so I just shake my head.

"I can't cage you. I tried to convince myself I could, but it wouldn't be right. There's still plenty of night left. Would you like some fresh air?"

I clear my throat to remove all the gunk tears and panic left in it.

"Yes."

We walk side by side to the cave exit and I take a deep breath. I appreciate the olive branch and I want to meet him halfway.

There's no actual need to go out into the night.

"I could just get fresh air here."

"Alright."

He sits back on his haunches and looks out. From the way he's scanning, I can tell he can detect details I could never pick out. All I see are the moonlit tops of trees.

Even those are vague.

I don't know what to say to him, so I just sit down, cross my legs and soak in the night. The calls of nocturnal animals and the cacophony of bugs is muted from up here, but still plenty loud.

More stars than anyone could ever imagine dot the sky.

This is what it must have been like back before we polluted Earth. I never thought much of only being able to see a few stars.

Looking out now it strikes me just how unnatural it was.

Safer. But not natural.

Thivoll's breathy whistle pulls me out of my musing. When he does it a second time I know he must have picked up on a smell he doesn't like.

"What is it?"

"There's a prey male upwind from here. He must be close."

I hum back in lieu of reply.

"You don't want to go talk with them?" he asks me.

"We must have passed a bunch of them earlier tonight. Why would this one be worth seeking out?"

He huffs. "Why not?"

"I don't know, Thivoll. It's starting to feel wrong to ask people to risk their lives for a bunch of women they don't even know."

"Is that what's been hurting your heart?"

"Partly. That and not feeling like I'm helping. And, well, because I've been risking you, too."

"Have you forced anyone?"

"No," I say, drawing it out.

I know where he's going with that question, of course, but it doesn't seem so simple.

"You haven't asked anyone to risk themselves. Just being here is a risk. One you didn't cause."

"But what if they—"

I don't get to finish.

"Stop. If they didn't want to help, they wouldn't. If I didn't want to help, I wouldn't. You can't be responsible for everyone, Ree. Let each of us be responsible for ourselves."

"You mean the women, too?"

"No, I think that is a situation where our help is needed. None of you are equipped to survive here."

I clamp down on the protest that tries to bubble up about him leaving the woman to float down the river.

Instead, I make myself listen.

To make connections. To think through my actions instead of continually repeating them. For once those impulses won't just lead to low sleep and money.

They might kill me or someone around me.

I've had a version of this conversation hundreds of times.

With my parents. As part of goodbyes from lovers, explaining why they couldn't stay with me. With friends.

The most recent person in my life to point out that I can't solve everyone's problems at my expense was Tamina. In almost every situation, it was said with care and love.

I ignored them.

The suffering in the world is great and the people willing to help with it are so few. Except... is that really true?

Now that I think about it, that sounds really self-important.

Damn.

What's the answer then? Just focus on what's in front of me? I don't know.

"I'm not sure I can send someone else out to risk themselves," I tell him. "Not tonight."

"Well, then how about we go looking for them and instead ask them to stay?"

I turn to him in surprise. "I didn't think you wanted to let anyone know where our cave was."

"At some point we need to trust someone. It's getting more dangerous. I'm not sure I'll be enough to protect you. And at some point I need to go track down the purple woman."

I realize with a start that he means the one from the river. "It was Amethyst?"

He nods.

"You would still go search for her?"

"Of course I will, Ree. I just need you safe when I do it. I know I overreacted before but—"

It's me who cuts him off this time. "No. I wasn't being rational. I've been struggling since... well, since they took me."

I'm trembling again.

I wipe away another tear and try to get myself under control. I'm sick of crying tonight.

There's a light pressure on my knee and I look down to see Thivoll's long, black scaled fingers tentatively touching me. Just the very tip, clearly poised to be snatched back if I don't like it.

I reach forward and grip his hand tight, my smaller hand no longer contrasting with his now that it's covered in the same black scales.

So strange, but it feels right somehow. And then I realize that all I have to do is pivot my hand and my white palm shows through.

I still have the same core.

Huh.

I can still help people, but maybe it's time I took a cue from my own shifting biology.

Maybe it's time to make sure I protect myself, too.

53

Thivoll

Once she grabs my hand, hundreds of tense muscles relax all at once.

I'm glad I didn't let my fear rule me. I'm hopeful she will be more careful, but if she isn't, I'll just have to do what I can to protect her.

Us not rushing off the moment I mentioned the prey male is a promising sign, though it might be a temporary lull in how hard she drives herself.

I suppose the best way to know is to ask.

"What do you want to do?"

She takes a deep breath, but doesn't answer right away. I take it as an excellent sign and keep myself still, careful to not rush her.

"Do you think you could get us close and scale a tree as I call out to them?"

"Sure."

"How about I take some supplies and offer them? I don't want to tell them where our cave is yet, though. I'd rather talk with them a couple times at least. Maybe even do a raid together first."

Apparently I had even more tense muscles than I thought because they loosen, too.

I approve of her new levels of caution.

"I think that is an excellent plan."

It doesn't take long to gather some items and soon we are galloping through the trees again.

Except this time it's as a team.

My fur puffs out thinking of that long run back and how much more terrifying it was when she lay limp against me, even though I had been pleading with her to be quiet.

I'd much rather be in our cave *teddy bearing*, but I think what's eating at Ree will just get worse from inaction.

I take a detour to check on the clearing Szhe'ka said he would return to. There's no sign of anyone there or evidence he has returned. I don't share this with Ree just yet.

Right now she needs good news.

I veer back toward the ridgeline, picking back up the trail of the male I detected earlier. He smells like exotic spices and something acrid, neither of which reveal anything much about his species or temperament, of course, but it's a pleasant scent that I hope translates to an equally pleasant ally.

He must be a quick one because we run longer than I expect, pushing farther into the mountains than ever before.

"Climb," Ree tells me and I don't hesitate to follow her order, though I don't hear or smell anything to prompt it.

I shift her around and start my hopping process to not leave any trace, but she interrupts me.

"No. Fast."

My throat constricts as I tear my claws into the tree, my tail whipping out to keep us balanced.

"What is it?"

She tenses in my arms, making the small sound of pain I recognize as a language shift. As I settle her against the trunk of a tree, caging her with my body so she is protected, I can see her throat and mouth moving, but I can't hear anything.

"Ree?"

She shakes her head at me, her eyes wide, and continues to move her mouth. She keeps talking in a language I can't hear, her body getting more and more tense.

"What's going on?"

Her mouth just keeps moving faster, and she tunes me out. A light scraping sound draws my attention and my ears sweep behind me. Then a branch snaps, this time even closer.

His heavy spice scent is dominant now, permeating the air. There's another snap and I open my mouth to demand answers, but she speaks before I can.

"He's coming to kill me."

I snarl and all of my claws extend. "Are you sure?"

"Yes."

There's no doubt in her voice. The sound of claws tearing into the bark below us startles me. How did he get close so fast without me hearing him?

I make sure she is secure and scramble down the tree to meet him head on.

I barely get down past the branch she is clinging to when I run into the male. He is covered in thick white fur, most of it stained with gore that I still can't smell over his heady scent.

I don't react in time to avoid the raking claws that swipe across my chest and down one arm.

I let out a groan and swing my tail around.

He flattens himself against the tree and I miss. It pulls me out of balance just enough that when he scrambles up higher and rams into me I'm not able to dig deeper into the bark of the tree to keep myself from losing my grip.

Headfirst was never an ideal way to climb down, and this is why. Instead of trying to cling to the tree I throw out one arm and dig my claws into the fur of the male.

He can't get to her, even for a moment.

He lets out a scream so high I can barely hear it. My ears throb in protest as I use my tenuous purchase on his hide to grab on with another hand.

Then I'm climbing up his broad back so I can start shredding him with my back claws.

I'm just about to clamp down on him with my mouth when he lets go of the tree and we hurtle backwards into the night.

I have just enough time to whip my tail around and deliver a load of venom before we hit the ground. A flare of pain across my back is quickly followed by the crushing weight of the male on top of me.

My ears are still throbbing from his screams as my mind tries to process all the layers of pain before they are thankfully muted by my nanites.

I'm still working on collecting myself, venom bliss and pain a nauseating mix, when his death throes end.

"Thivoll! Oh my *god*. Thivoll!"

I don't have enough air back in my lungs yet to answer her. She's making her eye leaking sounds.

I take a ragged breath in, then I see what parts of me are still working.

Everything, it seems, though painfully.

I wriggle and kick out until I'm able to get my head out from underneath the stinking hulk of fur.

"I'm alright," I tell her, though my voice betrays me.

"I c-can't get to you," she tells me with a hitch in her panicked voice.

"Just give me a bit. I'll come for you soon."

I'm not yet positive I can follow through with that promise, but continue to move out from underneath the dead male.

He's huge, with multiple sets of limbs tipped with jagged claws. I can't make out a head, then stop trying to make sense of the bundle of fur.

I'll recognize one if I see it again, and that's all that's really important.

My tail's stuck under him and I'm not as gentle with it as I should be in my need to no longer be trapped.

I can feel my instinctual response building up quickly. The last thing we need right now is for me to enrage.

I yank it out and tumble backwards into more of the bushes with a groan. One of them broke my fall from the tree. The puncture wounds seeping blood down my back are a small price for an intact spine.

In fact, when I shakily get back to my paws and fists I know I've been incredibly fortunate to come through that fight with no broken bones or missing body parts.

I realize Ree's talking again and I shake my head to clear it.

"… damn fucking liars. So much for blocks against hurting each other. Fuck!"

Despite it all, my whiskers jut forward. I love her fire.

I decide to give my nanites some time to catch up before I climb, which just leaves my usual burning curiosity.

"Why did he attack?"

She sniffs and lets out a huff of breath.

"He was completely deranged. Or that's just how his species is. I don't know. He was talking about feet when I first heard him. So I called out a greeting. Nicely, I thought. Then he was talking about how mine would taste. Over and over. I tried to reason with him, but by the time he started talking about cracking open my bones I knew there wasn't any hope."

"But he smelled nice."

I realize how stupid it sounds right after I say it.

A beat later both of us are chuffing, hers in her usual dulcet tones that soothe the last part of my rage.

"Do you think the slimes lied about prey not being able to hurt each other?"

I consider her question. "No. I think there's just some of us it won't work on. Unfortunately, we found one with a paw fetish."

We're chuffing again, this time with a manic edge to it. I decide that if I'm well enough to chuff, I'm well enough to climb, so I go retrieve her.

She doesn't balk for even a moment at the blood and grime coating me and starts running her hands over my chest and mane as soon as I'm within range.

Then she pulls herself to me in a tight hug.

"I'm so, so glad you're alright. When I heard you hit the ground, I thought my heart was going to break."

54

Ree

"Does that actually happen to humans?"

His voice is so sincere I can't help but laugh.

"Not exactly. Extreme sadness can kill us, but it isn't common."

"It is the same for my species."

My hands are still shaking and I can't seem to stop touching him. "I think I should use wound spray on those gashes."

He looks down at his chest. "You're probably right. No sense in making the nanites work harder. That male was disgusting."

"The smell is pretty overpowering, yes."

In fact, it's so bad my eyes are watering.

I get to work and it takes less than a minute, though I'm itching to use the stitch clipper.

So far his wounds have closed on their own, but he has several feet of gashes in five long, jagged rows.

"Are those too big to close on their own?"

He looks down at himself.

"No, but we should find a place to wash," he comments.

I nod absentmindedly as I continue my inspection of his wounds.

Then he's gathering me up and climbing down. He's much slower than usual. A testament to how much pain he must be in, even with nanites.

When I see the multiple punctures along his back I don't want to climb up on it, but he insists.

He walks us toward the nearest stream where I help him rinse out his fur in a deeper section of the frigid water before dunking myself for a quick scrub.

He shakes himself off, water flinging everywhere, leaving him with a profile I'm not used to seeing.

If he didn't look so beaten down, it would look comical.

"It's nice to be rid of that smell. It was overpowering."

He snorts out several times, then uses his hands to rub at his nose. I'm still scrubbing when his body tenses.

My heart races, wondering what additional trouble is headed our way.

"What is it?"

He takes in a long whistling breath. "I smell the one who took Silver."

My heart leaps at the news, and I scramble for the creek bank. I take in a breath to talk and think I might know what he means.

It's musky, but not in an unpleasant way.

"Really? Is it the musky smell?"

"Exactly so."

He whips his head over to me, his mane shaking from the speed. "You shouldn't be able to detect that."

I let out a groan. "My mouth has been hurting."

"At the top?"

"Yes..."

"We have a secondary scent organ there."

I let out a grunt. I've read about that. A vomeronasal organ. Great.

I take in another slow breath through my mouth and then cough it out, my brain completely overwhelmed and my stomach queasy at all the new aromas.

Some of them are highly unpleasant.

"I might throw up. Some things are best left unsmelled."

Not a phrase I ever thought I would need to say. Ever.

"You have to filter out what you don't like."

"What if I don't like any of it?"

"We'll have to work on it. For now, don't breathe through your mouth. He's been here multiple times. I could follow the trail."

I push aside my impending exi-scent-ual crisis—and how much I want to giggle maniacally in the grass over bad puns instead of dealing with my freakish new life—to focus back on Silver.

My hands are shaking and not just from the cold. This is exactly what I've been hoping to hear, but I don't like the timing.

"You're injured. I think we should go back to the cave."

He looks over at me with wide eyes. "I thought you would be running through the woods already."

"I'm not saying I don't want to be doing that. Just that we shouldn't."

He's purring now and the way he looks at me says it's one of pride.

"Let's go investigate, Ree. If it seems dangerous, we'll leave."

I huff out a breath. Now he's the one trying to convince me to go do something stupid.

Figures.

I'm shaking my head in disbelief as I clamber back up onto him, careful to avoid open wounds. Then we creep through the night. The terrain gets increasingly rocky as we go.

Thivoll pauses after a while, his fur standing on end. Not long after I hear a hissing language.

"Moon woman is mine."

My hands tighten in Thivoll's fur. "He's talking to us. He says she's his."

"I can smell her chamber, but not her. She must still be in it. There's no way for me to get her without killing the male."

I resist the urge to use my new super nose... mouth. Whatever. Now is not the time for puking.

I grunt, then switch to the lisping language. "She is not mine. She is not yours. She owns herself."

"She will decide," he responds.

"Will you let me see her? She's hurt."

"No. I will care for her."

"Please. I am responsible for her."

"No."

I let out a sigh. There's nothing to be done.

My chest tightens painfully at the thought of simply walking away. Except how much of this is for Silver and how much of it is for me?

She has a protector.

That's my primary goal. Isn't it?

"Will you keep her safe?" I ask the mysterious male. "It would be better if we were all in the same place."

"She is mine."

I open my mouth to keep pushing but realize it's futile. If we can't easily get to her, at least she has a guard.

I switch to Thivoll's language. "Let's go home. He won't give her up."

"We can check on her again."

I know he's right, but the tears spring to my eyes, anyway.

I sniff, but don't respond.

He turns around to go the way we came, stopping again at the stream for a drink and a snack. After that he steadily picks up speed until we are streaking through the forest at our usual pace.

The whole time we run I work through my grief.

My mind goes in circles wondering what I'll do now. I mean, she's safe, I suppose. But not where I can see her.

I just have to keep telling myself she's safe, but the tears still come.

We've left the mountain far behind us when he abruptly stops, tips me off of him into some moss, grabs me, and then scrambles up a tree.

I rub my wet face against his fur to clear my vision.

I'm pretty certain he's moving to other trees for a while, but I don't dare look to find out. I just cling to him. At least until I feel my back pressed hard against rough bark.

His hands are roving all over me. Squeezing, caressing, pulling through my long hair.

"I'm proud of you for leaving her. I know it had to be hard. Are you alright?"

"Yes, mostly. It felt right."

"Good. Now make your thread recede."

I do as he says, and he goes right back to touching me everywhere he can reach.

"Grab the branch above you."

"Are you sure you're well enough to—"

"Grab. It."

Damn. I'm not sure what's gotten into him, but it's hot.

I look up, then reach up to hold on to it with both hands. Thivoll's tail is wrapped around a couple different branches and then anchored back onto itself.

He moves a hand to my scaled throat, squeezing lightly and moves the other to support my weight. Then he uses his insane flexibility to lick my stomach and chest.

I moan at the feel of his nubbed tongue over my sensitive nipples.

His hands and tongue are rough, like he's staking a claim. Then he moves his hand from my neck between my legs and starts pumping his fingers into me, quickly adding more until he has three thick digits deep inside me.

The lurking danger of his unextended claws makes it a heady experience. My heart races and my breath is labored.

My own claws are extended and digging into the bark to maintain my grip as he roughly jostles me. He moves both of his hands to my hips, lifting me up and into him, then extrudes in one quick motion.

I gasp and throw my head back.

He wastes no time in claiming me. My breasts are bouncing with his pounding rhythm.

He's growling as he digs the tips of his fingers and thumbs into the flesh of my hips to ensure he is pulling me down onto his thick girth as hard as possible.

I tilt my head forward and just the sight of his violet cock pumping in and out of me is enough to tip me over. I cry out and he snarls and increases the speed of his thrusts.

He's still slapping into me as he lets out a thunderous roar.

Nothing held back, including the seed he spills that I can feel flowing out of me and onto my ass cheeks.

But he keeps driving into me, a dozen strokes past his release, something primal in his face. The thought of it and what it means brings another orgasm crashing over me and just like him I don't bother containing my cry.

When I come back to myself I realize he's licking my neck and chest again, then running his teeth over me.

"You're mine, sweet one. I'll never let you go."

I purr, that scared part of me finally receding. No longer overriding my good sense and once again secure in our growing relationship.

"I don't want you to let me go, Superkitty."

His purr joins my own as he continues to lick at my neck.

Then he reaches up to grab my arms, which still have the branch in a death grip. He wraps them around his neck as I feel him recede from inside of me.

We climb down as fast as we ascended and without another word I'm on his back and we're bounding home.

As we run, the events of the day plague me.

I keep seeing green blood all over me. I can't help but second guess my decision to leave Silver with that slithering, possessive male. I didn't even look him in the eyes to see if he seemed safe. Have I completely failed her?

Will I see her again?

Will I be able to keep myself together without her?

There's no answer, of course.

I can only move forward. Except this time I need to do it in a way that puts myself, and Thivoll, at less risk.

It's a miracle we aren't both dead already. I can't keep pushing the edges and expect it to keep working out.

I'm going to have to let some things go. Silver was a good start.

Maybe I need to let Amethyst go, too.

I clear my throat and ask Thivoll his opinion. "It's too much of a risk to get Amethyst, isn't it?"

He slows a bit, considering. "No. I think I should get her now."

"What? You need to rest. You aren't actually a Superkitty. You have limits."

"I still don't know what that means."

I quirk up a lip, but it's more fun to leave him guessing. "It's a mystery."

He chuffs. "You do realize that makes me even more invested in wresting the definition from you?"

I chuckle. "Of course I do, Fluff Brain."

I hear the crack of his teeth, then another chuff before he starts speaking again.

"I know my limits and we haven't passed them. I want her settled in our cave as much as you do. If I can't find her or if it's not safe, I'll just come back without her."

For once, I'm at peace with that possibility.

"That sounds like an excellent plan."

Soon after, we are back at the cave and Thivoll has me set up at the entrance with guns at the ready.

He disappears without a sound into the forest.

55

Ree

The shock of the day is waning, leaving exhaustion in its wake, but I keep myself propped up.

I killed someone. I let Silver go.

Both decisions were warranted in the moment, but they weigh on me. Luckily genali rations are gross enough to help shift my mind away from the remnant guilt and horror.

Just that little bit of space is enough for my brain to compartmentalize the experience, as I've trained it to do. It's an enormous relief, and it lets me turn my mind to far more important things.

Like, despite the danger and straight up surrealism of even being here, how happy I am.

And it's not just because of Thivoll, though of course that is most of it, but also how peaceful it is on this planet. If we could just remove the hunters from the equation, this would be a paradise.

Not that there aren't beautiful places on Earth, but I don't want them.

I wouldn't trade being home and safe for just how alive and cherished I've felt in my short time with Thivoll. I would go anywhere with him, but why not here? I haven't missed technology.

Or the oppressive expectations of culture.

Okay. I miss warm food. And human companionship. And probably lots of other things I'm ignoring right now in the moment's glow.

Those could be built here. There's just the slight problem of a bunch of sadistic aliens who think this is their blood-soaked playground.

I might not be able to get my own claws dirty making sure the blood on the ground turns into their own, but I know I can support others as they do it.

I'll start with supporting Thivoll. And then maybe Szhe'ka, Kuret, and others.

That reminds me we need to visit the clearing and ridgeline they said they'd return to. I'll be sure to mention it to Thivoll on our next run.

I stay alert during all my musing and so I see Thivoll as he scales the cliff. I'm relieved I don't have to shoot anybody.

It only takes him a few moments to get to me and I move to make room for him. I'm also thrilled to no longer be so close to the ledge.

"Do you have her?"

"Yes. Let's get her up. But I want you to stay up here this time."

I bite down on my tongue, something in me wanting to tear into him even though it is completely reasonable.

My aggression is what isn't reasonable.

It's something I'm still not accustomed to and assume it must be part of the genetic changes.

I nod. I know why he is feeling protective right now and being reactive to it isn't helpful.

I simply show him how to tie the knot, check the rope after he throws each end down, and then lay down so my head can peek over the ledge with less surging panic about the height.

It's a far more nerve-wracking experience to watch him this time, but he must have perfected his technique last time because it seems like he flies up the cliff face.

He moves Amethyst into the small chamber and my heart aches to see her in Silver's place. I hope the woman is okay. That the male is treating her like my Thivoll treats me.

My Thivoll. My lips twitch at how his idiosyncratic language is rubbing off on me.

I place a blanket over her to give her privacy, then gain her even more by using the hooks at the top of the opening to create a fabric door.

She isn't conscious, but it feels respectful.

Before we go out again, I'll figure out how to write her a note in case she comes out of cryo while we're gone.

Thivoll has replaced and fluffed up our bedding while I worked and beckons me over to it. I watch him as he settles in.

All those things about him that initially made him so strange and even frightening are just a part of what make him mine.

"Are you satisfied now, my Ree? I have plans."

I look him up and down. His long orange mane is puffed out, as usual. His tail is tapping impatiently on my leg and his hooded look is promising me all kinds of naughty things.

I still feel that spike of aggression and taking on my usual submissive role just doesn't appeal tonight.

"No, I'm not satisfied. But how about I tell you exactly what you can do to change that?"

By his surging purr I know he likes the idea.

I hope he'll like my plan, but I don't let any insecurities rise, quashing them with this newfound presence in my chest prompting action.

"Get in bed and lay on your back."

His tail dances behind him as he pads over to our pile of bedding, then he plops down on his side before rolling over onto his back, his large haunches and backward facing legs forcing him into a wide sprawl.

I stalk over to him, stepping one leg over his belly so I'm standing directly over the expanse of black scales of his belly and the slit of his sheath. I order my nanothread to recede and his eyes roam over me.

I move farther back and lower myself so I'm sitting half a foot down from his sheathe.

"Bring it out for me, Thivoll."

His whiskers droop, letting me know he's confused, but he does what I ask. My eyes widen when I see his massive violet dick.

It should never have fit inside my body, but it did. More than once.

I have to modify my idea to give him oral sex, but it's still doable. From his confusion, I'm guessing he's never had it done and so he'll never know I had to scale back.

The idea of being his first is exciting.

I start off by reaching forward and grabbing him near his base with one hand. It can't circle all the way around, so I add another. He's slick and a cooler temperature than I expect. I pull both hands up in a slow glide toward his tip.

The move elicits a low groan.

His tip is rough in texture, similar to his tongue, plus ribbing along the length, and now I know why him grinding into me felt so damn good.

I explore him with my hands for a few more moments, then am delighted when just that bit of stimulation makes pre-cum leak from his twitching tip.

I'm curious what he tastes like and lean forward, flicking my tongue on his tip and causing him to take in a gasping breath.

He's tart and spicy.

Not a combination I would've thought I liked, but it leaves me wanting more.

His eyes are wide, watching me raptly as I move my mouth closer to him.

I keep my eyes locked on his as I open my mouth as wide as I can and take him into my mouth.

56

Thivoll

I might die. Or be reborn. I'm not sure which.

I just know I never want her to stop. She's looking straight into the very depths of me as she moves her mouth over the end of my cock.

I know what she meant now about the unknown being difficult.

Part of me is scared, since no manticorid would ever think of extruding into three rows of jagged teeth. This is unfamiliar territory, but I trust her.

That trust is rewarded by sensations I never knew even existed.

Her blunt teeth lightly scrape me and her tongue explores what it can reach, spending extra time on the sensitive nodules at my tip, swirling around them in a way that makes me want to explode far, far too soon.

My own mouth drops open in shock and then I let out a long guttural moan when I feel a pulling sensation from her mouth.

Another thing my species is incapable of doing.

She stops sucking, swirls her tongue around me, and then pulls again. This time I feel the sensation all the way to the base of my tail and I have to keep myself from thrusting up into her mouth.

She can't take much of me inside it and I don't want to hurt her.

When she pumps her hands up and down my length in time with her sucking, my head drops back and I lose some of that careful control, my hips thrusting forward slightly each time I feel the pull of her mouth.

I'm existing in some sort of floating bliss state where I'm balancing the desire to embrace what she's doing while also holding back from pumping my seed into her mouth when she shifts again.

She crawls forward over me, my cock dragging over her wet heat, and then her breasts are dragging over my scales.

She moans at the contact and keeps crawling until she can reach my muzzle with her mouth. She leaves light *kisses* near my whiskers as she pets them.

"Put your hands on my breasts."

I shake myself out of my stupor and follow her orders. Squeezing each one together with a thumb on each side of her mounds.

She goes back to *kissing* me, each long stroke of her hands on my long whiskers making me want to bury myself deep inside of her.

Unfortunately, she's too far up my chest to accomplish that, straddling me with her knees in a way my species could never accomplish.

My hands are busy, but I realize my tail has just been laying limply to the side as I got lost in the sensations.

I snake it around behind her, pushing it between us so the side of the scaled ovoid pushes up against her wet heat.

She stops *kissing* me for a moment, looking down between us. I twitch the end of my tail in a steady pattern.

One that compliments the kneading of my hands on her breasts.

She shivers and lets out a moan, and then goes back to *kissing* me, the pressure of her mouth increasing.

Soon after she uses her tongue to explore the sensitive base of each whisker. My cock jumps and my tail picks up speed.

A moment later she makes her pain-pleasure sound, leaning back and tensing up. I'll never tire of how her face looks when I pleasure her.

Or the dazed look in her eyes afterwards, but she doesn't stay that way for long.

Instead she's moving backwards, leaning forward slightly and pushing herself back against my engorged cock.

I can still feel her twitching as I glide inside her. She sits back on me for a long moment and then uses her body to rock forward and back in a steady rhythm.

Each time my breathing gets ragged and I'm bucking my hips erratically she slows, pushing her weight back and grinding into me until I calm again.

On the third repetition I get impatient and move my hands down to her waist, prepared to keep her rocking.

She snaps her teeth at me and I hastily return my hands to her breasts.

She must like my idea though, because she changes her angle and starts slamming her rear down into me. I catch on to her rhythm and rise to meet her on each downward movement.

She loses her pace not long after, a keening sound coming from her and I take the opportunity while she's distracted to grab her hips.

I raise her up and down three more hard times as I pump myself up into her before I join her with a quickly cut off roar of my own.

She turns limp, melting down onto my chest with me still throbbing inside of her. I let my arms go slack at my sides, but use my tail to caress her back.

When I considered the possibilities afforded by her radically different anatomy I had no idea it could be this pleasurable.

57

Ree

I'm smiling as I move into his warm embrace.

He purrs as I wiggle into a suitable position. One that gives me access to his mane and whiskers and lets us see each other.

His whiskers betray his contentment and I bet I have one of those goofy looks on my face that instantly peg someone as newly in love.

I wish Tamina could see me now. Well, if she could even recognize me. It would be an endless conversation before it would even make sense.

If someone told me I would be holding an alien in my arms and thinking about love I would have considered referring them for a psych evaluation. Hell. I'm not completely sure I shouldn't be referring myself, but it feels right.

Everything about us feels right.

His eyes are half closed and part of me wants to let him drift off to sleep, but I have something to tell him. I tug on a whisker and his eyes open wide to focus on me.

"I love you, my Thivoll."

His purr feels like it might rattle me right out of his arms.

"I love you, my Ree."

It didn't seem like we could get any more intertwined, but somehow we manage it.

Our scales rubbing together is surprisingly soothing and nothing like what I would have expected. His golden eyes are just as enthralling as they were from the moment I wiped my eyes clear of tears and felt trapped in them.

Hooked in the best way possible.

My heart feels full in all the right ways. "I know this place is crazy, but I love being here with you."

His rumble dies back down and he looks more serious.

"It has been my greatest pleasure. But I also want to make sure our life together is long. You keep trying to cut it short."

I shift uncomfortably. "That's not fair. I'm not suicidal, I just need to protect them and this place is fucking insane."

He pats my butt. "You're a commander, not a common soldier. You can't be a leader if you throw your life away or run yourself into the ground."

I can't help the sharp bark of a laugh. "A commander? I'm barely keeping myself together. I'm incredibly ineffectual. I wish they had chosen Kira as the leader."

"Who's Kira?"

"How have I not told you? She has pink hair. I'm pretty sure she grew up with a knife in her hand or something. They only had her out of stasis for a short time and she was completely cool and collected. Pretty much told them she was going to kill all the fuckers. I was in awe."

He grunts at me. "Ree. Stop underestimating yourself. How long do you think someone with that sort of attitude would have lasted on a slime ship? She doesn't sound like a leader. She sounds like one of your soldiers."

"I don't want soldiers!"

He chuffs. "You already have three of them. At least. Others haven't spent enough time with their humans to realize that despite their bigger size they aren't the ones in charge. Silver, and it sounds like Kira, know about you. They will seek you out, even if they have to drive their poor male to near insanity to get their way. I know this for a fact."

I catch on to what he's saying and punch him as hard as I can on his shoulder. Then hiss and rub my hand until the sting goes away.

He reaches forward to help me, the cant of his whiskers betraying his amusement.

"You have someone either looking for or actively protecting all but four of your friends. In a few short days. How could you be anything but a commander?"

"It isn't enough. I can't rest until it's all of them."

"I understand that. We won't stop. We will win, but we have to be smart about it. You can't keep taking risks."

I let out a breath. I'm not sure why I'm still arguing. It's not like I hadn't already come to a similar conclusion, though without all the commander talk.

The title makes me want to retch but I don't deny that I will take all the necessary responsibility. And I suppose I can't really argue with him since the next prey male I see I'll be right back to working on recruitment.

Fuck.

That's exactly what the military does.

I'm a recruiter. We have a stockpile of weapons forming. Doing inventory is one step away from requisitions and fucking paperwork. I have people out on missions.

He's right, dammit.

Of course I don't tell him that, but the least I can do is agree to not fling myself into any more trouble.

"I know. I'll be more careful."

"I believe you. You've showed it recently, but I'm going to keep repeating it until the horror wears off. Let other people help you. I know you can fight when you need to, but there is a substantial cost for you. In your mind and your self-image."

My hands tremble just thinking about the cuts I made on the braceaaer. I never want to do that again.

I mean, I will if I have to, but it's wrong to expect him to do it all.

"It doesn't feel fair to let you take the risk alone, Thiv."

"Listen, sweet one. I will kill them until there is no threat left. I'll even enjoy it. It's no weight for me. Let me carry it. Let me be that for us."

I take in a deep breath and then let it out just as slowly. Just talking about what I did makes me shake and cry.

"You're right. I can't handle it. I just keep seeing his blood on me. Over and over, no matter how many times I tell myself that he planned to rape and probably kill me."

"You're a healer Ree. We'll find more allies and more of your friends and soon you'll have an outlet for how much you drive yourself. I know it's hard right now, but soon you'll be able to help in ways that are better suited to your personality."

"I'll go crazy if I stay in this cave all the time."

"I know. How about you run with me for the first part of the night?"

"That could work," I concede.

"I would rather not range far to look for your friends, but I know why it's important to you. You are going to be sitting near the entrance with guns loaded and at the ready until I return."

He lets out a low chuff, then continues. "If you have to kill a hunter, I will hold you while you face-leak again."

I laugh. "I was crying, not face-leaking, Fluff Brain."

My eyes fill up for a different reason altogether and I lean forward to kiss him near his whiskers.

"I believe in you, Superkitty."

He chuffs and runs his hands through my hair. I've never felt more cherished, and it wraps around my heart like a warm embrace.

"I'd be taunting genali from trees with no true purpose without you. It's me who believes in you."

Preview of Coral

Drasuk

The popping sounds grow louder as I continue my advance, my burning curiosity piquing with each burst of noise.

The sound ends as quickly as it begins, signaling the end of whatever conflict arose. With that realization, my claws dig into the soft earth as I lower myself to all fours, picking up speed.

As I sprint through the undergrowth, the forest becomes a blur of green and brown.

The first hint I get is the noticeable shift in the surrounding air, transitioning from its crisp quality to a sharper tone with a drier heat that contrasts with the usual humidity.

As I advance, the reason for the change becomes clear as the lush foliage gradually transitions, giving way to a strange, desert-like landscape.

Dark red soil crunches and puffs up dust motes beneath the thick pads of my feet, the air noticeably hotter.

I can't help but wonder how long it took them to terraform this planet to such extremes.

The process was refined by the manticorids at the height of their empire. After their decline, it was only a matter of time before the technology was stolen.

Other empires attempted to replicate the methods that ensured environmental variety, but had never done so. These limitations are clearly no longer relevant.

Fanciful thoughts to muse over Drasuk, but this is not the place.

I trample the errant thoughts and focus on my task.

The scent, that tantalizing blend of enemy and something else, guides me.

Ahead, I spot a crash site. A heap of warped metal juts out from the ground, the remnants of a larger ship.

I barely give it a second glance, my attention drawn to the bodies near a makeshift campsite. One braceaaer, one genali.

The corpses are fresh, their ballistic wounds still oozing.

But it's not their scent that draws me. No, there's something else, an eerily pleasant aroma that fills my nostrils.

How had this somehow become even more... exciting?

I move cautiously, scanning the area. A single crack of a gun rings through the air, replaced by an unsettling silence.

My instincts scream at me to be wary, but the scent is too alluring to ignore.

I draw nearer the bodies, examining the scene. The braceaaer's rigid stance indicates a struggle, while the genali's sprawled form doesn't leave much to analyze.

I crouch beside them, inspecting the wounds. Bullet holes, not energy weapons.

As expected, I suppose.

A vague memory surfaces about a hunting ground where technology ceases to work.

If nothing else, at least that narrows down the possibilities of where I am. Not that I could send out a distress signal or anything.

Focus, Drasuk.

I sniff the air again, trying to pinpoint the source of the enticing scent. It's not from the bodies, nor the campfire remnants. I close my eyes, focusing my senses.

It's strongest to the north.

I move away from the crash site, heading toward it. The ground shifts beneath my pads, the red soil giving way to rocky terrain. The temperature continues to rise, the sun burning along my rough blue skin.

Despite the discomfort, I press on, driven by an inexplicable need to find the source.

As I crest a rocky ridge, the landscape before me is a stark contrast to the lush forest I can still see from afar. A barren expanse stretches out, dotted with jagged rocks and sparse vegetation.

My eyes narrow as I see a tiny figure in the distance, leaving the desert biome and darting into the forest. The smell seems to waft from the direction the small creature took, so I give chase.

I drop to all fours again, feeling the muscles in my limbs coil and release with each powerful stride.

This one has a scent designed to trick me, like the carnivorous plants of my world that lure in unsuspecting animals.

Beneath that enticing layer, there's the unmistakable stench of the genali. No doubt a product of their body modification program.

That's enough for me to ignore the temptation the scent stirs in my loins.

Angry with myself for even entertaining such thoughts, I pick up my pace, crashing through the forest after the running creature. The foliage whips past me, branches scratching at my hide.

The chase is exhilarating. My senses heightened by the thrill of the hunt. I force myself to focus, to remember why I'm here.

Vengeance, not some twisted game.

The creature ahead is quick, darting around trees with an agility that belies its size. I am faster. My claws make deep furrows, propelling me forward.

The smell grows stronger, filling my nostrils and urging me on.

I push through the fatigue, my eyes locked on the elusive figure ahead. Glimpses of bright pink like a beacon drawing me toward it.

The forest thickens, and the undergrowth becomes denser. The creature weaves through the trees, but I am relentless.

With a burst of speed, I close the gap, my breath hot and heavy in my throat. The figure glances back, its eyes wide with fear.

It knows it cannot outrun me.

I leap, my claws outstretched, ignoring the impotent bullets the creature sprays me with as I feel the blood rush triumphantly through me.

About the Authors

This pen name represents a collaboration with the goal of creating stories just like we prefer: spicy slow burn, strong character arcs, and all about the... shall we say delectably different.

Ky is our public face...

the one of us who posts on social media, who decided it was *smart* to get a PhD in History (and so now regales you with the book related historical mythology in our newsletter), who tends to have all the wild ideas, the writing voice we follow, and who keeps all of it moving (sheesh, that's a lot... thanks, Ky!)

On a typical day you can find Ky hanging out with her own Mr. Delectably Different, loving on her fur babies, or convincing her two kids that she really is funnier than they'll admit.

She's a musician, sculptor, graphic designer, and lover of weirdness. Most of the time, she's either working her 9 to 5, writing, or running out in the wild.

Legends Start Somewhere

Want to read more stories in the Alien Hunting Grounds Universe?

Join our newsletter for a free prequel short story! You can access it at kylabreene.com

Myth Awakened: Vimala and Jentoll

Vimala

I was once a courtesan for kings... until a rival sent an attacker in the middle of the night. One moment. One coward with a blade. I lost everything.

My beauty no longer sustains me, but I refuse to simply fade away. And yet it is hard to maintain hope after so much loss. Will this otherworldly avatar of Vishnu be my salvation?

Jentoll

I've given more than enough to my people. To my failing empire. I gave an eye. My tail. Pieces of my sanity... far too much precious time. And now it's crumbling to dust. Falling to a far different sort of rallying cry. One for peace.

Let the next generation bear that task. This is my chance to flee. To find a new home.

Two wounded hearts, both seeking refuge.
Will they find it in each other?

Join our newsletter to find out: kylabreene.com

www.ingramcontent.com/pod-product-compliance
Lightning Source LLC
Chambersburg PA
CBHW060440310726
48977CB00001B/264